ADVENT

The countdown has begun

DAVID MILLER

Published in 2013 by DMBOOKS (Singapore)
First edition eBook – June 21, 2013 (V III)
First edition print – June 1, 2014
Revised edition print – September 28, 2015

For publishing or media enquiries please log on to
www.dmbooks.org or email admin@dmbooks.org
ISBN (paperback): 978-981-07-6390-9
ISBN (ebook): 978-981-07-6389-3

Cover design by DMBOOKS

PRODUCT OF SINGAPORE

FOR MY LITTLE ONES
DASHER, BOVRIL, BLITZEN
SNOWFLAKE & PRANCER

I believe that even the smallest prayer will still be heard

The fifth angel sounded his trumpet,
and I saw a star that had fallen
from the sky to the earth.
The star was given the key
to the shaft of the Abyss.
When he opened the Abyss,
smoke rose from it
like the smoke from a gigantic furnace.

– Book of Revelation

PROLOGUE

Every jolt along that rough dirt track frayed his nerves even further. Gingerly he turned to look back into the cargo bay of the old van.

She was still there, lying peacefully, looking almost serene in the stillness of the darkening evening. The thick nylon straps held her securely in place as the firm styrofoam base cushioned against the frustrating bumps of her final journey into oblivion.

On her main control panel, the little red light continued to blink reassuringly. Her heart was beating strong and all was well.

Saif felt better now knowing that his task was almost over and scanning the dark track before him, he knew that the end would soon be literally in sight any minute now. Taking a deep breath which helped to steady his nerves, he whispered to himself: "It is almost done."

While understandably nervous, he still enjoyed this time of the mission best of all – the advent to a kill, stealthily stalking the unwary foe, savouring the seconds before pushing that button. It was like a drug and Saif knew he was a hardcore addict who could never get enough of a fix.

Once again he turned to look out the window. All his senses were on alert – waiting and watching for anything that was out of the ordinary, anything which could upset these carefully laid plans. The element of surprise was after all, one of his greatest assets. But here, his target area was empty and there would be no one to stop him now.

They were less than a kilometre away from their objective – a desolate area of reclaimed land. Beyond the little trees planted along the fence in the distance lay their prize – the Changi Naval Base. In the hours to come this scrubland, if anything still remains of it, would be infamously known as Ground Zero.

These past few weeks had been a long and dangerous journey. The task was formidable, fraught with peril and uncertainty and yet he had done everything that was asked of him. He had done it well as a soldier should and now the mighty *Saif al-Haidar* with its plutonium core was finally ready to explode brighter than a star in the heavens above.

Thinking back over the short time he had spent in Singapore, Saif was proud that he had been chosen, destined really, for this mission. The history books would tell of this night that changed the world. It mattered none to him that those same books would probably never record his name or his role in it all. Simply to be picked from among all the others to be that singular instrument of total annihilation, that was enough of a reward for him.

This mission would surely eclipse even his greatest accomplishment to date – the crushing of the American Embassy in Nairobi, Kenya back in 1998. But that was many years ago – many years spent waiting in hope for his next assignment and the intoxicating adrenalin rush that came with it. Hiding in the shadows, this was simply the nature of the world he lived in – the world he belonged to, if only briefly.

Saif had waited a long time for this opportunity to prove himself yet again and tonight he was sure that everything would go as planned. He could see it all in his mind's eye – the brilliant flash of light that would unleash the unspeakable vaporising power of a nuclear firestorm. Unlike Nairobi, this time the fire and the glory will burn much brighter. And after it was all over, nothing would matter anymore. His job would have been done – his sacred mission complete.

A sudden bolt of lightning tore through the black sky and reflected off the calm surface of the sea in the distance. They were very close now. He could smell the salt in the air and straining his neck to see beyond the trees, he caught his first glimpse of the American warships anchored in the distance, oblivious to their fate.

Through the side mirror, Saif spied the subdued headlights of the second van with the other men travelling far behind them.

"Cowards!" he thought to himself. "Keeping your distance

will not save you from this. Nothing will ..."

1

One month earlier …

Police Headquarters, Singapore – October 23, 1132 hours

"Initial testing has confirmed that the polonium recovered is extremely refined – it is certainly of a weapon's grade," Assistant Superintendent of Police Gerald Loh told his audience seated around the conference table in Police Headquarters. Projected on the screen in front of them was a picture of the small metal disc, no larger than a medium-sized coin, which had been seized earlier that day.

"What are the chances that this disc has some kind of a dual use?" asked the Police Commissioner.

"That remains an outside possibility,' said Gerald. "Polonium does have a few industrial applications such as to eliminate static electricity in machinery or used in brushes to remove dust and other airborne impurities from photographic films but I'm afraid these appear to be very remote possibilities. The size and shape of the metal and the fact that it is too well refined for industrial applications …"

"So it's part of a trigger for a nuke then," cut in Colonel Brenton Wong, Assistant Director for Military Intelligence.

"Yes,' said Gerald. "It would seem so."

The group had already been briefed on the sequence of events that led to the discovery of the polonium disc earlier that morning at the Keppel Container Terminal just south of the city. The *Ovation Maria II*, a Panamanian-registered container ship had arrived in port at dawn. As fate would have it, one of the off-loaded containers was subjected to a random security x-ray and radiation screening test – something which only less than five percent of the thousands of containers passing through this busy port each year have to undergo.

Radiation, simply defined, is energy in the form of waves or streams of particles. The types and levels of radiation vary considerably. Some, such as sunlight and cosmic rays, occur naturally. Even certain foods such as bananas, are sources of naturally-occurring radioactivity. But the radiation detection portal at Keppel was designed to sniff out the more ominous types – in particular those which can be used to fuel nuclear weapons.

The security portal is made up of two four-metre-high panels that are anchored to the ground and placed wide enough apart for a container to be driven through. One part of the device quickly scans the contents using a form of x-rays similar to those found in airports to screen luggage. The other samples the air to detect the presence of radiation. Should any be found, the computerised detector would quickly determine its type and intensity.

The positive hit that morning immediately triggered a security alert involving the island's police, military and civil defence forces. Following strict emergency protocols, the container was driven to an empty building located a distance away from the rest of the port operations. There its contents were carefully unloaded and searched by civil defence officers in their white anti-radiation suits.

Eventually the polonium was traced to a small but heavy stainless steel tube just 30 centimetres long and 11 centimetres in diameter. Its two ends had been welded together and the shiny silver polonium disc found inside was further sealed within a protective casing of lead to reduce radiation leakage and therefore, detection.

Analysis later revealed that the tube contained just 124 grams of this rare heavy metal – a tiny amount by any standards but more than enough in which to fashion part of a trigger device for a nuclear weapon.

"So what do we know of its origins?" asked the Commissioner.

"The consignment came from Kuwait according to its end-user certificate," replied Gerald. "The container carried an assortment of industrial metal pipes destined for an oil exploration company in Jakarta, Indonesia. The documents, if they are to be believed, indicate that the container came from one of the most reputable oil-drilling outfits in that Gulf state.

"With the exception of the polonium container, the rest of the shipment seems to be bona fide equipment for oil exploration. The other metal pipes and assorted equipment have no dual usage so they can be ruled out as possible bomb components.

"We have alerted the US State Department and they are checking out the Kuwaiti company. We may have to wait a while for the interim results of their investigation but so far the company doesn't appear to have any known terrorist links. Likewise, the Indonesian authorities are checking out the receiving company on their end and we hope to hear from them in a day or two."

"So Gerald, are you working under the presumption that this container and its contents were only on transit here?" asked Associate Professor Viviane Then, Head of the Department of Epidemiology at the Singapore General Hospital.

"Well the shipping documents would tend to indicate that. The container was off-loaded here from the *Ovation Maria II* at 6:47am and it was due to be transferred to another ship bound for Jakarta tomorrow at 6.35pm. Since the container was kept here in a very secure transit area at Keppel ..."

"Hmm I just don't buy it," interrupted Viviane. "I mean come on, think about it. Polonium is not only highly radioactive but it's also very rare stuff. If it's indeed a terrorist group behind this, they are well organised and well funded. They would have gone through every detail of this operation weeks if not months in advance. I have a hard time believing that they would take the risk of this

8

shipment being interdicted here. They would have done their homework and know that we have advanced radiation detection equipment here. Jakarta doesn't have anything close to our capabilities in their ports. If Indonesia was the final destination, why not ship it directly there rather than let that container sit on its ass here for 36 hours?"

"I tend to agree with Viviane," said the Commissioner. "We should not … we cannot afford to exclude the worst case scenario that this polonium disc was meant to be received by a contact in Singapore for a bomb that is being assembled here."

"Commissioner, I certainly have not excluded that possibility. All possible scenarios are still on the table and until we know more, nothing is going to be excluded."

"Alright good, and now what are the follow-ups?"

Continued Gerald: "My guys are still at the shipyard interviewing the vessel's captain and crew. This disc is just one small but critical part in assembling a nuclear weapon. We are checking all containers here from Kuwait and from other countries in the region for other possible bomb components. The most essential and dangerous will be the fissionable payload – that's probably either Uranium 235 or Plutonium 239.

"As you can appreciate, we have thousands of containers both in transit within our port and those which end their journeys here. And to top it off, we also have dozens of container ships and other cargo vessels anchored just off-shore stopping for refuelling or resupply. I've got teams with mobile radiation detectors checking these as well."

"Sounds like this is pretty much a hit or miss affair," chipped in Brent.

"Well," continued Gerald, "we are doing what we can but this is like looking for a needle in a giant floating haystack. We can put more men on the job but I'm also concerned about affecting the operations of the port. Any delays in moving these containers could cost Singapore thousands of dollars if not more. But costs aside, we also have the equally dangerous issue of leaks. As far as possible, we are trying not to tip our hand – the longer the culprits are in the dark that we have interdicted this shipment, the greater our chances of getting them. Also we need to keep this operation out of the press at all costs. All our officers will be wearing overalls of the Port Authority and we are using unmarked police and military vehicles at the scene."

"Yes, keeping a lid on this is critical. We need to contain word of this discovery right from the very start. We certainly don't need public panic to add to our list of the urgent things that we need to see to at this time," said the Commissioner.

Gerald continued: "As part of this operation which is codenamed Archangel, we are also looking into who had access to this container on shore. This is working on the premise that the terror group responsible intended to smuggle out the polonium from the port while that container was in transit.

"If this is indeed the case, then it is reasonable to assume that the culprits would soon be aware, if they aren't already, that their container has been intercepted. This raises two possible reactions – they may have a Plan B which is to bring in a replacement trigger or they may cut their losses – just panic and run. Either way, all entry and exit points are on high alert for both the replacement disc as well as the people behind it."

"Since the polonium required is so small and mobile, what are the chances that a replacement disc may simply be carried on a person?" asked Brent.

"That's always a possibility, but without proper protection against the polonium, he'll be dead in a week from radiation poisoning. Still, as a suicide courier, well we can't rule out that possibility. Our intelligence people are also monitoring the 'airwaves' – emails, text messages, mobile phone calls – for any suspicious chatter. And as I mentioned earlier we are also pressing the Americans, Kuwaitis and Indonesians for updates on their respective investigations."

"Brent, your team is working on the polonium angle, what have you got?" asked the Commissioner.

"Our Defence Science people are trying to narrow down its area of origin. The metal itself in its natural state does vary slightly from region to region but it's a long shot because it has been so well refined but we are still trying. I'm also in touch with the US State Department. Unfortunately we need to go through them to get to the National Security Agency guys who may know more. It's just bloody politics and lots of red tape. We will also be tapping, very quietly, other intelligence leads both here and abroad to see if anything turns up."

"What do we know of known terror groups who may want to get their hands on a nuclear weapon?"

"Well Commissioner," continued Brent, "there are over 200 identified terrorist outfits worldwide and more than 30 have publicly expressed interest in some form of WMDs – nukes included. Al-Qaeda is the most obvious one and then closer to home, we have our very own Jemaah Islamiyah."

Turning to Gerald, the Commissioner said: "What about Mas Selamat? Might he know something about this?"

"Our Internal Security guys are sitting on him now," replied Gerald. "But as you know, he's as hardcore as they come. We are turning up the pressure on him and on all known associates in custody, but he's been locked up for some time now so he may be out of the loop on this one."

Mas Selamat, now in his fifties, is Singapore's most dangerous terrorist. He was part of the Jemaah Islamiyah (JI) terror network which had planned a series of attacks on embassies and other targets both civilian and military in Singapore in 2001. The plot was uncovered in December that year and some 15 suspects were arrested in Singapore within a month.

The Indonesian-born Singaporean fled the country in the wake of the government crackdown but was arrested in January 2006 by Indonesian authorities and deported back to the island state. He was suspected of plotting to damage Singapore's Changi Airport in 2002 by crashing a civilian airplane into it.

In 2008, barely two years after his arrest, he escaped from police custody by climbing out of an unsecured toilet window at a detention centre in Singapore. This severely dented the country's tough security reputation and initiated the largest manhunt in the nation's history. After staying with relatives for a few days, he fled to the neighbouring state of Johore in Malaysia. There he was able to remain undetected for about a year before he was arrested by Malaysian authorities and eventually extradited to Singapore.

"What about his visitors?" asked Viviane. "Has he had any?"

"Very few," said Gerald. "Visitors are restricted to his immediate family and a few religious teachers as part of his rehabilitation process. The teachers have been thoroughly screened. Still, we are now reviewing all the transcripts of these meetings just in case there may have been some coded communications that we missed earlier. And until we know more, I have ordered a halt to all external visits to Mas Selamat and his associates in custody. Each one is now in an isolation cell and they will remain there until we know more."

"Has he been cooperative all this while?" she asked.

"Mas Selamat comes off pretending to be all meek and humble but he's well trained in defeating most interrogation techniques. After all these years of frequent questioning, he is still proclaiming his complete innocence," said Gerald.

"Okay Gerald, keep at it and let's turn the pressure up on

this guy. Get our Internal Security interrogators to do whatever it takes to break him down. The stakes now are just too high. Brent, back to this issue about these terror organisations, can the Americans give us any indication if any groups are known to have WMDs or are in the process of acquiring one?"

"Our defence attaché in Washington is talking to their State Department people and I've been on the line, unofficially, with a contact from their NSA. So far we've been getting the standard official line that no groups are known to have or are close to getting their hands on a nuke or its main components. But it's early days yet. I'm pretty sure they will be more forthcoming over the next couple of days. This case is bound to ruffle some feathers in Washington especially with their elections around the corner. We know that their State Department is on the alert so we'll probably hear more soon. They have as much to lose as we have."

"Quite right," said the Commissioner. "What about the trigger itself? Can the amount of polonium recovered give us any indication of the possible weapon's yield?"

"My guys say that's a tough call," said Brent. "There is no direct correlation between the amount of polonium seized and the size of the blast it could initiate. That would depend largely on the quantity and quality of the fissionable payload used, how well the weapon was designed and how it would be deployed – be it an air-burst, surface or sub-ground detonation.

"The blast could range anywhere from a small dirty bomb with minimal explosive force and radiation, to a crude atomic weapon, to a full military-grade thermonuclear device with a killing power … maybe up to 20 times that of Hiroshima if not more."

"But would a terrorist group have the technology to put together something as complicated as an atomic or a nuclear weapon?" asked Viviane.

"Modern thermonuclear weapons," replied Brent, "are obviously a lot more intricate in their missile design, tracking and telemetry systems and associated fail-safe components. However you can certainly download detailed plans from the Internet for a basic atomic device of a World War II design. It would be extremely rudimentary by today's military standards but it could still work. The tricky part is not the technology or even the building of the bomb itself but rather it's getting your hands on enough fissionable materials for the trigger and the nuclear payload."

"How much would it have to be – the nuclear fuel that is?" asked the Commissioner.

"It wouldn't take much to fuel a small bomb – probably anywhere between seven and 20 kilogrammes. Uranium or plutonium are both very heavy metals so we are talking about a relatively small package – perhaps the size of say, a small melon and that's something that can be smuggled in quite easily," said Brent.

"I take it that interdicting this core shipment is at the top of our priority list assuming that it hasn't already been smuggled in," said the Commissioner.

"Yes sir, at the very top of our list. All entry points have been placed on high alert."

"Alright, keep at it. Viviane, what about you, what have you got?" said the Commissioner.

"Well all this is a bit away from my area of expertise but from the environmental healthcare front, we have teams stationed in and around the port and at other strategic points across the country taking air readings for ambient radiation. But we are critically short of these mobile detectors. Through the Ministry of Foreign Affairs, we have asked the Americans and they have agreed to loan us some units ASAP. Hospitals have also been placed on alert for anyone displaying symptoms of radiation poisoning.

"I fear, given the huge manpower we are devoting to Archangel and the fact that much of this work is being done in public, it's only a matter of time before something leaks. And yes, just to be on the safe side, it may be a bit premature but I'm also dusting off our medical contingency plans for a nuke … event – just in case," concluded Viviane.

"Good and I expect our military, police and civil defence contingency plans to be re-evaluated as well in the light of this morning's development. We need to keep these emergency procedures current and flexible. As for leaks, well, we'll tackle that if, or more likely, when it happens. As of today I'm activating Operation Thunder. Gerald you have the lead as usual, Viviane and Brent will both assist you. We don't have much to go on yet so work your teams hard and let's meet up at 4.30pm for an update."

Operation Thunder is the codename for the Singapore Government's emergency crisis plans. Painstakingly developed over years, it details reactions to a variety of possible scenarios from mass casualty accidents, to terrorist attacks to full-scale offensive military engagements.

Before he ended the meeting, the young Commissioner had these final words for his team leaders: "I want all of you guys and your respective teams to stop thinking about this as just another case to be cracked and the culprits to be caught. If we do have the makings of a rogue nuclear weapon out there – and we can't exclude this possibility – that means we are all on a war footing. Let's be careful, let's be thorough but for God's sake, let's be quick."

2

ANG MO KIO INDUSTRIAL PARK, SINGAPORE –
OCTOBER 25, 1037 HOURS

Being quick was not a virtue for Saif al-Adel. In his world
as a professional engineer and more recently, as a self-
taught bomb-maker, being careful was much more
important. There was simply no room for mistakes here
and Saif was not a man to make one, especially not now –
not when the stakes were this high.

The office that Saif had been given was a second-storey
unit in the middle of the Ang Mo Kio Industrial Park. This
small commercial hub was made up of six two-storey
buildings and it was home to numerous car workshops,
electrical component firms, automotive spare parts dealers
and a mix of other small businesses. A mere 20-minute
drive from the city centre, this enclave was a hive of
activity throughout the day and occasionally into the
evenings.

On the ground floor directly below Saif's office, was *Hoi
Kee Car and Accessories* – a non-descript automobile repair
garage. It was owned by Halim bin Kader, a Singaporean

Malay and a sleeper member of the local branch of Jemaah Islamiyah. Although he had been a member of the group for more than three years, his only involvement had been in attending a few religious talks.

But all that changed about eight months ago when he was given his first assignment. He had been instructed to set up a front car repair business. The money was provided and the necessary equipment was brought in. A Chinese name had been chosen deliberately for the garage to blend in with its surroundings where most of the businesses were run by the local Chinese community. Halim made sure only reliable Chinese mechanics were hired. Beyond this his job was to ensure that the car repair business kept up a busy appearance and that no one – save for a select few people that JI would send down – entered the office on the second floor.

Since the workshop started operations six months ago Halim was hardly ever there but the business had been surprisingly good. With astronomical prices of new cars in Singapore, many locals were turning to the second-hand car market and this meant fixing up some of these older vehicles.

The spacious second floor office remained largely bare with the exception of some cheap office furniture, an old sofa and a brand new laptop. Halim knew not what work would be done in this office. It was not his job to know these things and he was only too happy to remain oblivious and just do his part for the cause.

Despite the air-conditioner running at full blast in his office, Saif could still feel the heat seeping in from the outside. This heat was different from the dry desert temperatures of the Middle East that he had been used to. Here it was not just the hot weather that made it unbearable but also the high oppressive humidity that sapped his strength.

Walking to the window, he looked out into the street below and watched in fascination as people went about their lives totally oblivious to the struggles of his world. There was a small coffee shop just across the street from his office. At any time of the day, the placed seemed crowded. Singaporeans were clearly fascinated by food. He was constantly surprised to see so many overweight people here, a sharp contrast from many of the cities in the Middle East where he had lived most of his life. The trappings of such indulgence were a clear sign that this was a country which had known peace for much too long.

Taking the train to work in the morning, he had observed many of the country's young conscripted soldiers presumably travelling to their camps. Plugged into their expensive smart phones, they seemed too comfortable and content, lacking that aura of hardened warriors. But maybe all this would soon change he thought.

As an Egyptian, Saif held nothing against Singapore or its people. But in supporting the infidel Americans, by sending her support troops to the Middle East to help the Americans suppress the struggles of his brothers, the Singapore government had written its own fate. In helping to callously spill blood in the Middle East, much more blood would soon be shed here.

In his office window, Saif could see his reflection. He looked so much older now with his greying temples and the fine wrinkles around his eyes. The stress over the years had certainly exacted their toll on him.

Abruptly he snapped out of his wandering thoughts, realising that it was time to get back to work. Slowly he walked back to his desk and sat down. As he had only arrived here a week ago, his desk was still relatively clear of clutter. Besides the laptop, a telephone which he never used and some miscellaneous stationary, the only other thing on the desk was a photograph in a simple white frame. He had left it there several days earlier, lying face down. It still hurt to look at it but today he felt he had to.

Slowly he placed the cheap plastic frame upright and the two familiar faces smiled back at him. They were both so young, so innocent and so dead.

October 23 1983 – he would never forget that day when he died inside. He had been working in Lebanon as a young engineer. Two truck bombs exploded earlier that day at the American barracks and what followed was a series of random shootings in the streets of Beirut. His wife who was accompanying his daughter back from school, was cut down in the crossfire as they walked along a small street just minutes from their apartment.

He had found them some 20 minutes later, lying on the pavement where they had fallen. They had simply been left there like a mistake that could not be undone and so they were ignored by the people walking by. Saif did not know who was responsible for the shooting and that mattered little now. His wife was already dead. Her body was cold, lifeless and drained of colour. Shielded by her mother, his daughter was severely injured but still alive. Bleeding from a wound in her stomach, she had somehow clung on to life. In what must have been pain beyond all description, the little child's eyes were wide open looking at her father as he lifted her small limp frame from the stained concrete pavement.

He carried her and ran to a US Aid Station close to the bombed barracks. The doctors there were busy caring for their own soldiers injured in the suicide attack hours before. They only took a cursory look at the four year old and told Saif that there was nothing they could do – she was in shock, she had lost too much blood and was already too far gone. Still he pleaded with them to try – he begged them on his knees to try anything they could but they told him he would have to wait. The doctors were just too busy.

Staring into her unblinking eyes, he felt more helpless than he had ever been in his entire life. He watched her eyes as life slowly drained away leaving behind only a vacant, accusing stare.

Four hours later Saif buried his family in a small grave,

their bodies lying side by side. The preacher from a mosque nearby hurried through the prayers. It was getting dark and it would be dangerous to be out in the open at night. Everyone had expected that American soldiers would soon be out to vent their anger over the suicide attacks that morning which killed almost 300 US and French servicemen.

But Saif was not afraid. His new hatred for the Americans had engulfed his very being. He would never forget nor forgive the Americans. For all their power and technology, they had refused to help him – they had simply turned away a child, a dying child – his child. Ten minutes after he had laid his family to rest and buried his past along with them, Saif, his clothes still covered with their blood, followed the preacher back to the mosque a short distance away. There he offered his services to fight the Americans. He was already a dead man, one who had nothing else to lose.

And so today sitting alone in his office half a world away, he looked at the photograph again. He thought he would be consumed by grief but in reality, he felt nothing more than guilt. He had failed them and cold, blind revenge was all he had left.

Already most of the components he would need had been delivered to his office and awaited his expert assembly. Sitting at his desk, he read the email yet again.

Greetings Bro,

Things have been busy on our end and arrangements for the wedding are in full swing. The invitations have yet to go out. John is still trying to confirm who from his side can attend. Gramps is sour-faced as usual. Walks around looking like he just swallowed an unripe grapefruit! Guess he'll only be happy when all the family has arrived home and everyone is OK.

John finally managed to get a replacement of his suit – the right colour this time. LOL. We are still trying to decide what music to play. We have a bunch already burned on a compact disc. Any suggestions? Jill should be on her way too. Gloria and her husband are away for their anniversary.

Okay I better run. Lots of stuff to get out of the way. See you soon.

Andy

On the surface, the message looked benign enough until he applied the decoding formula. This was simple yet ingenious. Saif had been given an envelope containing 31 code keys each consisting of a set of random numbers – one key for every day of the month. As the message had been sent on the 25th, he looked at the corresponding numbers in the 25th key. It read: 29, 50, 61, 66, 73, 102, 108, 119, 133, 147, 182, 201 … and the numbers went on.

Carefully he began counting and soon the decoding was done. He looked at the words that he had highlighted:

confirm grapefruit arrived ok
replacement disc on the way

Yes the grapefruit had indeed arrived safely in its protective steel casing – all 11.3 kilograms of highly enriched plutonium. Smuggling the core into Singapore had always been his biggest worry – probably the most risky part of the whole operation.

Just how it was brought into the country, he himself was not sure. It was after all, not his job to know these things. Two men delivered it a day earlier and there it sat quietly in a corner of his office hidden behind some empty boxes. He had resisted the temptation to open the protective steel casing to see the prize for himself but now was not the time for that. The time for assembly would come soon enough once all the pieces were in place.

The discovery of the polonium by Singapore police two days earlier was a setback but just a temporary one. This email confirmed that a replacement was already on its way and all he had to do now was to wait.

He began composing his reply. It would essentially contain just one word to let them know that all was going to plan.

Hey Andy,

Great to hear from you again. Happy to know that the wedding arrangements are on schedule. Yeah things have been busy on this end too. So have you confirmed the date for the wedding? Do let me know yes so I can book my flight.

Cheers

John

Pleased with himself that he was able to draft his reply in record time, he counted the words yet again. The 29th one was the only word that mattered. CONFIRMED – yes, the 'grapefruit' was in his hands and all was well.

3

PRESIDENT'S DAILY BRIEFING, THE WHITE HOUSE, WASHINGTON D.C. – OCTOBER 25, 0932 HOURS

Outgoing US President Theodore Monroe adjusted his reading glasses once again before he scanned the next document in his leather-bound folder.

"Yes James … please continue."

"Mr President, it would appear that the polonium while interdicted in Singapore, was destined for a terror cell in Indonesia. Over the past three months we have detected increased chatter over the Internet and in intercepted cell calls. There are indications that a terror group is planning a major strike, possibly directed at US or other Western interest in the country."

"Is this al-Qaeda again?"

James Carron, the director of the National Security Agency (NSA) cleared his throat discreetly before continuing: "Sir that's a possibility, but it could also very well be any number of associated terror outfits operating in and around Indonesia.

"Following the killing of Osama bin Laden in May 2011, al-Qaeda has been without a figurehead leader to rein in its different factions. Each group seems to have its own pet cause and geographic area of interest. The global network is still there – crude and fragmented for sure, but alive. Just who is actually pulling the strings at this point in time is anyone's guess."

"What about this Hassan guy? He's been in the papers quite a bit pontificating about the plight of the Palestinians. Is there any connection? What do we know of him?"

"Mr President, Hassan Ahmad Khan is an astute businessman of Iranian descent. He was born and raised in Bandar-e Abbas – a small fishing community bordering the Persian Gulf. His father was said to be a poor fisherman but not much else is known of his family background or his early years.

"It was only in recent months that he has gained greater prominence. He seems to have his fingers in a number of industries especially the oil trade where he allegedly made his fortune. He appears to be well educated, charismatic and politically-attuned in galvanising local support for the so-called Third Palestinian Intifada which seeks an all-out Arab uprising against Israel. The guy operates out of Saudi Arabia and is quite a media whore, frequently making political statements but his political connections are unclear. He's got a well-oiled PR machine to back him up and he certainly knows the power of the media and uses it well. And he's also well-versed in using social media to reach out to the masses – not just to his followers, but his YouTube broadcasts and blogs appear to be directed at the English-speaking world at large."

"And what's his message?"

"His verbal attacks seem to be aimed at Israel alone and not us, at least not directly. Regarding the US, he talks incessantly about increasing economic cooperation to raise the quality of life for the Palestinians."

"Hmmm, is he going to be a problem?"

"That seems unlikely Mr President. Our analysts feel that while he plays up the Palestinian card to garner local support, he's still a businessman at heart, driven by money."

"His speeches aside, have we got anything else that might link him to this possible rouge nuke in Asia?"

"There doesn't seem to be any obvious connection between him and the situation in South East Asia," replied Carron.

"If I may sir," said William Baldwin, director of the Central Intelligence Agency (CIA), "we have intercepted a few cell calls allegedly from al-Qaeda operatives in Asia. They mentioned something called the *Saif al-Haidar* which roughly translated means Sword of the Lion. As far as we can tell, this sword may refer to some kind of weapon, possibly even a WMD. But there was nothing specific in the intercepts linking this to a weapon or even to Indonesia. We are still working on it.

"While this *Saif al-Haidar* may possibly be a codename for a weapon of sorts – it could be nuclear or another type of WMD or it could just be nothing more than another rallying cry for their Third Intifada."

"Yes, yes, Bill, all this seems to be a lot of speculation and guesswork. What facts do we have?" said the President with more than a touch of derision.

Director Baldwin shifted uncomfortably in his seat yet again. "Sir the intercepts only offer very fragmented pieces of information, disjointed scraps really and much of it is still coded. We are working on it as best we can, as fast as we can."

"Let's leave this for now. Back to this nuke trigger, what else have we got?"

"It's still early days into the investigation but we are not totally convinced that it is a nuke trigger to start off with," said NSA's James Carron. "It could just be another red herring to make us think that they are further along in their development and deployment of a nuke, assuming they even have the makings of one to start off with.

"Mr President you would recall back in 1990 we foiled an attempt to smuggle American-made krytron nuclear triggers to Iraq. That formed the basis of public opinion that Iraq was on the verge of attaining a nuclear weapon just months before the start of Desert Storm. The fact was that Saddam Hussein's nuclear programme was barely in its infancy. The terrorists in this case could be using the same tactic – trying to scare us into thinking that they are assembling a bomb that in fact does not exist."

"It wasn't public opinion! It was the Bush Administration just groping for another reason to go to war with Iraq. Anyway, does CIA concur that this is another deception ploy?"

"Well Mr President, it is difficult to give a definitive assessment at this point in time. Our best intel would indicate that neither al-Qaeda nor any terrorist faction is anywhere close to assembling a nuke of their own or acquiring one from an ex-Soviet republic or Pakistan or even North Korea," said Baldwin.

"Our intel from the computer documents seized during *Neptune Spear* tends to indicate that al-Qaeda was interested in acquiring fissionable materials from Pakistan. They had attempted to infiltrate some elements within Pakistan's Inter-Services Intelligence, the ISI, and its military for years.

"It appears that al-Qaeda operatives also downloaded from the Internet massive volumes of research materials and weapon design plans of 'Fat Man', the second atomic bomb that wiped out Nagasaki. By today's military standards, that's a pretty crude bomb but well within the capabilities of a modern terror group provided of course that they can get their hands on enough fissionable materials. So we know that they are interested – keen even, but there is nothing to suggest that this plan to get their hands on a nuke has advanced beyond Stage One of the drawing board."

Operation Neptune Spear was the codename of the military operation which terminated Osama bin Laden in Pakistan on May 2, 2011. Navy SEALs of the United States Naval

Special Warfare Development Group which conducted the pre-dawn raid on the terror leader's compound in Abbottabad, Pakistan, found more than 6,000 computer files on five computers, dozens of hard drives and more than 100 external data storage devices in bin Laden's hideaway.

"But what can they hope to gain by pretending to have a nuke or the makings of one?" asked the President.

"Sir, touting a nuke in hand," said Baldwin, "would give any organisation some measure of respect from its own people and rival groups as well. In al-Qaeda's case, a faction with a nuke could easily assume control of this still headless network. Even the suspicion of a nuke has its own benefits as it would make us a little more cautious in hitting any of their bases. Besides, even if it's a bluff, it will take our intelligence people a lot of time and resources to confirm it one way or the other."

"Yes and our intel has been faulty many a time …" said the President without even looking at his CIA director. "Alright gentlemen, the stakes are just too high for us to sweep this one under the rug and hope it comes to naught. We have to assume that the possibility exists that a terrorist organisation is putting together the bomb. Who or what are the likely targets? Are they going to hit Singapore? It's a small country but we have a lot invested in it. If it gets vaporised we lose a strong ally and the political and military fallout will bite us all."

"Sir assuming someone is in fact putting together a nuclear weapon, the most likely target would still be Indonesia rather than Singapore – that's where the container was heading to according to all the documents seized by authorities in Singapore," said Baldwin.

"Indonesian terror cells especially the JI – Jemaah Islamiyah are active. They bombed Bali in 2002 and two hotels in Jakarta in 2009 so they have proven their ability to organise on home soil at least, large-scale attacks and coordinated ones at that.

"The organisation has yet to demonstrate its ability to pull off a complicated kill ops outside of the country. Besides, Indonesia has a huge Muslim population – the largest in the world, so religious radicals can count on some measure of local support. And it's a big rural country – impenetrable jungle with lots of places to hide. Their police and military … well let's say it appears that they can be compliant for a price.

"Singapore on the other hand, would be a lot harder to hit. It's a tiny speck of an island nation run by super boy scouts – all clean, efficient and no-nonsense. Those guys are fanatical about security and their intelligence people – very much just like our Israeli friends – are up to scratch. The chances of such a plot being discovered in Singapore where such a group would lack home-ground advantage are much, much higher. The fact that the Singapore police could find such a small amount of polonium hidden in a container at one of the world's busiest ports – shows just how serious and capable they are."

"Yes but Singapore," countered Secretary of Defence Jeffrey Brown, "would be a better high-value target – it certainly has a higher global profile than Indonesia.

"Singapore is Asia's financial hub – hit the banking infrastructure and the computer records of daily transactions worth billions of dollars could be erased. The country also has close ties with the West with lots of foreigners working there, not to mention the presence of tourists in their thousands. There was a JI plan a few years back to bomb simultaneously half a dozen western embassies over there. Singapore is a small but juicy target Mr President.

"With bin Laden out of the picture, JI could be coming of age on its own. It may want to move away from hitting small soft local targets like pubs or hotel lounges to something more substantial and Singapore, I fear, could be very much in the cross-hairs. To put it bluntly Mr President, Singapore would be a perfect target for a terrorist nuclear strike."

"Mr President, with all due respect to Secretary Brown, NSA tends to disagree," countered Director Carron. "We have known for a few months now that JI is planning something big targeting Jakarta. This could be it. We have our people on the ground and we have detected increased chatter over the Internet and in intercepted cell calls that plans are underway for a major strike possibly directed at Jakarta's international airport or perhaps against US or other Western interests in the country. To date we can't nail down any details but we are still working on it. So we can't discount Indonesia, Jakarta specifically, as their prime target."

The President thought for several seconds before continuing: "Until we get a better picture of what's going on, we have to keep all options open. Work closely with the Indonesian authorities – let's press them hard and get some answers. Ditto our checks in Kuwait and the region regarding this possible nuclear trigger. I need good intelligence not speculation from both NSA and CIA as well as State and the DOD. I want all of you guys to work together and with Homeland Security. If I find anyone holding out for a shot at personal glory or inter-department one-upmanship or a place in the next administration, I'll personally ensure that he lives to regret it. I don't want the mistakes of 9-11 to be repeated here and now – not while I still occupy this seat. Clear?"

The room became instantly silent.

"State … do you have anything to add?"

"We've been in close contact with the Singapore authorities," said Secretary of State Kelly Yee. "They have asked for our help in checking out the Kuwaiti connection. State is coordinating the probe with input from our agencies. Singapore has also requested for mobile radiation detection equipment. Seems they need a lot more than what they have …,"

"Give them whatever they need. Singapore hasn't asked for any favours and they are a strong ally so get it to them quick," ordered President Monroe.

"The Air Force is flying them out as we speak," replied Secretary Yee.

"Good – anything else?"

"That's about it for now Mr President."

"Remember people," stressed Monroe, "this one has priority. I have a bad feeling about it. There are far too many unknowns and the timing, with our elections just round the corner, it's too much of a coincidence. Let's work fast and get some answers quick. This office cannot and will not make decisions of such magnitude based on Ivy-League academic opinions, conference room deductions, and hairs-standing-on-the-back-of-your-neck guesswork! I need solid, actionable intel from grunts down in the field on who's behind this, the target, the plan and the timeline. The candle is burning in the wind people so kick some asses and let's get a move on. Am I clear?" said Monroe as he surveyed the room.

"Okay now let's return to this morning's agenda and the situation in Iran. Bill, what have you got?"

4

Riyadh, Saudi Arabia – October 31, 1043 hours

The killing of Osama bin Laden in 2011 was really a blessing in disguise not just for the Americans but also for the enemy they had hoped to decapitate.

In the grand scheme of things, bin Laden had simply outlived his usefulness and his continued presence was more of a stumbling block for the organisation – a liability that the Americans were only too happy to take care of. It only took one carefully engineered leak to tip off the eager Americans and the rest as they say, is history.

In truth, bin Laden had very little to do with the actual attacks on 9-11. He was a convenient scapegoat for some rogue elements within Corporate America and some others to launch another money-making conflict following the end of the very lucrative Cold War. For the Arabs, bin Laden became a unifying symbol of their political plight. But in reality, he was nothing more than a talking head, full of schemes and plans but directed by seven powerful men who made the real decisions behind the scenes. Now it was time for others to step forward but before that, bin

Laden needed to be removed. He had served his purpose but had far exceeded his shelf-life.

The tide had indeed changed and bin Laden – an old man hiding and hunted with no real plan of moving forward, was not the leader these times now called for. Still his betrayal to the Americans and his ultimate demise had worked in their favour, helping to fuel the widespread Arab resentment against a dominant and belligerent adversary.

Despite being a successful businessman, Hassan hated working in the confines of an office. He conducted most of his business meetings and deals from the sprawling grounds of his villa on the outskirts of Riyadh with its manicured gardens, Italian fountains and relaxing Koi ponds. Here he could think better and plan – for planning was what he was best at.

His business was oil and money. Terrorism and the growing wave of religious extremism sweeping the region were getting to be too much of a distraction and this was hurting the economy of the entire region. The American withdrawal from Afghanistan and Iraq helped little in bringing stability to the region. The terrorist network as it stood in a post-bin Laden world was still much too fragmented and insular to move forward with any sense of purpose or mission. These people needed a masterplan and a leader around whom they could rally. Hassan knew just the right man for the job.

He understood better than most that terrorism and religious fundamentalism, while blunt motivational weapons, still had their distinct advantages in advancing a business objective but only if they were used effectively to sway hearts over minds. And for this to work, timing was everything.

The oil reserves of the region were bleaker than most people realised. The flowing crude would be gone is less than 20 years. Action had to be taken now to protect the fortunes of the few families who controlled the oil. Waiting for the day the wells were reduced to a trickle would be much too late. By then, the region and all the oil wealth that went with it would be doomed. The key to survival lay in fighting the Americans and the American dollar which controlled the world economy. Hassan knew he needed to act now, quickly, before it was too late.

There was much work still to be done and the time to set the plan in motion was fast approaching. The groundwork had been laid well over the years since September 11. All the elements had been drawn together and each piece had fallen into its appointed place.

He knew his role too would change from a lonely voice crying out in the wilderness for Arab unity to becoming a bridge which would herald a new world order.

The invasion of Afghanistan and the driving out of the Taliban incensed his Arab brothers who saw this as yet another example of US subjugation – of one wrong being replaced by another. The American-installed democracy in the country was a farce for the people of Afghanistan as it offered neither the peace nor prosperity promised by the armed invaders. The Americans had miscalculated once again. Beyond putting bread on the table and giving peasants the right to vote in highly-skewed elections, what the people really wanted was respect and pride for their faith and way of life – all of which had been stripped from them in generations past. This was all they truly craved for – this and to be left alone.

But the seeds of insurrection had been planted in the region a long time ago. And it was this unquenchable yearning among his Arab brothers for respect and pride that triggered the latest wave of uprising which became known as the Arab Spring.

It began on Saturday, 18 December 2010 in Tunisia with the self-immolation of Mohamed Bouazizi in protest of police corruption and ill treatment. This single act triggered an unstoppable wave of unrest spreading to Algeria, Jordan, Egypt, and Yemen, Libya, Syria, Saudi Arabia and most recently to Iran. Almost all of North Africa and the Middle East – save Israel, were engulfed in this new political and spiritual awakening. But even Israel would wear her deserving crown of thorns soon enough thought Hassan.

He turned away from his television screen which had been a running series of movies to celebrate Halloween. It was now time for more serious stuff. Yusman should be arriving any minute now and today he had to ensure that his faithful but misguided friend was ready. The time of his betrayal was close at hand.

Yusman bin Iranto rose quickly when Hassan entered the room. Grasping the elder man's hand, Yusman bowed down low to kiss it in a humble and age-old sign of complete submission.

Hassan had hand-picked him for his current role and Yusman had proven himself to be as dedicated a soldier and a servant as they come.

Born into a wealthy family that made its fortune in the oil palm business in Indonesia, he was schooled in the best institutions in Jakarta before he attended the Universitas Syiah Kuala in Banda Aceh where he read engineering.

It was there that he was caught up in the religious fervour which was sweeping the country. He soon joined a small radical splinter group dedicated to the eradication of Christians from the country. His family's wealth and his agile intellect soon caught the attention of Jemaah Islamiyah – the largest terrorist grouping in South East Asia.

JI was formed with a jihadist vision of establishing, through armed revolt and subversion, an Islamist state in the region encompassing Brunei, Indonesia, Malaysia, Singapore, the southern Philippines and southern Thailand. It would be the second pillar of Islam – second only to the Islamic Caliphate al-Qaeda was seeking to establish in the Middle East.

Yusman had worked hard over the years rising through the organisation's loose and convoluted hierarchy to emerge over the past year as the undisputed head of the organisation.

At that time, he did not know that he had been singled out and groomed by Hassan for the most important mission of his young life. It had taken much time but Hassan, working through a number of intermediaries including some well-known clerics, had simply exploited Yusman's complete and blind devotion to his faith.

In a series of carefully orchestrated meetings in Indonesia by local religious leaders, Yusman was told that Hassan had been quietly financing a number of terrorist groups to hit back at his eternal nemesis – the United States and plans were underway for a major strike which would simply change the rules of the game.

This was only the second time that he had met Hassan in person although they had communicated often through a series of coded letters and emails, all of which he destroyed promptly as instructed.

"Sit," said Hassan, "we have much to discuss and very little time. So tell me of your progress."

"It is all ready. The carriers have been identified. The documents will be in place to ensure that all seven vehicles leave at the appointed time. The routes each will follow to their targets have been mapped out and I have personally done a few trial runs to get the timing perfect. The strike has been calibrated for Jakarta's rush hour traffic. The drivers will soon know their individual targets when you give the order. Everything is ready – set to go on your instructions."

"And what of the second parcel?"

"Almost all the components are in. Saif will be arriving in Jakarta soon to put it all together once he has finished his business in Singapore."

"Good, good. And your people … what do they know?"

"I have told them only what they need to know for now. They are as devoted to our sacred cause as I am and each is eager to do his part. Everything has been coordinated. They will be told their destinations only closer to the date. There will be no leaks, no mistakes."

JI had time and again proved its mastery of striking its targets with unwavering resolve and cruel lethality. In October 2002, it orchestrated a triple bombing in Bali which killed over 200 people. Barely a year later in August 2003, it carried out a suicide bombing at the J.W. Marriott Hotel in Jakarta. And in September the following year, it struck the Australian Embassy killing 10 and wounding hundreds. Yusman had been involved in the planning of all three hits and now he was ready for his swansong.

"Yes," said Hassan, "they will not have long to wait. Are you sure your holy warriors are committed enough … ready to die if necessary?"

"They all firmly believe in our cause and will gratefully die for our faith if needed. Each is ready to strike the infidels and enter paradise."

"And you my friend? You do realise that this will be the beginning of the end … for you and for JI. There can be no turning back once the wheels are set in motion. The Americans will hunt you down and with my help, they will get you eventually. There is … there can be, no other way."

Yusman nodded, his eyes downcast. He had long accepted his fate. "Yes, and you? Will you be taking over?"

"Oh no, no. JI has run its course. When the Americans strike back, it will be over for JI. As an organisation, it would simply cease to exist. Something much more important will be ready, waiting in the wings to take its place. It will be a very different type of war. The plan calls for many sacrifices and many martyrs but rest assured, through your sacrifice, many of your brothers will live on in a more secure world. This plan, once executed, will change everything."

Hassan paused to let the gravity of the position facing his young friend sink in. "Yusman, I know the price will be high for you and your army but none of you will be forgotten when the dust has settled."

Then returning to the business at hand Hassan continued: "We need to keep up the noise as a distraction for as long as possible."

"We've been doing that for months now, dropping a keyword here and there over certain handphones that we know have been compromised. False rumours have been leaked to the Americans by some people on the fringes. I have sent some of them as part of the recon teams to Jakarta's airport and the fuel dumps there. Others have been on surveillance at the arrival halls and outside the control tower. I've got people trawling the Internet for maps of the airport, the emergency vehicles stationed there, flight schedules, traffic conditions – everything.

"Already there have been whispers among the lower ranks of an imminent attack on the airport. I've let these go … hopefully it will get back to the Americans. We know that for past two weeks now, airport security has been stepped up so someone must be listening."

"Good you have done well. Now, your speech … is that all ready?"

"Yes, I have brought a copy of the video just as you asked."

"Good, let's watch that. Drink up my friend. Celebrate now 'cos you need to return home soon. Your long journey is almost at its end."

5

OFFICE OF THE SECRETARY OF STATE, WASHINGTON
D.C. – OCTOBER 31, 1023 HOURS

Kelly Yee ran over her speech once again. She knew that
this could well be the decider in her race to the White
House. Her nomination as the Democratic Party candidate
six months earlier had not been without numerous
reservations.

The press and many even from within her own ranks
believed that her campaign as it stood had focused far too
heavily on US foreign policy at the expense of local issues
especially on the rebuilding of Corporate America after a
series of crippling economic recessions.

Her Republican rival Senator Harrison Coal, had been
milking his domestic agenda for all it was worth, playing it
up for Middle America which was growing increasingly
disillusioned under the weight of high taxes and
mortgages, unaffordable health care and the weakening of
the US dollar which had been driving up inflation at home.

But Kelly had stuck to her guns firmly believing that the

key to pulling America out from its economic slump lay in a robust foreign policy. America, she had explained many times before, needed to look outwards to solve its domestic woes.

"Why can't they understand that we need to engage the world to build a stronger America," she mused to herself. She had already outlined her plans for a more equitable trade balance with China, advocated tighter monetary controls within the EU, gaining a stronger foothold in the emerging economies of South America and forging closer economic alliances with ASEAN – the Association of South East Asian Nations, a region she believed would dominate world economic growth over the next decade.

One of the sharpest points of contention with her Republican opponent had been on defence costs. She and her current boss President Theodore Monroe had advocated maintaining defence spending at current levels of about US$700 billion a year.

But Coal had proposed a deep 20 percent cut in the defence budget and diverting the money saved to shore up American healthcare and public housing expenditure while reducing taxes on the middle and low income groups. This trendy view appeared to have gone down well with many voters who believed that America cannot and should not continue to play the expensive role of the lone global policeman.

President Monroe's decision to withdraw the remaining US forces from Iraq and Afghanistan a year earlier was well received at home, but many still questioned America's need to spend billions of dollars on maintaining the country's First Strike military options around the world.

Voters were also simply tired of the constant terrorist alerts all of which had in recent years, proven to be false. The killing of al-Qaeda's leader Osama bin Laden in 2011 and the lack of any retaliatory response had some Americans convinced that the sorry chapter of 9-11 can and should be closed once and for all.

"If America only knew about this possible renegade nuke in Asia, maybe they would see things differently," she thought to herself. But the Administration had gone to great lengths to ensure that the press never got wind of it.

It was a popular myth that Washington was unable to keep its secrets. While there were leaks aplenty over the years, the powers that be had jealously guarded its most prized secrets and the surfacing of a nuclear trigger in Asia was kept tightly under wraps.

Finishing up her now cold cup of coffee, Kelly returned to drafting her speech yet again.

6

SINGAPORE – NOVEMBER 2, 1642 HOURS

The white van stopped by the side of Robinson Road in the heart of the country's Central Business District. It was still an hour before the evening rush home but already the traffic was heavy.

In the cargo bay, two men sat hunched over their equipment. Dressed in black military fatigues, they were members of the Nuclear Emergency Support Team (NEST) – a highly secretive unit within the Singapore Armed Forces. Several teams just like this one had been combing the city, street by street, for more than a week now checking the air with their ultra-sensitive detectors, looking for any signs of suspicious ambient radiation.

With the press of a button, one man raised the 'nose' – an innocuous detector shaped like a 30-centimetre-long pipe – from the roof of the van that would sniff the air.

An impeller within the device began spinning, drawing a small amount of air through a special filter. This was then examined by the gamma ray spectrometer which tested the sample for man-made radioactive elements. The automated test was completed in less than two minutes and the flashing green light told the men that this was yet another negative result, just like the hundreds the team had been getting over the past few days.

Ticking off this sector from their checklist, the team moved on to their next location about a thousand metres away and there they would conduct yet another test of the air.

It all seemed so futile but the men knew the importance of this mundane task and it was a race against time. Every green light meant that this part of the city was safe, at least for now.

7

HOTEL DE BILDERBERG, OOSTERBEEK, NETHERLANDS – NOVEMBER 2, 1000 HOURS

Hassan freshened up quickly after his long flight. Stretching out on the sofa in his hotel suite, he was anxious to catch up with the latest news on television about the upcoming US elections in three days time.

Yes the Americans were absorbed with their domestic concerns about taxes, unemployment and soaring healthcare costs. And the common denominator for all was money. That was what it boiled down to. It was the US currency that greased the wheels of international commerce and it was this blind faith in the strength and stability of the mighty US dollar that kept the world as we know it spinning. This was the fatal weakness of the world's financial system and it was this that Hassan intended to exploit.

He had listened intently to the long, meandering speeches made by the two presidential hopefuls – Senator Harrison Coal and Secretary of State Kelly Yee. He paid more intention to Yee's address to the American people, jotting down carefully some of her statements concerning America's foreign policies and her proposals to rejuvenate the ailing US economy. He would use these notes later when the time came.

The pundits were predicting a close fight. Most had tipped Senator Coal to win the White House. His 'America First' policy of shoring up federal aid for the common man resounded well with the wide populace and contrasted sharply with Kelly Yee's tougher focus on strengthening America's economic ties with the world. Yes, it would be a close fight but only on television. The outcome had long been decided.

Checking his watch, he saw that it was time to head for the private conference room he had booked on the second floor of the hotel for his meeting. His special guests should be arriving in a few minutes. They were simply called the Seven Heads for that is what they were – the seven most powerful men in world. Only two were of Middle East origin but that did not matter now even as they were meeting to decide the fate of the Middle East. World conquest was their true objective. These men wielded not political authority nor military might but they possessed something much more commanding – money and influence – and each man had an almost endless supply of both.

This would be the sixth and final meeting that Hassan would have with the Seven Heads before at least part of their plan was announced to the world.

Each man had his fingers in a number of strategic businesses ranging from banking to shipping to manufacturing to the media. But all had made their early fortunes in crude – crude oil that is. They had owned or had been entrusted to manage either directly or by proxy the giant oilfields in Saudi Arabia, Kuwait, Iran, Bahrain, Iraq, Qatar, Oman and the United Arab Emirates.

With these men, Hassan could drop any pretext that his plan would be for the greater good of the world or be helping the Palestinian cause or even be advancing a faith. These were businessmen, pure and simple. None of them were interested in religion – any religion for that matter. If they had any devotion to a singular cause – it would be to the pursuit of money and the unadulterated power and influence that came with it.

Heavy drinking was the usual preamble to their meetings and it was an hour before they got down to business. The bulk of the work – all the planning and coordination, had already been done months before. Each man had in turn recruited several others – all close, trusted associates who would assist in this global operation.

They ranged from influential politicians, senior government economists, heads of regional conglomerates, bankers, media professionals, social media activists and equally important, a significant number of clergymen. It was this second diverse group that would do the bulk of the selling and persuasion when the time came.

8

OUTSKIRTS OF JAKARTA, INDONESIA – NOVEMBER 6, 0410 HOURS

Yusman knew he was early so he waited patiently in his car parked two hundred metres outside the refinery gates in Segarajaya – a province about 13 kilometres northeast of Jakarta. The order had been given and the operation that he had waited all these months for was finally about to get underway.

Soon he spotted the first tanker leaving the complex. The other six, all painted in the company's trademark white and green colours, soon followed along obediently forming a small convoy through the deserted streets.

They turned to the east heading further away from the city. This was their scheduled route which would take them to their original destination in Surabaya, a town about 600 kilometres away. This routine journey made once a fortnight, was expected to take some eight hours because of the country's speed restrictions on such heavy vehicles.

It would give him until noon at the latest to accomplish his task before someone would raise the alarm when the convoy failed to arrive at its destination. But Yusman knew that he would need only about half that time.

After travelling for about 15 minutes, the vehicles each loaded with 34,000 litres of petroleum, turned south and headed to a disused warehouse located on the outskirts of Jakarta.

Steel doors were shut and locked as the last tanker entered the old building. Yusman and his team were already there waiting eagerly as the drivers lined up their vehicles.

The men wasted no time in getting down to business. First the vapour vent cover on top of each tanker was removed. Slowly and with great care, the men using a long PVC pipe began pouring in just over 200 kilogrammes of assorted heavy nails, screws, industrial nuts and steel ball bearings. These had been coated earlier in heavy oil to prevent them from rubbing together causing a spark. Soon they covered the base of each eight-metre tank filled with light petroleum. These metal objects would form the deadly shrapnel for the mobile bombs increasing their anti-personnel lethality.

Next the men tackled the engine compartment placing a small canister filled mainly with potassium chlorate and several other chemicals. A small pull-action primer was inserted to initiate the device which was then encased in insulating foam to prevent overheating from the engine which could cause a premature detonation. The device was fastened to the engine block and a thin wire connected to the primer, was threaded into the driver's cabin. It would take just a simple tug on the wire to active the device. The primer would then spark causing the chemicals inside to burn producing a constant stream of black smoke.

Finally the explosives were put in place. A single kilogram block of RDX, a stable military-grade explosive, was attached to the underside hull of each tanker. Shaped into the letter V with a thick metal underplate, the explosive was then rigged to be detonated remotely using the microwave signal from a handphone. Because of its more complex design, the microwave triggers were built and tested several days earlier. All that the men had to do now was to insert the electric detonator into each explosive block.

The V shape of the charge would direct the force of the explosion upwards towards the body of the tanker blasting it apart and igniting its flammable contents.

The men rigging the vehicles had practiced their jobs well and by 6:50am, all seven tankers were primed and ready. The two explosive experts who had supervised the work, examined each truck one final time making sure all was in order.

Meanwhile Yusman gathered his drivers and their attendants for a final briefing. Each man wore a dark blue company jacket over his civilian shirt and a blue baseball cap pulled low. Yusman went over in detail the plans they had all heard many times before. Using a large map of the city, he pointed out to the drivers the alternate route each team could take to reach its primary target should it become necessary to deviate from the original plan.

Each team also had a secondary target. If the men felt they

could not reach their primary objective in time perhaps because of heavy congestion, the team would then head to their alternate kill zone. Timing he stressed, was everything. They would not have far to travel but each tanker had to be in place at exactly 8:30am.

Traffic on the outskirts of Jakarta was already starting to build up as the morning rush hour approached. Still the men waited patiently. As each team had a different destination, their start times were staggered accordingly to ensure that all seven vehicles were in position for a simultaneous attack. This too had been practiced many times over the past two days so that each man knew exactly where he had to be at precisely the right time.

This operation was not expected to be a suicide mission and the men could reasonably expect to return safely but only if everything went exactly to plan.

Just as he ended his briefing, Yusman handed each attendant a grenade. These along with the RDX explosives, had been stolen two months earlier from a military barracks in Banda Aceh on the western tip of Java. He warned the men that the grenades were only to be used as a last resort should the main explosives fail to detonate.

Yusman showed them exactly where the grenade should be placed under the most vulnerable part of the tanker if it came to that. He did not have to tell them that should the use of a grenade become necessary, given its short four-second fuse, the men would almost certainly be caught up in the resulting blast and survival would be near impossible.

With the briefing over and final prayers said, the teams mounted their respective vehicles to await the order to leave. Most were consumed with their own thoughts about the carnage soon to be unleashed but a few seasoned hands seemed unperturbed by the real dangers they faced.

At 8:02am the first truck called Tanker One began rolling out of the warehouse. Over the next nine minutes, the remaining vehicles began their short one-way journey into history.

Yusman watched them go in a heady mix of excitement, apprehension and also a tinge of sadness. This would be his biggest and most complex operation to date – and also his last. For it to work perfectly, the teams needed to follow their instructions to the letter.

He checked his watch again. It was time for him to leave and head back to his safe house a six-minute drive away. From the balcony of this 10th storey apartment, he would be able to see his final mission live and in person.

Tanker One headed to Blok M, a business cum shopping centre located in Kebayoran Baru in South Jakarta. Built some 20 years earlier, the area was always packed with locals and tourists out for some bargain hunting. The narrow two-lane roads around the area, all one-way traffic, were frequently congested and today it was no different.

The driver expertly manoeuvred his cumbersome 10-wheeled vehicle through the chaotic traffic as the attendant checked his watch. At precisely 8:27am as they passed the front of Blok M, the driver veered sharply from the left lane to the right narrowly missing an elderly motorcyclist before mounting the curb and hitting a small tree. With the tanker stopped at an angle, the entire road was effectively blocked off bringing all traffic behind it to a grinding halt. As the vehicle mounted the curb, the attendant triggered the smoke canister in the engine compartment, causing a small but constant stream of black smoke to emerge from the engine bay.

A crowd of curious on-lookers soon gathered to get a better view of the apparent accident and the traffic build-up was almost instantaneous. Amidst the blaring horns from disgruntled motorists, both men alighted from their seemingly immobile truck. The attendant picked up his handphone making a show of calling for assistance. As they walked through the swelling crowd, they casually discarded their distinctive blue jackets and caps which helped them blend into the background.

Barely 60 seconds later, both men had disappeared into the crowd as the attendant punched in the activation number on his handphone. When they were 200 metres away and shielded by a large concrete wall, the attendant crouched down, checked his watch and hit the green call button.

The time was 8:30am – precisely.

No one could discern the double explosions as the first

happened a fraction of a second before the following blast. The RDX tore through the hull of the tanker instantly setting aflame the 34,000 litres of petroleum. This was only about a third of the fuel carried by American Airlines Flight 11 – the first plane to hit New York's World Trade Centre in the terrorist attack on September 11, 2001. Still the effects were no less chilling.

The huge fireball fuelled by the petroleum reached over 300 metres into the sky as the pressure wave blew out windows up to half a kilometre away. The thick smoke shielded for a time, the utter devastation on the ground. Vehicles next to the tanker had also exploded and were left burning, leaving behind the charred and blackened remains of their occupants still strapped in their seats.

Further out from the immediate blast zone, scores of people, many of them onlookers, lay dead in an untidy heap of dismembered body parts burnt beyond recognition. Those fortunate enough to be further away from the immediate kill zone of Tanker One were hit by shrapnel blasted out from the exploding vehicle.

The effects on office workers, tourists and ordinary folk going about their daily business in this busy district, were no less horrific than being caught in a merciless hail of bullets. Some were decapitated instantly, their now lifeless bodies still moving forward a step or two before crumpling to the ground. Others were cruelly torn apart by the shrapnel which exited their bodies with still lethal force.

Large glass shards falling from the surrounding buildings also took out more innocent victims as the flaming petroleum flowing across roads and through drains, started a rolling series of building fires that would continue to burn well into the evening.

The intense fires coupled with the grid-locked roads, prevented ambulances and other emergency vehicles from reaching the victims still clinging to life. Those who were still conscious would hear the approaching sirens but help for them would never arrive in time.

Tanker Four was tasked with a more symbolic hit – the American Embassy. This fortified building was set well away from the busy boulevard it fronted.

As the vehicle neared the front of the embassy, the driver braced himself for the impact as he gunned his engine. The tanker lurched forward crashing into the rear of the van he was following. Immediately on contact, the attendant triggered the smoke device sending a cloud of black smoke billowing out from the engine.

Stopping by the roadside 70 metres away from the embassy's guard post, the 'accident' had already triggered a security response. With two armed guards running to the scene, the attack team dismounted from the vehicle. The embassy's security men with weapons drawn, ensured that no one was hurt before escorting the driver and attendant back to the guard post.

A small crowd of about 20 people were lined up at another gate close by, waiting to enter this highly-protected building to apply for US visas. More security guards were arriving by the minute as the attendant, who had already keyed in the attack code, pressed the green call button on his handphone.

The time was 8:30am – precisely.

The resulting explosion mirrored the others that were taking place all over Jakarta this morning. This blast tossed several passing vehicles into the air and they came crashing down on the road which was already engulfed in flames.

Both team members, who were still well within the kill zone, knew that there was no way out for them. There was barely enough time for a silent prayer as a rain of deadly shrapnel tore through their bodies with ease. Five security guards and most of the crowd outside the embassy were also struck down, many fatally.

The embassy itself suffered no significant damage apart from some broken windows caused by the pressure wave from the explosion. Only four employees were injured by the flying glass but all would live to recount the horror of November 6.

In planning the hit, JI knew that the damage to the embassy would be light but still the message would be delivered loud and clear to the Americans that they were still in the crosshairs.

But it would be Tanker Seven that would deliver the most horrific example of pure terrorism to the Americans and the rest of the watching world.

The men of Tanker Seven pulled their vehicle over to the side of the street just before a road hump about 200 metres from the entrance to the Indonesia American School. It was far enough away so as not to arouse suspicion of the school guards and yet be close enough to their approaching targets. School was due to start at 8:45am and the buses loaded with the first and second grade students should be arriving any minute now.

The tanker driver made a show of opening the hood of the engine bay and fiddling with the cables. He checked his watch. It was 8:26am. Leaving his hazard lights on and the hood open, he and his partner began walking away. The latter had already keyed in the telephone number into his handphone. Now all that was left for them to do was wait.

Three minutes later, the two yellow school buses turned the corner and slowed down as they approached the road hump. They were driving just three metres apart now and were right on schedule as they neared the tanker.

The attendant waited from his vantage point 300 metres away until both buses were aligned with the tanker. From his left, he heard the first sound of an explosion a few kilometres away. The attack had begun as he keyed the call button of his handphone.

The white flash and deafening blast caught the man by surprise and it took several seconds for him to regain his senses. Instinctively he checked his watch. It was 12 seconds after 8:30am and his job was done.

The blast ripped through both buses as they were tossed on their sides and sent spinning like giant tops across the road by the pressure wave. Burning oil soon engulfed these vehicles drowning out any final screams from those children trapped inside. There would be no survivors.

One press photographer who happened to be nearby

would soon take a picture that the world would remember for years to come. Amidst the smoke and burning embers, the small blackened hand of a dead child – with the flesh charred almost to the bone, reached out from one window of the overturned bus as if pleading for help – an innocent, silent cry that the world failed to hear.

9

He counted them again. From his apartment high above the city, Yusman had heard the multiple blasts that occurred within seconds of each other. There were seven ugly columns of black smoke rising across the city. Each team it seemed had found its mark and the mission was complete.

He wondered how the American President would react. "See we too can hit back with deadly precision. So how does it feel to have Shock and Awe turned on you, Mr President?" murmured Yusman to no one in particular.

Shock and Awe was the tagline the Americans had used to describe their surgical air strikes during their initial invasion of Baghdad in 2003. Revenge had been a long time coming but it tasted sweet now as he viewed the spreading destruction across Jakarta. Sirens from emergency vehicles could be heard in the distance but it would be too late.

There would be no need for him to call Hassan and report the success of his mission. In a few minutes, it would be all over the news.

The exhaustion of the past few days hit home and Yusman slumped in a chair by the television waiting to hear the first news broadcast. Now his job was to lie low at least for the next few days.

It was all going to plan exactly as it had been envisioned but Yusman knew that he was already a dead man.

10

With Washington 12 hours behind Jakarta, news of the attack in the Indonesian capital first flashed across US television screens just as many Americans were still settling down to dinner on the eve of Election Day.

Kelly Yee was at her campaign headquarters in a hotel across the Potomac when her handphone buzzed – the Secretary of State was need back in the White House ASAP.

Seven minutes later she was escorted by Secret Service agents to the underground Situation Room where the President and several of his senior advisors were already present. The four television screens mounted on the far wall were all showing scenes of the carnage in the Indonesian capital. Only one had its volume turned up and that was the English feed from the Arab news network Al Jazeera.

"I'm sorry to drag you away from your campaign at this

time Kelly …," said President Monroe.

"This is still my job Mr President."

"Yes, quite right," said President Monroe. "Mr Baldwin, please continue …"

"As I was saying earlier, the Indonesian authorities are reporting at least seven major blasts all over the capital Jakarta," said the CIA Director. "Each was triggered by a petrol tanker rigged with explosives. Two exploded in crowded shopping districts, one outside the capital's main courthouse, two more outside two western-owned hotels. And of course outside the Indonesia American School and the US Embassy.

"All blasts occurred within seconds of each other at 8.30am local time. Initial estimates put the casualty numbers at more than 200 dead and just under 700 injured. We can reasonably expect those numbers to increase over the next few hours. So far American casualties are 42 dead – all 36 children in the two buses and at least six in the explosion in Blok M – one of the shopping centres hit."

"So they are deliberately targeting children now," said President Monroe, his face bright red with anger. "Please tell me we know for sure who did this."

CIA Director William Baldwin and James Carron, the director of the National Security Agency exchanged nervous glances before Baldwin continued: "No one at this time has claimed responsibility but it's still early. These attacks bear all the hallmarks of a JI hit … very similar to the Bali bombings back in 2002."

"And why the hell did we not have any intel warning? You guys said a hit would mostly likely be targeted at their airport and instead they were out to kill our children!"

"Sir we had suspicions that a terrorist group was planning an operation in the Indonesian capital but we could not get a handle on the specifics. We had issued a travel advisory two weeks ago warning Americans in the country to be extra vigilant. Security at the embassy and US-owned assets had also been put on heightened alert ..."

"And that's all that we seem to be doing all the time!" exploded President Monroe. "Giving out warnings after warnings – yellow alert, orange alert, red alert – without really knowing what's going on. Do you expect me to tell the parents of those dead kids that they should have been more careful?"

No one spoke for several seconds as the television sets continued to display gory images of the blackened victims lying dead in the Jakarta streets. Again they repeated footage of one of the burnt school buses with the charred hand of a child reaching out from a broken window.

Regaining his composure, the President continued: "Tell me what we know for sure ... the facts!"

"All seven tanker trucks came from an oil refinery in Segarajaya, that's on the outskirts of the capital. They were each transporting more than 30,000 litres of petroleum destined for a station in Surabaya. Indonesian authorities believe that the convoy was hijacked and each truck was subsequently rigged with explosives and possibly foreign objects – nails, bolts and ball bearings were added to the load as shrapnel …" said Baldwin.

"Sir, looking at the target spread,' continued NSA Director Carron, "it would appear that the culprits were going for soft hits to maximise civilian casualties. There appears to have been no attempt to breach the compound of the US Embassy and exploding the vehicle some 200 metres away from the building, was probably a more symbolic gesture rather than an effort to destroy or cripple the embassy as in the case of Africa in '98."

In a coordinated attack on August 7 1998, two trucks loaded with explosives exploded outside US embassies in Dar es Salaam, Tanzania and in Nairobi, Kenya in East Africa.

The attack in Nairobi involved a truck with about 500 cylinders of TNT along with explosive aluminium nitrate and aluminium powder which had been packed into wooden crates and triggered with an electric detonator. The Dar es Salaam explosion used TNT attached to fifteen oxygen tanks and gas canisters which were surrounded with four large bags of ammonium nitrate fertilizer.

That morning at about 10.30am, suicide bombers detonated their trucks as they tried to enter the compound of the embassies. More than 200 people were killed and 4,000 wounded in the Nairobi attack. In Dar es Salaam, the attack killed a dozen people and wounded 85 others.

These bombings marked the eighth anniversary of the arrival of American forces in Saudi Arabia for the Desert

Storm offensive. Following these attacks which were linked to al-Qaeda, Osama bin Laden was placed on the FBI's Most Wanted list.

Continued Director Carron: "Our guys from the embassy have positively identified traces of RDX in the explosion there ... military-grade. It was probably used to trigger the secondary blast with the petroleum. CCTV footage showed the driver and another man walking away from their vehicle seconds before the explosion outside one of the shopping malls. One of the suspects was using his cell phone so it was probably radio-controlled. We can assume that the other explosions were triggered in the same way."

"I just don't believe that someone can hijack a moving convoy of seven large vehicles in the city. It has to be an inside job. What do we know of the men in those vehicles?" asked Vice President John McKenzie.

Responded Carron: "Both men involved in the embassy hit were killed in the blast. Of the others, we still don't know. Our people have their names from their employer at the oil refinery and we are working it through the system but so far there have been no red flags. If they are part of the terror group, they were probably too far down the totem pole to have been registered with the NSA as known terrorists."

"Well one thing seems obvious," said Secretary Kelly Yee, "the timing was meant to disrupt our elections. They knew that we would up our terror threat warning during election time – that's no big secret, it was all over the news – so they want to show that they can still hit us even when our guard is supposed to be at its highest."

"And we still have the unresolved issue of that nuke trigger from Singapore. Is that connected with this mess in any way that we know of?" asked VP McKenzie.

"That is highly unlikely," responded Defence Secretary Jeffrey Brown. "The polonium won't work as a trigger in such an explosive device. It is possible that the polonium was simply meant to throw us off the scent while they planned this hit."

"I don't have the luxury of taking that risk, that it was just a red herring," said the President looking at the television monitors which still showed scenes of devastation with the burnt-out shells of the two school buses lying in the Jakarta streets. "It was a miracle that the Singapore authorities found it in the first place. No, we still have to assume that there is a rogue nuke or parts of it somewhere out there. With the election in just a few hours, we need to show the American people that this attack has not shaken us or our democratic process in choosing a new leader.

"Alright, first things first – John, get the FBI to coordinate with all state and federal law enforcement agencies – I want security beefed up at all polling stations. I do not want this to be just a preamble to a hit on American soil. I'll talk to the nation at 8.30 tomorrow morning and give them some assurances. At all costs, we have to stop this from turning into another religious divide. That would tear this country apart.

"Kelly, as you are a candidate, I can't have you making any policy speeches on this even though you are still the Secretary of State – well at least not before I do. I don't want our good friend Senator Coal and his Republican hacks crying foul that you used this attack to sway voters. I'm sure the conspiracy theorists are already having a field day with the timing of these hits so be extra careful in dealing with the media tomorrow.

"In the meantime John, I need you to arrange an urgent meeting for me with the Indonesian Ambassador in say … two hours. We need to press him to get their investigation speeded up. Those Indonesians have been dragging their feet with the polonium investigation and now we have this new chaos to deal with. I'll try to pressure him to accept some US investigators so James and William, get your teams set to move. I want all our people and contacts out probing this aggressively – we will need all the fresh intelligence we can get.

"John, I also want you to get our people at the embassy working on establishing the identities of the American victims. See if Indonesian medical authorities need help identifying those … dead kids. Their families – give them all the assistance they need and I want planes on standby … military or civilian I don't give a damn right now, just get them ready. We need to bring … to bring those children home as soon as possible. See to it now, please," said the President choking back his emotions.

"I'm on it Theodore," said the Vice President as he stood up to leave. Walking past his old friend, he patted the President on his shoulder. Inwardly the VP was glad that he had declined to run for the post of Commander-in-Chief. He was far too old and his heart was far too weak now for all of this.

"Mr President, I can help, it's still my job," offered the

Secretary of State.

"No Kelly, your job now – for today and tomorrow at least, is to win this damn election. Focus on that and then you can take over this seat … and this burden of responsibility. It will be in your hands to continue the work that we have been doing all these years to rebuild America. That's your job."

Kelly nodded to her Commander-in-Chief as Monroe stood up and began to pace the room. Being deep underground in the Situation Room he could not see them or hear them but he had been told that they were there – a small but growing crowd had gathered just beyond the gates to the White House – a hurt and angry mob intent on seeking bloody retribution for the killings in Jakarta that day. The American people were demanding action from their President as the lights of the White House would continue to burn late into the night.

A group of 30 US Marines in full battle gear waited in their underground barracks out of sight within the White House grounds ready to confront the growing demonstration outside the gates should the situation turn ugly. Police in Washington already stretched with the security preparations for the presidential election just hours away, deployed more uniformed officers outside the Indonesian Embassy. Still more policemen were sent to be conspicuously present outside the city's main mosques.

Tension in the capital was on the rise as more office lights in the Pentagon were turned on and the carpark outside began filling up. The military was gearing up, awaiting new orders from the White House.

The seconds ticked by as the President paced the room lost deep in thought. The others shifted uncomfortably in their seats. Everyone knew what was to come next. Finally the President stopped and wiped his reading glasses again. With a deep breath, he retook his seat at the conference table.

Finally he said. "America and the world must be assured that this senseless act of violence is not going to derail our democratic electoral process. Nor will it make us cower in fear when cowards wage war against defenceless civilians … against innocent children. This cannot and will not go unpunished. We have made that mistake before."

Turning to his Secretary of Defence Jeffrey Brown the President asked: "Am I right to assume then, that until we uncover any confirmation to the contrary, all evidence as of now points to this being the work of JI?"

"It would appear so sir," said Brown.

"And does the NSA and the CIA concur with this assessment?"

"Yes Mr President," said NSA's Director Carron.

"It certainly looks that way as of now," said CIA Director Baldwin.

"Alright what do we know of the JI leadership and it's command structure?" asked the President.

NSA's Director Carron checked his notes on his laptop before he began: "As a domestic terror group, JI's grew out of the Darul Islam sect in the 1940s. That was a radical

Islamic organisation opposed to Dutch colonial rule in Indonesia. It formally came into being as JI sometime in 1993 and it opposed the oppressive Suharto government which was in power at the time. Towards the end of the 1990s with the end of the Suharto regime, Jemaah Islamiyah began colluding with al-Qaeda. While al-Qaeda strove to form an Islamic Middle East, JI's aim was to establish an Islamic confederation of nations which included all of Indonesia, Malaysia, Singapore, parts of the Philippines and the southern provinces in Thailand.

"Initially their terrorist activities were mostly domestic violence – mainly bombing and a few political killings. In recent years with the spread of radical Islam, JI shifted its focus targeting US and Western interests in Indonesia. In October 2002, it bombed a night club in Bali killing more than 200. Later that month, JI was put on the United Nations watch list of terror organisations. The group was thought to behind a series of other later attacks around Jakarta – the 2003 bombing of the JW Marriott hotel, the Australian embassy explosion in 2004, the 2005 Bali terrorist bombing and the JW Marriott and Ritz-Carlton hotel blasts in 2009.

"JI was also believed to be responsible for planning a series of bombings hitting Western targets in Singapore, but these were foiled by local authorities."

Monroe nodded in silence as he was briefed and scribbled a few notes on the pad before him. "What do we know of their command structure?"

"Until quite recently – maybe two or three years back, the hierarchy was very fragmented with a number of subgroups operating with much autonomy. In early 2011 our sources confirmed that command of JI is now in the hands of this man – Yusman bin Iranto."

From his laptop, Carron flashed a picture of Yusman on the main television monitor.

"He is aged about 35 but this picture was taken about eight to 10 years ago. Information on him is sketchy at best. We know he came from a wealthy family and was believed to have been indoctrinated during his university days when he was studying to be an engineer. Our sources say he was in Jakarta until about a month ago when he disappeared from the radar. He may have been travelling abroad under false papers but that is just a rumour."

"So if our sources are right," commented the President, "and this attack was carried out by JI, then this would have been his first major operation in charge. Is this man capable of pulling off something this big?"

NSA Director's Baldwin answered: "As Director Carron said earlier, this Yusman character is still an unknown entity … untested. Going by JI's track record, major attacks like this one are usually sponsored by another group. Their banker used to be al-Qaeda or ISIS but our operatives in the theatre say it's highly unlikely that al-Qaeda had a hand in this one. So the money was probably fronted by someone else, but as of now we just don't know who that could be."

"Have there been any claims of responsibility so far?" asked the President.

"JI, as with several other terror groups including al-Qaeda," said CIA Director Baldwin, "never publicly claim responsibility for attacks. They may allude to it, make some oblique references to the hit, but they don't come right out and claim responsibility."

"Are there any other groups that we know of capable of pulling off something of this scale?" asked President Monroe. All three men shook their heads. "Okay, we have to assume that while there may be other accomplices, JI is behind this. What do we know of their bases or training camps?"

Replied NSA's Director Cameron: "JI's stronghold used to be Banda Aceh on the north-western tip of the main island of Sumatra. Their main command elements and top-ranking members tend to be spread around the country. They usually congregate in mosques and use a number of religious schools for meetings. The only known concentration of JI members are at their training camps. These are located in remote jungle areas. They are usually small and make-shift operations, moving every couple of months to avoid detection."

"Do we have people … I mean reliable people in their organisation who would be able to give us accurate and timely information on these camps?" asked the President.

"It's been messy and difficult getting our people in and they have to start at the bottom. Most of our intel comes from paid informants. So far, for the right price, they have proven to be quite accurate," said Cameron.

"And are these the same '*reliable sources*' who told us that the attack would be directed at the airport?" spat the President.

Intervened Kelly: "Mr President, for all we know that information could have been accurate at the time. In consultation with the Indonesian authorities, security at the airport was almost doubled. Indonesian security made it very obvious that they weren't taking any chances with airport security. We may never know for sure but these measures may have prevented an attack at the airport."

"Okay let's give them the benefit of the doubt on the airport. Still I would have expected that our multi-billion dollar intelligence agencies would have picked up on at least some of the actual targets that were hit. There were seven for God's sake and we didn't even have a hint of one!"

Without looking at anyone in particular, the President paused for a moment before he continued: "Look I know it's difficult … maybe damn near impossible to know about every single attack that is being planned. I know we may have deterred tens maybe even hundreds from happening, but every time we screw up … every time we miss one ... it ends up like this!" he said gesticulating to the row of television sets which were still showing the stark scenes of devastation across Jakarta.

Regaining his composure the President continued: "Keep … keep putting more pressure on whatever sources we have in the country. We need to know the whereabouts of their camps and their leaders. I don't want this to be just a token hit – sending in some cruise missiles to bomb a few empty buildings in the jungle. I have no intention of going to war but we need to strike back hard and at the right people."

Turning now to the Secretary of Defence, the President directed his next question that everyone in the room dreaded but expected: "Jeffrey, what military assets do we have in this region?"

11

GRAHA MEDIKA HOSPITAL, JAKARTA, INDONESIA –
NOVEMBER 6, 1242 HOURS

It had been some four hours since the first casualties
began arriving at the Graha Medika Hospital, one of
several medical facilities around the city that were still
receiving a steady stream of the injured.

The wounds of many patients at the hospital were horrific
but at least these lucky ones were still alive with a chance
for eventual recovery.

Surgeons rushed the most critically injured straight into the
operating theatres. Many suffered traumatic blast
amputations along with major shrapnel wounds. Scores of
others were branded with disfiguring third degree burns
and doctors fought valiantly to fight off infection. The
slow healing for many would take months if not years but
still those scars would remain, scorched into their
memories and their nightmares.

The scale of the disaster had simply overwhelmed the hospital's ability to cope but weary trauma teams struggled on for hours without rest as more victims were brought in.

Even before public appeals were made over television and radio, traumatised civilians and hundreds of soldiers began lining up to donate blood and plasma to help the injured.

Singapore was one of the first countries to respond offering its world-class medical facilities. Three C-130 cargo planes from the Republic of Singapore Air Force with medical teams and a large quantity of supplies on board were dispatched to help their Indonesian counterparts and ferry the most severely injured back to hospitals on the island.

But for most of the victims, there was little that could be done. Many had lapsed into shock while waiting at the scene for help to arrive. They had clung on to hope for as long as they could before their weakened bodies simply gave up the fight.

At the hospital's morgue, scores of bodies covered with black plastic sheets lay on gurneys against the wall as space in its refrigerators ran out. The nauseating stench of burnt flesh and lingering gasoline was overpowering. Even more grotesque were the large white plastic containers stacked chest high. For want of a better description, someone had scribbled on the accompanying tag 'TBI' – meaning To Be Identified. These contained an assortment of barely recognisable arms, legs, torsos and blackened clumps of human tissue retrieved from the various attack scenes.

Soon more doctors would arrive. These were the

pathologists. With many victims dismembered or burnt beyond recognition, they would have the grim task of matching body parts and identifying the dead through dental records and DNA analysis.

At the attack scenes, police and firemen were still pulling out one smouldering body after another from the wrecks of the burnt out vehicles littering the streets. Most of the victims were dead. Occasionally they would find one still barely alive. As they carefully lifted the injured out, their hopes would soar that perhaps they were not too late.

But as the hours came and went, it became apparent that this was no longer a rescue mission but a recovery operation.

Indonesian investigators swarmed the seven crime scenes intent on recovering whatever evidence was still left behind. Chemical swabs taken from the twisted chassis of one tanker confirmed the presence of RDX explosives. At another scene, small fragments of the mobile phone detonator would be found.

12

SOUTH CHINA SEA – NOVEMBER 6, 1501 HOURS

He was still 15 nautical miles out and the *George Washington* seemed tiny, like a little grey island in the distance amidst the restless sea of emerald green water.

Making slight corrections on the throttle in his right hand, Lieutenant Commander Robert Green or Foxbat as he was better known to his crew, watched intently as the crosshairs on his Heads-Up Display (HUD) began to move.

The Instrument Landing System had been activated as Green lined up his Boeing F/A-18E Super Hornet for landing on his carrier, the mighty *USS George Washington*. He was now 45 seconds away from touchdown. Easing back on the throttle while extending his flaps, the ship loomed larger before him. He had done this manoeuvre hundreds of times before – perfecting the delicate art of a carrier landing. Still it required all his concentration. He tried not to think of why his flight of seven fighter jets had suddenly been recalled home to their ship abruptly shelving their scheduled bomb practice runs that afternoon.

Just a few minutes earlier, Green had been circling high overhead as he watched one by one the other six fighters in his formation land safely. Now as the flight leader, it was his turn to bring his bird back home.

Instinctively he patted his left thigh where in a pocket under his G-suit, Green always carried a laminated photograph of his family. Just before any carrier landing, arguably the most dangerous part of the most dangerous job in the world, he would tap that photograph for luck. Call it superstition but Green didn't care, as in all his landings even those done in a storm at night where the black pitching deck was barely visible, he had always brought his prized Hornet and himself home in one piece.

Now he was just seven seconds away from touchdown and adrenaline was pumping through his system. His tailhook was extended, ready to catch one of the four arresting wires strung across the flightdeck. Confirming that he was lined up perfectly on the glide slope, Green gunned his engines to full military power – the maximum thrust of the jet without engaging afterburners – instantly accelerating some 13,000 kilogrammes of aircraft, fuel and ordinance.

While naval aviators had to slow their jets down on approach to the carrier, in the last seconds before touchdown, they would need to open up their throttles to full power. Should their fighters fail to catch any of the four wires, or if they needed to abort the landing for any other reason, they would need every bit of that thrust from their twin engines to launch themselves into the air again.

Despite the thunderous roar of the engines, the Hornet seemed to float down gently to the carrier's deck. Bracing himself for the landing, he was thrown forward violently in his harness as wheels screeched meeting tarmac and his mighty F-18 was brought abruptly to a deadstop within just a few short metres. Catching the elusive third wire, it was a textbook return to ship landing and Green expected nothing less of himself.

Cutting the engines and releasing his canopy lock, he could already feel the carrier starting to turn starboard. Crew members were running about the flightdeck hastily securing the jets still parked topside. Clearly his ship was in a hurry to get moving.

Looking out towards the horizon, he could see the two grey escort frigates churning up water as they revved their engines and began their starboard turns in tight formation. Further ahead, he caught a faint glimpse of one of their attack submarines just as its black conning tower slipped below the water. The entire Task Force 70 battlegroup was on the move as the wind picked up speed across the carrier's flightdeck.

"Commander, Air Boss wants to see you now," shouted one of the yellow-jacketed crew members who climbed up on the Hornet just as Green was releasing the straps of his harness.

The pilot sensed that something major was brewing as adrenaline once again began flooding his system.

13

ANG MO KIO INDUSTRIAL PARK, SINGAPORE –
NOVEMBER 6, 1626 HOURS

Turning away from the television that was still showing
scenes of the terrorist attack in Jakarta a day earlier, it was
now time for Saif began the delicate task at hand.

Even though he knew by heart how to put the device
together, he still painstakingly sketched it out on paper,
paying careful attention to the delicate timing and trigger
mechanisms. It was just his way of running through every
step of the process on paper while he rehearsed it in his
mind's eye.

With the sketch done, Saif scrutinised his hands carefully
turning them over trying to detect the slightest shake or
quiver but they were steady. He was almost ready to begin
but first he rolled out his small prayer carpet to seek divine
blessings for his work over the next few hours.

He knew that in fashioning this nuclear weapon, thousands
maybe up to a hundred thousand people would be killed in
the blinding flash and the rolling blastwave of super heated

winds that would certainly obliterate anything in its path. He did not see himself as a cruel man, a crazed religious fanatic or a brainwashed suicide bomber as the Western media had often portrayed his brothers who made that ultimate and supreme sacrifice.

Saif had thought long and hard about the work that was asked of him. He had watched the television news reports of his last mission – the destruction of the US Embassy in Nairobi back in 1998. He had seen the bloodied and torn bodies, some of them women, carried away on stretchers – the results of the bomb that he had designed. Those scenes which he replayed in his mind over and over again had caused him intense pain and anguish. He had searched his heart and his soul many times, weighing his actions to see if the ends justified these means. And each time the answer was a sad but resounding yes.

In his heart he knew that everything he had done had been thrust upon him and that it was the government of the United States that had forced his hand. They had bullied and bloodied his brothers and then robbed them of the sacred lands of Palestine when the state of Israel was created.

In the decades that followed, his people had been beaten, raped, humiliated and murdered and yet the world looked the other way. It was nothing less than another holocaust that went unacknowledged.

He thought of his own family and how they were killed, just innocent bystanders who were in the wrong place at the wrong time. The world had simply gone on, taking no notice of the plight of the Arabs or the systematic and continued oppression of the Palestinian people by Israel and its American protectors. And yet when his brothers fought back, taking up arms and fighting a guerrilla war to reclaim the land which was rightfully theirs, they were branded as terrorists to be hunted down, tortured and killed by a technology superior foe.

Over the years, the United States kept up its military occupation and subjugation of much of the lands of the Muslim brotherhood. From Libya to Syria, to Iran, Iraq and Afghanistan – it was not just their historic lands that were being attacked and plundered for their mineral wealth, it was their faith as well that had been placed in the bombsights of western weapons.

Striking back with bombs of their own was the only way to extract a measure of revenge for his family and halt what Saif saw as another Christian crusade out to knife the very heart and soul of his faith.

But with the sheer magnitude and horror of this bomb, the West will be stopped. Saif knew of no other weapon that would cause his eternal foe to pause and retreat. America itself had rationalised its decision to drop atomic bombs during World War II on Hiroshima and Nagasaki – both essentially civilian targets, as the only way of preventing the deaths of thousands of American soldiers who would be killed in a frontal assault on the Japanese mainland. And these bombs, they argued, would shorten the war saving the lives of many civilians. Saif felt the same rationale still applied. A nuclear bomb or two would stop his enemy and save the lives of thousands of his brothers.

The *Saif al-Haidar* would be just one of the two weapons

that he himself will be assembling. It would come as no surprise to him if there were others like himself who would be working on building even more such colossal weapons around the world. But this one, the Singapore bomb, this would be the first to be detonated as an example of the power he and his brothers now held. The rest, he assumed, would be held back and used as threats to curb America's growing aggression against his faith and stop the continued plunder of Arab oil.

Of the plan to use this weapon, he had been told little, not even the actual target, but still it was enough for him – enough to justify the task he was about to undertake. His conscience was clear and his hands would remain steady.

Kneeling on his prayer mat, Saif had already turned to the north-west to align himself with the Holy Land. Slowly he bowed his head till it touched the ground and he began his prayers. Once again he prayed for peace, peace that he hoped would come soon.

The design and construction of a nuclear weapon is not as formidable as it may seem. A number of these plans and their intricate circuitry can be culled from the Internet these days. The main stumbling block is in getting enough of the fuel.

The two main fuels for a nuclear weapon are uranium and plutonium. Both are highly radioactive which simply means that they are constantly shedding subatomic particles including neutrons. However only certain isotopes of these heavy metals – Uranium 235 and Plutonium 239 – would consistently give off neutrons of such high energy that are capable of splitting atoms and releasing its raw power.

A nuclear weapon essentially compresses its radioactive fuel into a supercritical state, triggering the release of a sudden and massive burst of energy – a single colossal detonation of heat, blast force and lethal radiation.

The weapon that Saif would soon be putting together was that of an implosion design. It would be somewhat more complex than the crude gun method used in the first atomic bomb dropped on Hiroshima.

In that design, a hollow uranium bullet is fired by conventional explosives down a long tube commonly referred to as a gun barrel. It would then collide into a 'spike' of fissionable material. If timed correctly, the two nuclear components will be brought together and held long enough to cause a chain reaction. The combined fuel mass would then go supercritical, triggering a nuclear explosion.

However the biggest weakness of the gun design is in holding both nuclear parts together long enough – just micro-seconds – for the entire fuel mass to reach a supercritical state at one go. Typically, as the two fuel sections come within a few centimetres of each other, they will begin to exchange neutrons. This could initiate a premature explosion, simply destroying the weapon before it reached a supercritical state for a nuclear blast to take place.

In the more sophisticated and reliable implosion design that Saif would be using, the plutonium fuel at the heart of the device, would be shaped into two halves of a perfect sphere. This highly radioactive core would sit inside another sphere made of conventional high explosives. The latter resembling a soccer ball, is made up of 32 individual shaped explosive charges.

An implosion bomb requires a nuclear trigger or initiator to flood the plutonium core with neutrons during detonation. This trigger, made up of discs of beryllium and polonium separated by thin gold foil, is placed in the centre of the plutonium core.

When activated, the shaped explosives contained within a hardened titanium sphere, will create a massive shockwave radiating inwards squeezing the nuclear core into a dense supercritical mass.

The layers of beryllium and polonium together with other components including a 'pusher' which is designed to increase the implosive shockwave hitting the core, a 'tamper' to prevent the core from blowing apart too quickly once the detonation is initiated, and a 'reflector' which is composed of materials which will reflect neutrons back into the core increasing the amount of fission – these together will greatly enhance the explosive yield of the nuclear device. The devastation would be complete and absolute.

14

ONBOARD THE *USS GEORGE WASHINGTON* IN THE
SOUTH CHINA SEA OFF THE PHILIPPINES –
NOVEMBER 6, 1518 HOURS

The Task Force 70 battlegroup of the U.S. Seventh Fleet
led by the nuclear-powered CVN-73 *George Washington* with
its 78 aircraft had completed its sharp turn to the
southwest and began picking up speed.

The Task Force itself is made up of two components – the
surface combat force which is comprised of cruisers and
destroyers and the carrier strike force centered around the
USS George Washington and Carrier Air Wing 5 (CVW-5).

Christened in July 1990 with the motto 'Spirit of Freedom',
the *George Washington* with its crew of more than 6,000 had
seen regular deployments to the Persian Gulf. On
September 11 2001, the carrier had just completed major
upgrades to its digital combat management systems at the
Norfolk Naval Shipyard and was operating off the coast of
Virginia when the World Trade Towers and the Pentagon
were struck. It was immediately diverted north and arrived
in New York the next day. There it provided near

continuous combat air patrols over the injured city and the surrounding areas in those tense days following the attacks.

Today, just as what was done on September 11 2001, the battlegroup's commanders and senior officers were summoned to the carrier's Ready Room. They watched as a television mounted on one wall replayed the scenes of carnage in Jakarta which took place some seven hours earlier.

A closed-circuit security camera mounted on a building opposite the school had caught the attack on film. It showed in chilling detail the tanker exploding in a huge ball of flames just as the school buses passed by. They were tossed in the air like toys before they landed on their sides and were spun across the road engulfed in fire.

Task Force commander Vice Admiral Cyril J. Forrestal surveyed the room trying to gauge the reactions of his senior officers. Some winced when Indonesian television crews filmed close-up shots of dismembered bodies lying outside the bombed shopping centre. Scenes of the charred school buses and the hand of the little victim reaching out from the shattered window were watched by the officers in what seemed like silent awe or more likely, cold anger.

He let the pre-recorded news footage continue for several more minutes until the tape ran to a stop. Then rising from his seat, Admiral Forrestal began speaking: "As you are all aware, this terrorist attack coming just hours before our presidential elections was timed to be a slap in the face of what America stands for – freedom and democracy. It is clear from the footage you have just seen, that the terrorists are not just targeting civilians but specifically children – American children.

"Our Commander-in-Chief has directed that we, the Task Force 70 battlegroup led by the *George Washington* be moved into an attack position and readied for an offensive, surgical strike if and when that order should come."

Forrestal noted the murmurs and nods of approval around the room. His men were ready, eager for payback. He waited a few more seconds allowing the murmurs in the room to settle down before he continued: "For some time now we have been cruising here,' he said pointing to a map on the wall, "in the Luzon Straits just north west of the Philippines keeping an eye on that Chinese carrier battlegroup. As you well know, we were due to end this rotation in a few weeks and head on back to our home port of San Diego in time for the Christmas holidays but now, all that has been changed.

"The Pentagon has ordered that we move here, about 215 nautical miles north east of Singapore. When we are on-station, we will begin a series of night-time low-level precision bombing workups as well as covert heliborne SEAL insertions for a possible strike on a JI training camp deep in the Indonesian jungle.

"And while we are stationed off Singapore – the timing has not been confirmed as yet – we will also be conducting joint military exercises with the Singapore air force and her navy. That will be our cover, allowing us to remain in position for much longer.

"Understand this, we could be here well beyond Christmas

and the New Year so let's examine our logistics and determine what resupplies are needed. We may, if possible, make a brief port call to Singapore just for resupplies. I also want all weapons and munitions topped up and an airtight screen placed around this carrier. We are heading into some shallow and unwelcome waters so we need to be prepared.

"Gentlemen brief the men and women under your respective commands. What has happened in Jakarta is nothing short of an act of war. Training over the next couple of weeks is going to be very intense. The President will be addressing the nation soon and he will make it clear that these terrorist attacks will not go unpunished. We will be that mighty hand of vengeance when the enemy has been identified and his locations are known. Until that time comes, we need to get all our people and equipment ready for the fight. That is all."

15

WASHINGTON D.C. – NOVEMBER 6, 0702 HOURS

As doctors continued to fight through the night to save the lives of the injured and pathologists worked to identify the remains of the dead in the Indonesian capital, America was waking up to a new day.

Millions watched in silent horror as the events on television the previous evening had been repeated many times over the past hours. The initial shock and disgust over the attack on the two busloads of American children had long since given way to anger.

The crisis just hours old, had already left the nation divided. Many, as on 9-11, felt utterly helpless as they watched replays of the terrorist operation in Jakarta. But today something was different. The attack was timed to disrupt the elections and many Americans including those who had never voted in years, felt compelled to cast their ballot slips today. It would be a small measure of participation, of defiance in the face of cruel terrorism.

And so the crowds began lining up at polling stations

across the nation well before the doors were opened. It was a sight unseen across America in decades. As cars passing these voting centres sounded their horns repeatedly in anger and frustration, ordinary Americans were determined to show that no attack, no matter how horrific, was going to undermine the democracy that this nation cherished above all else.

A group of young protesters had remained camped outside the White House overnight. 'Death to the Child Murderers', 'Kill the F****** Cowards', 'Strike Hard – Strike Fast' read their placards.

Demands for justice grew even louder as fresh supporters joined in with the rising sun. Already two mosques in San Francisco were burnt to the ground the previous night in an early display of mob violence. The anger of a nation was just beginning.

Another group of older demonstrators gathered quietly in Lafayette Park just across the road from the White House. Many here were war veterans, from Vietnam to Afghanistan. While not directly opposed to war, these men who had suffered in the field of battle did not want to see history repeat itself yet again, to see their nation rushing off to invade yet another country without sound achievable objectives and equally important, a clear exit strategy.

They gathered together seeking comfort and direction. These weary knights of battle talked quietly among themselves – worried that even more blood would soon be wasted.

Republican candidate Senator Harrison Coal was out at the polling stations early, shaking hands with his many supporters amidst the jostling of the press contingent following in his wake.

He realised that his campaign strategy of massive defence cuts and curbing the power of America's military was about the blow up in his face following the Jakarta attacks. He knew many voters if, in nothing more than just a knee-jerk reaction, wanted revenge however bloody it may be. But it was too late to change strokes now on the morning of Election Day. He had to find a way to use the events of the past hours to his advantage.

Responding to the inevitable media questions, Senator Coal gave his take on the reasons behind the Jakarta attack. "This is just another example of how President Monroe and his current Administration have failed the American people yet again.

"By our unwarranted meddling in the affairs of other countries, we have put a target on the heads of all Americans. This then forces us to spend billions of dollars trying to protect our citizens. And even though we have thousands of our brave young sons and daughters in uniform stationed across the globe, even though we have the best technology and the most formidable weapons at our disposal, this present Administration has failed in its most basic function of defending America and Americans. If we can't protect our people, our children, what does that say about our role as a world superpower?

"We have spread our resources too thinly across the globe. We have allowed ourselves to be drawn into unnecessary wars and into domestic conflicts that we had no legitimate right to interfere in. Has any of this made America stronger? No! Our enemies grow in number and resolve because of our actions. And as our attention is focused outward trying to be a global cop and solve all the ills of the world, who pays for this? It's you – the American people in high taxes, less funds for healthcare and higher mortgages. America is growing weak economically as China and the rest of Asia gets stronger. We need to get back to basics and rebuild this country, rebuild our industries from within, create more jobs and strengthen our economy and domestic demand by putting more money back into the hands of Americans.

"Today America will choose – do we continue sacrificing the lives of our brave men and women in uniform meddling and fighting in conflicts overseas, do we continue to put the lives of Americans on the line as we play global cowboy, do we allow our children to die, slaughtered in the streets half a world away or do we take a new path where America puts Americans first and …"

Presidential candidate Kelly Yee muted her television set, cutting off her rival in mid-sentence. "If only it were that easy to shut him up in real life," she thought.

She had decided to remain at her party headquarters inside

the Washington Plaza Hotel instead of hitting the streets trying to the very end to sway the undecided voters. It had been a calculated risk but she felt it was the right thing to do. The President had wanted it that way and it was only proper that as Commander-in-Chief, he should address this grieving and angry nation first. He would be making his televised speech at 8.30 that morning. Only when that was over would she step out – back into the political fray. And this time, she would be speaking for herself.

Restoring the volume of her television set, Kelly listened intently as political pundits gave their opinions on how the voting would go. In the two weeks leading up to Election Day, both she and Senator Coal seemed to be locked in a dead heat. But as her campaign manifesto had always advocated a tougher defence posture for the country, her numbers in the final poll started to pull ahead. The full horror of the Indonesian massacre was just setting in and the real dangers facing America were becoming only too apparent.

"It all boils down to the sentiment of the voters at this, the final stage of the campaign," said one analyst. "If yesterday's terrorist atrocities in Jakarta have scared the American people into re-examining our foreign policies, they would surely gravitate to Senator Coal's conservative domestic camp. If, on the other hand, this senseless slaughter of innocent American children on the streets of Jakarta has galvanised the US to say 'No More' to half measures in dealing with terrorists, then Secretary Yee's no-nonsense stance on defence would surely make her the woman for the job of President and Commander-in-Chief."

Oval Office, The White House, Washington D.C. – November 6, 0830 hours

"My fellow Americans," began President Monroe as he faced the television cameras in his office. "We have all witnessed in chilling horror, the senseless and unprovoked attacks that happened in Jakarta some 12 hours ago.

"Terror forces of evil have once again targeted civilians in an act of violence beyond the comprehension of any civilised society resulting in the deaths of hundreds. Among them were 42 Americans, of which 36 were children innocently travelling to school.

"To the families of the dead and the injured, I offer to you, on behalf of the American people, my condolences and my prayers in this time of deep sorrow and anguish.

"I have directed Vice President John McKenzie to take personal charge in ensuring that everything we can do as a nation to help these families, will be done. We will bring our dead home and we will grieve with you through the pain, through the dark sadness.

"This attack half a world away, was directed at the heart of America and what America stands for – a beacon of peace, justice and democracy. It was timed to disrupt the elections for the American presidency. These evil men are out to scare the American people to withdraw into a shell, in the illusion that we would be safe there. They will fail in this as they have always failed before. Do not be cowered.

Voting is not just a right or a duty – it is a sacred oath that we make to each other, to our families, to our friends, to our community and to our country. It is in voting that we pledge to stand together as one – one people, one nation under God. So my fellow Americans, I say to you today – go out and vote for the candidate of your choice – man or woman – that you feel is best to lead this great nation forward in these perilous times.

"Our initial assessment tends to indicate that this attack was carried out by members of the outlawed Jemaah Islamiyah (JI) terrorist sect in Indonesia. This was not an attack by Muslims upon America. It was undertaken by a group of cowards who are hiding behind a great religion of peace and mutual respect, to camouflage their murderous intent.

"Today, as your Commander-in-Chief, I have directed that all our defence forces be readied to respond to this attack. To the evil men behind this slaughter, I say this to you – there will be no place for you to hide and swift justice will be done. We will, with all the military might we can muster and all the economic and political avenues at our disposal, oppose any country that offers support, help or sanctuary to these cold and heartless murderers.

"Significant military assets are being moved into position even as we investigate those behind this wanton act of aggression. It will not go unpunished; the guilty will never be free. We will hunt you down…"

Kelly Yee stood up and prepared to face the media gathered in the hotel lobby below. As ridiculous as it seemed, she could not shake that nagging suspicion that in some twisted way, this entire attack had been staged just for her benefit.

16

RIYADH, SAUDI ARABIA – NOVEMBER 6, 1409 HOURS

Hassan nodded repeatedly as he watched Kelly confidently handling the media in a live broadcast on television. The political analysts were already beginning to predict a landslide victory for the Secretary of State making her the first candidate of Asian descent and the first woman president of the United States.

As Hassan stretched out on his plush leather sofa, his aide Abdalla Saeed was also engrossed with the images on the screen. "It is all happening just as you predicted. It looks like she is really going to win!"

"And why do you sound so surprised?" replied Hassan.

"Because she is a woman and so she is naturally weak … and just a few months ago, she was far behind in the polls."

"The polls," said Hassan, "like people, can be manipulated. People are swayed by their emotions more than their heads. If you know how to push the right buttons at the right time, you can get anyone to do just about anything. A weak woman? No, she is not weak. She was picked for her strength and her intellect … to make the tough choices that would scare most men."

"So is this woman, is she part … a part of the plans?"

"A very big part, yes. She does not know it yet but her time will come soon enough."

"But what are these plans you keep talking about? You have only mentioned bits and pieces of it. Is there going to be a war in Indonesia?"

Hassan paused for a few seconds as he felt that old burning sensation start again in his chest. His young aide was indeed curious and perhaps it was time that he revealed some of his knowledge. Saeed, like Yusman, had been his faithful servant for a long time. Soon Saeed too would be called upon to pledge his life to the cause – it had all been preordained and nothing could stop what was simply destined to occur. Maybe he should tell him now … now while there was still time.

Just like Yusman, Saeed had been hand-picked for this job. While Yusman was singled out because of his bravery and command skills, the younger Saeed was more an academic who had just completed his master's degree in political science. Thus far he had been a discreet sounding board for Hassan and being a computer geek, one of Saeed's few responsibilities was to film and upload YouTube videos of Hassan's speeches and to maintain his website, blogs and Twitter feeds. But soon, he too would be destined for much greater things.

"A war in Indonesia? No, that is not going to happen. But there will be much violence and bloodshed in many places for different reasons. A world war will come very soon thereafter and when it does, no one would know it for not a single shot would be fired."

"But I don't understand. How can there be a war without a shot being fired? Do you mean there will be another cold war?"

"A cold war? No. Your university days and your history books have taught you much but you have been reading all the wrong books. The future of the world has been written a long, long time ago and that story will be played out to its bitter end."

Gesturing to the television set which was again carrying a story on the Jakarta attacks, Saeed asked: "So this, this all was done to help her get elected?"

"In part yes, but more importantly, it will set the scene for the next great distraction."

"And what ... what will that be?"

Hassan picked up a copy of the US daily *The Independent*. Its bold headline screamed: 'Terrorists unleash the fires of hell' as it splashed gory colour pictures of the incinerating fires that had swept across Jakarta and the bodies it left behind. Rubbing his chest again, he could feel that burning sensation spreading outwards from his heart. The time of fire was indeed drawing near.

"All this," said Hassan, "as terrible as it seems now, it will soon be forgotten when a star is born. And only the faithful who follow that star, will learn the truth."

"Star? Huh … what star? Boss, you are speaking in riddles again. I don't understand at all."

"Don't worry. You will … in time."

17

WASHINGTON D.C. – NOVEMBER 7, 0107 HOURS

The unusually high voter turnout had kept polling stations across the nation open for an extra hour.

Despite the months of arduous campaigning and the endless debates about improving healthcare and shoring up America's financial systems, the Jakarta attacks simply overshadowed these domestic concerns and preoccupied the minds of many voters as they proceeded to elect a new leader.

Once again Americans were reminded that they were being singled out by terrorists. Lofty ideals of free speech and democracy were set aside, replaced by the primal need for self-preservation from a faceless enemy that seemed able to strike at will. For many, the attack on the two school buses was the final straw.

All across the US, Americans gathered to watch their President promise to strike back, to pull out all the stops and hunt down those who would threaten their safety. They wanted to believe him; they needed to believe in him.

As they headed solemnly for the polling booths, old party allegiances were tossed aside. All that mattered today was choosing which candidate would be better at keeping America and their families safe.

The inward looking Republican candidate Senator Harrison Coal promised much in the way of domestic reforms. He dangled temptingly the juicy carrots of improved healthcare, lower taxes and changes to the volatile banking industry which had caused so much global woes in recent years. But he had also pledged to pay for this by making steep military cuts and shrinking the size and reach of America's defence forces, essentially pulling them back to protect the home shores.

They remembered the last Republican President and his cronies who had side-stepped answering the many haunting questions about the 9-11 attacks. Millions had watched the Internet documentaries that followed and questioned why the most powerful nation on earth had been caught so unprepared to defend itself at home. They felt lied to and betrayed as the nation was dragged into a bloody and unnecessary war in Iraq on the basis of unfounded accusations that Saddam Hussein was on the verge of developing nuclear weapons.

Perhaps at best, Senator Coal may be a good president in times of peace. But the horrific images on television reminded the voting public that dark ominous clouds were once again on the horizon.

Secretary of State Kelly Yee on the other hand, had promised little in the way of freebies. She had cajoled and sometimes bravely lashed out at Corporate America to shake off its apathy and fight – to compete headlong with the economic powerhouses of China and the rest of Asia and the rising industrial might of South America for its share of economic success and to stem the downward spiral of the American dollar.

Kelly had pledged to scrutinise reckless defence spending while keeping America's defences strong. The speech she had given just hours before was still ringing in their ears.

She said: "The horror that has occurred in Jakarta is yet another reminder that the world we face today is much different.

"The bitter Cold War is long dead. Eastern Europe is free. The once-reclusive China has emerged as a superpower which threatens to engulf this nation. The economic fate of the European Union still hangs precariously in the balance and with terrorists getting increasingly ruthless, the fight continues. These are the cold realities of today's world.

"Just as the era of empire-building is over, the political and economic dominance of one nation over all others is also a thing of the past.

"The only way forward for America is not to go down a protectionist road or worse still, retreat inward into Senator Coal's little shell. Now, more than ever before, America needs to be united and strong – economically and militarily. To cure all that ails America and suppress all those who threaten our peace, requires the commitment and dedication of every citizen.

"We need to band together and compete head to head with other nations for our fair share of economic prosperity. And we will be successful not by dominating others but by cooperating with our friends and allies for mutual benefit, stability and growth. It is the growing rift of economic imbalance among countries rather than any perceived religious divide that is the true cause threatening world peace.

"Formulating fair and sustainable cross-border business practices, helping the developing world evolve, showing mutual respect and tolerance for all religions and beliefs – this is the path to success not just for America but for the world at large.

"We will always need a strong military to oppose all those who are jealous of our freedom and the success that it brings.

"And America needs a strong, committed and resolute government to make all this happen. Today voters like you are turning out in numbers larger than we have seen in a generation, to pick a new leader whose vision would guide this great nation forward.

"I say to you then, be not afraid. Stand by me as I shall stand by you and together, we shall keep this country strong. Together we will engage the world and banding together, we will do what needs to be done to protect our children, our families, our country and our future."

It was not even a close fight as pundits had predicted months earlier. In the hours that followed her speech, 'Kelly-mania' as the media dubbed it, had swept the nation as the country welcomed its first woman to the highest office in the land.

18

POLICE HEADQUARTERS, SINGAPORE – NOVEMBER 8, 1232 HOURS

Far removed from the heady excitement gripping America following the election of Kelly Yee, the police in Singapore had made another chilling discovery in their investigation of the nuclear trigger.

For two weeks now, the Singapore authorities had stepped up their checks at all entry and exit points across the island. It was a mammoth and yet discreet operation with thousands of vehicles, ships and airplanes scanned to detect the presence of any radioactive particles. And this morning, they finally stumbled upon the elusive radioactive trail.

A high-speed passenger cruiser plying between Singapore and the holiday Indonesian island of Bintan one hour away was berthed at the Tanah Merah Ferry Terminal waiting to take on its next load of passengers. Using a hand-held detector, officers from the Police Coast Guard nailed their first positive sign of radiation.

"They were scanning the starboard side of the vessel when they got the spike. It was very faint but it's definitely 239 – weapon's grade and it has to be the core," said Associate Professor Viviane Then to the other members of Operation Thunder as they gathered behind locked doors in the conference room of Police Headquarters three hours later.

Plutonium 239 is a rare isotope of plutonium and like Uranium 235, it is used primarily as fuel for a nuclear weapon.

"We couldn't detect any other traces until we had the ferry towed and dry-docked at the Changi Naval Base," said Viviane.

"And that's when my people took over," continued Colonel Brenton Wong of Military Intelligence. "We had a much stronger hit about a metre or so below the waterline. There were some scratches on the ferry's side at that spot and we detected some residual magnetism.

"It would appear that the plutonium core was probably encased in some protective container which was then attached using strong electromagnets to the side of the ship. It would have gone completely unnoticed as it was well below the waterline. A scuba diver could come in to port, retrieve the container and get out without anyone ever detecting him. If it was done at night, even his bubbles wouldn't be visible."

Said Viviane, "We got the hit only because the core had irradiated part of the ship's metal hull where it had been attached. But even then, the trace was very faint meaning all of this could have happened days or even weeks ago."

"So the million dollar question is which way was it travelling – Singapore to Indonesia or Indonesia to Singapore?" said the Commissioner.

"With all due respect sir," said Brent, "I don't think that makes a whole lot of difference. If this is a do-it-yourself nuke and if it is detonated by terrorists in Bintan, Indonesia, with the monsoon season we are in now and the direction of the prevailing winds, the radioactive plume is still likely to drift over to Singapore."

"Where are we in checking on the passengers and crew of that ferry?" continued the Commissioner.

"We have impounded the vessel and detained the six-man crew – all Indonesians," said lead investigator ASP Gerald Loh. "We are also tracking down the names of the passengers over the past month but they could number up to several hundred at least. We'll run their IDs through the computer all the same."

"These passengers, could they have been exposed to radiation while on board that vessel?" asked the Commissioner.

"Highly unlikely," responded Viviane. "Judging from the small amount of radiation detected, the plutonium core was probably quite well shielded. Anyone who had direct, physical contact with the container such as the scuba diver may receive a small dose of radiation – but probably not enough to kill unless he is stupid enough to open the container and handle the core without protection. But as for the passengers on the ferry itself, it is highly unlikely that they would have received any significant exposure at all."

"Well at least we can be thankful for that," said the Commissioner. "So where are we in the investigation now?"

Viviane was the first to give her update reporting that a number of undercover operatives disguised as port workers were continuing to search the giant Keppel Container Terminal with hand-held radiation detectors for other nuclear components.

"So far we've got absolutely nothing," she said. "But following this morning's development, we have to assume that there may be a nuclear core somewhere on the island. We still have our four NESTs patrolling in a grid pattern sniffing for airborne radioactive particles using the equipment the Americans sent us. They are working shifts, 24 hours a day, but that as you can imagine this is still a long shot."

Suggested Brent: "Ever thought of using helicopters? It will be a lot faster and we can cover more ground."

"That wouldn't work in an urban environment," countered Viviane. "You would need to fly low and slow and even if you got a hit, it would be hard to pinpoint the source. Besides, the prop wash from the rotor blades would make it nearly impossible to get an accurate analysis of the air."

"And low flying helicopters are going to make a lot of people jumpy," added Gerald. "The terrorists could just set the nuke on a timer and run or turn themselves into suicide bombers if they thought the police were closing in on them."

"But Viv, what realistically are the chances of your detectors getting an airborne hit?" asked the Commissioner.

"To be honest, pretty slim," said Viviane. "As long as the core remains well shielded in its protective casing, very little radiation will leak out. And to then detect such minute airborne traces in a passing vehicle … well …" and her voice trailed off.

"Okay but keep at it. Gerald, what about you?"

"Well Commissioner, despite intensive probing, neither the Kuwaiti company which had sent the container with the industrial metal piping nor the oil exploration company in Jakarta which was the intended recipient, appear to have any links to terrorists according to American intelligence. That's also the assessment of the Indonesian authorities.

"We have questioned over 100 port workers here – half of them foreigners.

The locals, apart from some traffic violations and petty juvenile offences, all appear clean. The background checks on the foreigners are taking a lot longer as expected. Still we are running all the names through the CIA to see if anything pops up."

"Any progress with the interrogation of the JI detainees we have in custody?"

"That is still on-going," said Gerald. "Mas Selamat as expected is not saying anything. We know that he spent a considerable amount of time in Indonesia. Of course he is denying even knowing the JI leaders, Yusman bin Iranto and the others.

"We are still working on another 24 detainees we have locked up as well as 39 others on home supervision. Sixteen from the latter group had visited Indonesia in the past three years but these appear to be short holidays taken with their families. We have all of them under surveillance and our Internal Security Department has made it plain that if any of them even appear to be less than fully cooperative, we will revoke their home detention orders and they'll be back behind bars indefinitely."

"Yeah we need to get a lot tougher with these people especially now that we seem to have traces of a core about. Okay Brent, what have you got?" asked the Commissioner.

"The metallurgical test on the polonium disc has narrowed down the probable area of origin to be somewhere in Central Asia or Eastern Europe."

"Russian?" said the Commissioner.

"Possibly, but it's really difficult to be sure. It could have been mined there originally and refined to a weapon's grade level in anyone of half a dozen countries."

"And what are the Americans saying?"

"When we first told them about the polonium, they were of course concerned but they appeared to be more focused on other foreign threats including a possible terrorist hit in Indonesia. I guess they were right there.

"But today when I notified their State Department about the traces of the Plutonium 239, that got their attention. They said they would be tapping their sources 'vigorously' and will let us know if they hear anything. They will also be questioning their detainees at Guantanamo to see if those guys know anything."

"Anything else?"

"Yup Commissioner, one more," said Brent. "The US Navy is deploying a carrier task force to the region. It's going to be based in international waters just outside Singapore. I guess they want some military assets in place for a counterstrike in Indonesia if the targets are known. They have also asked for our help in trying to pinpoint the JI bases, its training camps and the whereabouts of its leaders."

"I assume we are cooperating?" asked the Commissioner.

"Fully – these are things we need to know too, now more so with this plutonium hit. Our air force will also be conducting joint military exercises with the American task force. These war games were scheduled to be held early next year but given the recent events, they were pushed forward. Also it makes a good cover story for the fleet to remain in the region," said Brent.

Questioned Viviane: "Hang on … assuming this nuke is meant for Singapore, wouldn't that make us an even bigger target if there is some giant US aircraft carrier round the corner?"

Countered Brent: "That's possible but then again, with the presence of an offensive carrier task force breathing down their necks, it may just give these terrorists pause to think twice."

"Well either way we can't do much about the Americans if they want to park one of their aircraft carriers in international waters even if it's just outside our doorstep," said the Commissioner. "It's all politics and way over our heads. Let's focus on the investigation here."

"If they were to hit us, what would be their high-value targets?" said Viviane.

"Viv, you have to understand that we are talking about a nuclear weapon," said Gerald. "You don't need to get close to your target to wipe it off the face of this earth – just getting within a kilometre or two would be good enough."

"How big of a bang are we talking about then?" asked Viviane.

"Well as I've said before, we can only speculate," replied Brent. "There are many factors to consider. It is not just the size of the bomb and the timing of the attack but also the location of the device at the point of detonation, be it sub-surface, surface or an air burst. Air-burst detonations just like Hiroshima and Nagasaki will of course be the most destructive."

"Exactly what kind of post-blast destruction are we talking

about?" asked the Commissioner.

"I've discussed this with my defence specialists," continued Brent. "They feel a terrorist group would probably only be able to put together a small nuke, perhaps about 20 kilotons. Still, with an optimum air burst detonation like in Hiroshima, the initial blast would destroy most buildings within a radius of 1.2 kilometres and ..."

"Hang on," interrupted the Commissioner. "You can't really compare old Japanese cities of the 1940s with a modern day city like Singapore. Our buildings are bigger, taller and stronger with reinforced cores."

"You are right up to a point," explained Brent. "Sure the technology of modern buildings has progressed a lot over the years. But that wouldn't really make a whole lot of difference if you are at Ground Zero when a nuke goes off.

"In fact, with our buildings constructed so close together, these tall structures would trap and funnel the blastwave increasing its destructive power. So the overall impact will probably be worse. One collapsing building will topple others like a stack of giant dominoes.

"If it is a surface detonation, the thermal energy released into the ground from the explosion could trigger a moderate, shallow earthquake. Our buildings here are simply not designed to withstand that. Remember a lot of our buildings are constructed on reclaimed land that for the most part, is soft marine clay and sand. It's far from being as stable as solid bedrock. So when the ground gives way, those buildings, as strong as they may be, will certainly come crashing down.

"The superheated air blasted out by the shockwave would cause third degree burns on unprotected skin and start fires within a radius of 3.2 kilometres. Then of course there are the blast injuries and radiation to consider …"

"A radius of 3.2 kilometres – that's enough to destroy half the Central Business District …" interrupted Viviane.

"… or an entire satellite town or Changi Airport," said Gerald.

"… or take out any number of military units or our airbases," said Brent.

"But … I still don't understand. Why would anyone want to target Singapore? What the hell have we ever done to them?"

"Viv, as much as I hate to say this," said Brent, "Singapore is the perfect target for a terrorist nuclear strike. We've known this for years … it's one of the hot topics for strategy debates at our military Command and Staff College."

"Huh? But why?" said Viviane.

"Because terrorists know that if you strike at obvious targets in the US, the reprisals will be swift, overwhelming and simply crippling to their organisation. They learnt that the hard way after 9-11 and the war it triggered in Afghanistan. You see, al-Qaeda under bin Laden didn't have much of a plan for growing the organisation after the strike on the US. He simply assumed that Muslims from all over the world would take up arms and join in his so-called Holy War. Sure some did, but without a solid post-9-11 plan to keep the momentum going, it simply fizzled out and al-Qaeda itself was severely hurt in the war that it had essentially started.

"But now with bin Laden out of the picture, the operating strategies of terrorist organisations appear to have evolved."

"How? If they explode a nuclear weapon, won't that just make the Americans more determined than ever to crush them?" said Gerald.

"Well yes and no. Terrorists today aren't out to conquer the whole world. They know they can't. So they will probably be more than willing to settle for a stand-off with the US. With nukes in hand, they can blackmail the world to back off and give them some breathing space – perhaps even an area that they can govern on their own."

"And why would the US ever allow that?" asked Gerald.

"Because of MAD – Mutually Assured Destruction. Any country would think twice before going head-to-head against a terrorist organisation that has proven to have nukes at its disposal, the ability to smuggle them across borders, and the willingness to push that button.

"For almost half a century, we've lived in peace despite an ever-growing Cold War. Two mortal enemies – the US and the then-Soviet Union – both standing eyeball to eyeball, each bristling with nuclear weapons ready to fly at a moment's notice. But nobody pulled the trigger because of MAD. One country can't destroy the other without it being nuked in return and totally destroyed. It's a zero sum game."

"Brent, that's history! What does it have to do with this?" asked Viviane.

"Well the same principle more or less still applies. The Americans would be reluctant to strike if they knew that a terrorist organisation could detonate a nuke in any of its cities.

"But for this standoff to work," he continued, "the terrorists would first have to prove that they not only have the power of the atom at their disposal but also the willingness, the sheer audacity to actually use these weapons. And the best way to prove this beyond all doubt is to have a small, live demonstration.

"But of course you would first need to pick the right target. If you nuke California for example, the US will stop at nothing to hunt you down and bomb you back to the Stone Age if you are lucky, no matter what the consequences for America may be. You are also not going to hit somewhere like Timbuktu in the African Sahara because it's too remote for a demonstration and the world doesn't have much vested interest in a place like that.

"You need to pick a small, juicy and highly visible target – a tiny nation that after being struck would be too decimated to respond militarily. A small country hosting lots of 'foreign talent' and foreign investments so the effects will reverberate across the globe. You need to find one that is a global banking hub so millions of dollars can be wiped out when the EMPs – the Electromagnetic Pulse – radiating out from the blast, fries every computer for kilometres around.

"If your intended target is also a major petroleum refining centre – then that's going to disrupt global oil supplies for months at least.

"Ninety percent of world commerce relies on shipping lanes so if your little glow-in-the-dark, highly irradiated target sits at a major choke point for global shipping – think of what that would do to the world's economy.

"You need to pick a small country surrounded by large Muslim nations where you can seek refuge after the attack – preferably one with impenetrable jungle that would bog down even the most advanced army. Given the harsh terrain with many places to hide, explosive religious tensions and the threat of more nuclear reprisals this time directed at major American or Western cities – all this would make the US or any other country for that matter, think twice about starting another war.

"Singapore as a target fits the bill in every category – and that's why we are the perfect sitting duck for a nuclear strike!"

"So you mean to say that if they were to strike Singapore, these terrorists would face no reprisals at all?" asked Viviane.

"Sure there will be the expected saber-rattling and the thumping of chests and the long political speeches and the usual ineffective overtures by the UN – but just about every nation would know that if terrorists can take out Singapore with one nuke, any one of their cities could equally be at risk if they try and start another war. It will be a whole new ballgame, a stalemate, and everyone is gonna be scared shitless waiting for the next move to happen," said Brent.

19

ONBOARD THE *USS GEORGE WASHINGTON* IN THE
SOUTH CHINA SEA NORTH-EAST OF SINGAPORE –
NOVEMBER 15, 0202 HOURS

Lieutenant Commander Robert Green braced himself as
his Super Hornet was catapulted off the *George Washington*
reaching its launch speed of 288 kilometres an hour in just
1.5 seconds.

Safely free of the carrier, he banked his jet sharply to port
and pulled into a steep climb to regroup with his fighters
waiting overhead. Within two minutes, the carrier was a
barely-visible speck of light in the blackness of the sea
below him. He could feel the air bladders in his G-suit
begin to compress around his legs as the jet, straining
against the force of gravity, pushed him ever higher into
the night sky.

Punching through the cloud bank, he soon caught sight of
the blinking navigation lights on the other fighters. Green
eased off the throttle as he reached his cruising altitude of
8,000 metres. There he took up his lead position at the
head of the seven jet formation and together they headed

out to the horizon for yet another night practice run.

As they flew in silence, Green had time to think about the mission and what they were practicing for. He had no qualms about striking the terrorist camps in the jungle and killing those who had caused so much death and suffering in Jakarta.

With these camps far removed from civilian areas, the chances of collateral damage and injuries to innocent bystanders were much reduced. But still the mission would be fraught with many dangers and uncertainties. They would be violating Indonesian air space and risk being shot down. They would have to fly low, at almost treetop level to evade radar and they would be flying at night in uncertain monsoon weather.

Intelligence analysts in Washington had assured them that the chances of encountering 'significant anti-aircraft capabilities' on their approach to the target were remote but Green knew full well how faulty such intelligence reports can be. If his aircraft was crippled by hostile fire, bailing out over thick jungle could in itself be fatal. And even if he could parachute safely to the ground, his chances of survival in such a harsh and unforgiving terrain would be slim at best.

But he would worry about all this later, if and when that time came. For now, Green needed to focus all his skills and concentration for the practice mission at hand.

Far ahead of him was his quarry – a three-metre-long floating platform bobbing harmlessly on the surface of the sea. It had been towed there by another ship which had since moved off to a safe distance but it remained close enough to film the mock bomb run with its high-speed night-vision cameras.

The coordinates of the target had already been fed into Green's flight computer. On a small screen to his right, the targeting computer picked up the platform floating on the sea now sixteen kilometres away.

Locking it into his digital map, he turned to the monitor on his left and scrolled to the weapons payload screen. It displayed the various types of ordinance at his disposal. Although this was just a practice bomb run, as security for the task force had been stepped up, all the attack jets were loaded with live weapons as well including Air-to-Air Sidewinder missiles should they need to protect themselves or the carrier group now far behind them.

Navigating through the various weapons on display, Green made his selection – a GBU-32 JDAM [P]. This was a practice bomb which was fitted with a dummy 450kg Mark 83 warhead.

JDAM or Joint Direct Attack Munition is a guidance kit that converts unguided or 'dumb' gravity bombs into all-weather 'smart' weapons. JDAM-equipped bombs are guided by an integrated inertial guidance system coupled to a Global Positioning System receiver, giving them a range of up to 15 nautical miles or 28 kilometres. An upgraded version which was used extensively for precision bombing missions in Afghanistan and Iraq, also featured a laser seeker which vastly improved its accuracy to within five metres of the target.

Although this training mission was to be done under strict radio silence, the only exception to this rule was the Forward Air Controller who would communicate directly with the attack pilots.

Circling high overhead in another plane, a twin-turboprop Grumman E-2 Hawkeye, the controller codenamed Nightmare would ensure that the target was set in place correctly and that the area was clear of all civilian shipping traffic. The FAC would then contact each pilot in turn giving him permission to proceed with the night's exercise.

Green was concentrating on the indicators in his Heads-Up Display when his headphones suddenly crackled to life.

"Exercise, Exercise, Exercise – Foxbat One – Nightmare … Launch envelope is open. You are cleared to proceed with mock bomb run. Go weapons hot on practice JDAM – Target Vector 24. Good hunting," said the Forward Air Controller.

"Nightmare – Foxbat One, Roger … Exercise confirmed. Foxbat One going weapons free on practice JDAM," replied Green as his Super Hornet entered the launch envelope and dived to 4,200 metres – the optimum height in which to release his weapon.

With the Hornet's laser designator locked on to the target, he waited as his on-board computers calculated continuously his speed and position for the exact point in time and space to let loose his chosen ordinance.

On his HUD, Green watched as the target range began closing in. His gloved finger moved to the launch switch.

Seconds later, the word 'FIRE' flashed in green on his HUD. He hit the pickle button releasing the JDAM from under his right wing.

"Nightmare – Foxbat One, weapon released," said Green as he banked hard left. The nose of his jet rose slightly as the heavy warhead left its rack. From the corner of his eye Green caught sight of a flash of grey as his wingman flying to his right, followed his evasive manoeuvre.

Together, still flying in perfect battle formation, the two jets circled waiting for the results of their strike to be reported.

Unlike most missiles, the GBU-32 JDAM has no internal power source to propel it forward. Instead it uses gravity and the speed of the jet at the point of launch as forward momentum to reach its target.

From the moment it was released, electronics in the weapon's tail using GPS coordinates, adjusted its flight fins making constant corrections to guide the weapon home. The bomb would fly the track on its own and in complete silence following the invisible laser beam all the way to the target.

Infrared cameras on the ship nearby and radar recordings on the carrier tracked the weapon as it streaked silently across the sky and splashed harmlessly in the sea just two metres from its target. It was another perfect hit.

"Foxbat One – Nightmare. Splashdown confirmed … Sierra Hotel … copy, over?" came the confirmation from the Forward Air Controller.

"Nightmare … Sierra Hotel … roger … Out," replied Green as he smiled to himself. Sierra Hotel was the phonetic abbreviation for 'Shit Hot' – high praise indeed for a pilot who was dead on target.

Still flying in tight formation, they egressed out of the target zone as the next pair of fighters waited patiently for their turn to attack and once again the cameras would be rolling.

20

ANDREWS AIR FORCE BASE, WASHINGTON D.C. –
NOVEMBER 14, 1440 HOURS

As Lieutenant Commander Robert Green led his
formation back to the USS *George Washington* after another
successful practice run, it was a bleak and bitterly cold
November afternoon back in the US capital.

Flags at Andrews Air Force Base on the outskirts of
Washington D. C. were flying at half-mast. The Marine
Corp's band waited silently on the tarmac with their heads
bowed as the wheels of the giant Lockheed C-5 Galaxy
aircraft of the US Air Force rolled to a stop.

President-Elect Kelly Yee stood with her husband Victor
and their two teenage children Lauryn and Jordan
alongside the President and the senior members of his
Administration as they witnessed the bodies of 47
Americans including 36 children killed in Jakarta being
unloaded from the plane.

As the band played that haunting song *'I Believe'*, the
children were brought out first. Their remains, hermetically

sealed in cold white metal coffins with shiny brass handles, were carried out reverently by Marines wearing their crisp ceremonial uniforms. On each coffin, someone had placed a plush toy bear carrying a small American flag in its tiny paws.

Last off the plane were two coffins, each draped with the American flag. A lone bugler played 'Taps' as the caskets were carried into their awaiting hearses. These were the remains of two Marines who were killed in the first blast outside the Blok M shopping centre. The men had been escorting a visiting diplomat when they were caught in the traffic jam moments before the explosion. Suspecting a trap, the diplomat together with a third Marine hastily left the vehicle and moved away from the scene on foot while the other two remained in their unmarked car. Both Marines were killed instantly when the fireball from the blast tore through their vehicle barely two minutes later.

Ironically the diplomat, Under Secretary of State Michael Collins was visiting Jakarta to meet with some government officials to discuss the possible terrorist threats facing the country. He and his escort were only slightly injured by falling glass shards.

It had taken almost a week, far longer than most people had expected before the bodies of the dead could be released by the authorities in Indonesia. Gathering forensic evidence at the scene, performing the autopsies and making positive DNA identifications on all the victims had taken time and tension was mounting in the US to bring its dead home.

Four days earlier, President Monroe had personally called

the Indonesia premier urgently requesting that the process be speeded up as much as possible as the C-5 Galaxy transport plane was dispatched to Jakarta.

Between filming scenes of the coffins being unloaded from the plane and placed in hearses, the cameras of the media shifted between tight shots of President Theodore Monroe and President-Elect Kelly Yee. And the differences were stark.

The President, a widower, stood alone looking impassive and resolute. The eight years that he had occupied the White House had taken a toll on him, ageing him prematurely with the heavy burden of his office. The Commander-in-Chief stood stoically still only raising his right hand slowly in a final salute when the two flag-draped coffins were carried past him.

He had always been uncomfortable with the pomp and ceremony that came with the job but today, on this cold November afternoon, it was different. He could not remember a time when it was harder for him to stand here alone without flinching and be seen as a pillar of strength to the nation as he felt a president should. His heart wept bitterly when the little coffins were carried out one by one in a line that seemed endless, but still he stood tall. As hard as all this was, this was still part of his job – at least for the next two months.

He knew in his heart that it was his intelligence agencies that had failed him and the nation once again by not uncovering this plot in time. Maybe their job was an impossible one given the few clues that they had in hand. Monroe had long since accepted the fact that his presidency would be forever marred by this one single tragic event and all the good that he had tried to accomplish over the past eight years would largely be forgotten. As president, he could not blame anyone for the buck as always, stopped with him.

Still, he did have some time left in office to help put this ugly situation right and Monroe, with anger swelling inside him, was determined to do just that. History and his own sense of unwavering righteousness would demand nothing less.

It was Kelly Yee's first public appearance with her family since her election victory barely a week earlier. This was not the way she had hoped it would be. Still she felt that it was important to have her family next to her. Beyond the senseless politics of this attack, the deaths of so many children were a tragedy for the American Family. Kelly's husband and children readily stood by her side as the nation still reeling in shock, mourned for its dead children.

As television cameras zoomed in, Kelly made no move to hide the tears that rolled down her cheeks. Like many mothers across the nation, this was a time to weep for those little lives so cruelly snuffed out, their innocent laughter to be heard no more.

Thousands of Americans lined the roads in complete silence. Many held candles, some sobbed quietly in groups hugging each other for comfort and strength as the lengthy cortege made its way from Andrews Air Force Base to the Washington National Cathedral at the corner of Massachusetts and Wisconsin Avenues for a brief funeral service. From there, the dead would be escorted back to their home cities across the country for burial by their families.

As expected, pictures of President-Elect Yee with tears rolling down her face were splashed across newspapers the next morning. Some political watchers wondered aloud if she really had the sterner stuff necessary for such an office and the difficult challenges she would undoubtedly face. But it was the netizens who rushed to her defence, proudly applauding her for not hiding her grief.

Kelly herself knew she risked being attacked in the media for showing her emotions so openly but she felt that it was a perfectly natural emotion and one that should not be suppressed for cheap political gain. There would be time enough for America and the world to judge her and her actions over the coming four years. This was a time to grieve with the rest of the country. But she also knew that the time of reckoning was fast approaching and for her, it could not come soon enough.

21

OVAL OFFICE, THE WHITE HOUSE, WASHINGTON
D.C. – NOVEMBER 18, 1410 HOURS

"And NSA is sure that this base is operational?" questioned the President as he gesticulated to the television monitor in his office. "I don't see any people, any signs of life."

The high-resolution satellite picture on the monitor showed a desolate clearing in the jungle with nine wooden buildings partially obscured by the surrounding trees. A bare winding path led from the buildings to the river nearby where two wooden boats were moored.

"Three separate sources have confirmed that this is an operational JI training camp," said Director of the National Security Agency James Carron. He explained that the camp was only used during certain months of the year. "It's basically a boot camp for new recruits to give them some paramilitary jungle training and to weed out the weak and the unmotivated. These camps are occupied from around November to January during the North-East Monsoon season. It rains heavily almost every day and the whole area turns into one giant muddy mess – lousy for mounting a military strike but excellent to get their raw recruits nice and dirty.

"As JI trains its people mainly for urban warfare, these jungle camps are used simply for their remoteness. There are no roads anywhere close by so the only way in or out is by boat and they have look-outs along the river. By night, the recruits sleep in these buildings. In the early morning there is some physical training and weapons handling is done at an improvised shooting range here, just north of the camp. Then its classroom lessons for the rest of the day," said Carron.

"The recruits are taught the basics of mixing explosives, prepping IEDs and making booby traps. We estimate that there could be up to 180 militants in the camp. Those who graduate, go on to attend more classes in a number of cities where they are taught other terrorist skills like communication, surveillance and logistics planning."

"What about the senior members of JI – those are the guys that we want not a bunch of novice, misguided recruits," said the President.

"Mr President," said CIA Director William Baldwin, "our understanding is that some senior members are at the camp now conducting the training. JI's leadership is spread out across a number of cities all over Indonesia. Most of their communication is done through couriers delivering encrypted handwritten letters, coded emails or disposable cell phones. This makes such communication difficult to intercept on any sustained basis.

"Our sources say the JI leader Yusman bin Iranto is still in Jakarta but he moves around a lot. He's been known to stay in over a dozen houses and apartments around the city and in the suburbs. To take him or any of his top lieutenants out, we need to expend a lot more time and resources on the ground and have snatch teams ready to pounce at a moment's notice. If we aim to detain them, it needs to be a well coordinated operation. When word gets out that we have grabbed one, the rest will simply go deep underground."

"And even if we do get them," said President-Elect Kelly Yee, "we can't just smuggle Yusman or any of the others out of the country. We would have to hand them over to the Indonesian authorities and work out an extradition process. That alone could take months if not longer."

"Remember we do have the option of a sniper hit or a drone attack. It's fast and relatively cheap. But with a UAV strike, the odds of collateral damage could be significant," offered Director Carron.

"I'll leave those options on the table for now until such time as we can ascertain the whereabouts of the JI leadership. But I can't afford to wait weeks or months before we act. Any prolonged delay will be seen as a sign of weakness – that our political renewal process," he nodded to Kelly, "makes us unable to be prompt and decisive when we need to be. More so now that Singapore authorities believe they may have a plutonium core on the loose somewhere in this area."

"That, Mr President, is still technically a matter of speculation," pointed out Defence Secretary Brown. "The radiation traces that they got from that Indonesian ferry were very faint and ..."

"Be that as it may," said President Monroe with more than a touch of annoyance in his voice, "when we have a nuclear trigger recovered from a shipping container and then traces of what could be a plutonium core are found two weeks later, we can't ignore the very real possibility of a renegade nuclear weapon being assembled somewhere in either Singapore or Indonesia.

"If this base is the only confirmed target we have now, then that's what we will hit. If JI has its hands on a nuke, we need to be aggressive. Strike hard and fast at any and all targets of opportunity. Now General, how will this be done?"

"Mr President, immediately following the Jakarta attacks," said General Bradley Myers, Chairman of the Joint Chiefs of Staff at the Pentagon as he clicked the mouse on his laptop to bring up a map of Singapore and the region on the television monitor, "we have moved the Task Force 70 battlegroup of the Seventh Fleet to an area here just north east of Singapore. Our Super Hornet strike team has been conducting a series of low-altitude precision bombing workups over the past week or so. We have also been working on mock SEAL insertions.

"But we are now running low on fuel for many of our ships and some urgent repairs are also required for two of our frigates. I propose we bring the fleet in to Singapore to be refuelled, repaired and restocked. We will do this on an urgent basis and it should only take two to three days tops.

"We then move the *George Washington* and the rest of the task force to our final staging point here – about 120 nautical miles south east of our target – that terrorist camp. The guided missile destroyer *USS Arleigh Burke* will then launch four Tomahawk missiles which would obliterate the target. As a backup, we will have the strike squadron ready to fly in for an air-to-ground attack with JDAMs if need be. We also have a third option of sending in a SEAL team to destroy the base in a ground attack. The SEALs will also be ready for a rescue operation if any of our planes go down.

"I'm proposing we strike on the night of the 24th. It would be moonless and the weather reports indicate that we should have a break from the thunderstorms which can affect the GPS targeting systems on our Tomahawks. A weather-break would also make it safer if our planes need to go in."

"What about civilians – any in or around the camp?"

"Mr President, it's too risky at this time to put eyes on the ground but our satellite pictures show the area is clear of any significant groups of civilians."

"But General,' said Kelly, "aren't we taking a huge gamble having all our ships at a Singapore port when we still have that unknown nuke factor to consider?"

"Yes Ma'am, but we don't have much choice. The Task Force itself was due to be rotated home just before the Jakarta attacks. Fuel and other supplies are low. I would assume that after this strike, those ships would have to remain on station for quite a while longer so we really need to see to the logistics now when we have the chance. Singapore is the only port in the region that has the repair capabilities. If we wait until after the strike, our presence in some ports may be well … less than welcoming," replied the General.

The President stared at the television monitor for several more seconds weighing his limited options. "Alright Bradley, move the battlegroup to Singapore and get your logistics sorted out quickly. Let's keep this operation as quiet as possible so make sure that there are no press leaks. Two days in port maximum and then I want the fleet out at their staging area. Until we have a better handle on this nuclear threat, I want to keep our ships far out at sea. That's the safest place for them to be."

22

SOUTH CHINA SEA, NORTH-EAST OF SINGAPORE –
NOVEMBER 20, 0917 HOURS

The constant fleet protection drills by day and the nightly bomb practice runs of the last week left the Task Force crew worn and on edge. So news that they were heading into Singapore for a few days was greeted with a great sense of relief.

Still, Task Force commander Vice Admiral Forrestal made it clear that this was not a pleasure stop but a quick repair and resupply operation. Only a quarter of the crew would be given a day of shore leave – a traditional concession when the fleet hits port.

But there would be no let up for Lieutenant Commander Robert Green, his fellow pilots and ground crew. They would fly out from the *George Washington* that night while the Task Force was still at sea and land at the Tengah Air Base on the north western side of Singapore. From there they would use the country's bombing range to continue their night practice workups but this time on land targets. The squadron would rejoin the Task Force in a few days time when it made its way to the final staging area.

As he packed his small overnight bag for his short stay in Singapore, Green had time to reflect on the strike mission to come. He knew that despite all their intense preparations of the last few days, he and his men would be a backup for the Tomahawk cruise missiles which would fly the strike mission and make the kill. Their Hornets would only take to the skies if something unexpected happened but the chances of that occurring were quite remote.

The Tomahawk was after all, an excellent weapon of choice. The long-range, all-weather, subsonic cruise missile was first flown in the 1970s and since then, it had undergone many significant improvements to its range, accuracy and payload. Flying low to the ground and following the earth's contours programmed in its electronic memory, it was virtually unstoppable. The main danger to a Tomahawk was damage by enemy ground fire or a lightning strike which could destroy its delicate electronic brain.

As a naval aviator who had seen his fair share of action in the recent *Operation Enduring Freedom* in Afghanistan and *Operation Iraqi Freedom*, Green was no stranger to combat. The fighter pilot in him longed to see action again in the upcoming strike. It would be swift and just revenge for the killing of so many civilians including children.

He removed the photograph of his family from his flight suit and looked into the faces of his two girls aged nine and five. The kids who were killed in that bus attack were probably around the same age. He would feel no remorse in striking that terrorist camp. Those guys would be dead long before they knew what hit them, he thought to himself as he stuffed the photograph back into his pocket.

He had made his weekly call home to Rachel, his wife, earlier that day. All he told her was that it was unlikely that he would be home for Christmas this year. Something had come up. He did not tell her of the possible upcoming mission but she must have sensed the tension in his voice. "Just do what you have to do, then come home 'cos we'll be waiting," that was her standard line. She never asked for details about his job and he would never tell her the horrors and near-misses during some of his missions. That single sentence said it all. It was enough to reaffirm their bond.

Slamming his locker shut, Green headed down the steep metal stairs to the maintenance deck to check on his Hornet which was being prepared to fly yet again in just a few hours.

23

ANG MO KIO INDUSTRIAL PARK, SINGAPORE –
NOVEMBER 20, 2237 HOURS

Saif checked his email once again and this time his heart skipped a beat. The message that he had been waiting for had finally arrived. The last two weeks since the attack in Jakarta had been long and mentally torturous for him as he knew his time was fast approaching.

Like any soldier, he hated the waiting for the mind goes into overdrive and the imagination replays scenarios of everything that could possibly go wrong. He had been tempted a number of times to email his handler in Riyadh to check if the plan was still on schedule. But he knew better than that. His orders had been explicit – no unnecessary communication unless something goes wrong. He had to sit tight and wait for further instructions.

Clicking on the email he read:

Greetings Bro,

Hey how have you been? Over here things are busy as usual. Looks like all the wedding plans are set to proceed on schedule. John did a final fitting for his suit and surprisingly, he looks quite good! All the parts for the reception tent have arrived and are sitting in the backyard creating a mess. Just waiting on the workers to start their final assembly.

We are hoping for some good weather so keep your fingers crossed. It should start at 6pm and hopefully everyone will arrive on time. Mum has everyone doing something and we all have to keep to a strict deadline. Yeah things here are going a little crazy. I can't wait until Saturday when it will be over! Take care.

Andy

Saif walked to the back of his office and retrieved the brown envelope he had taped to the underside of the third shelf. Pulling out the 31 coded sheets, he looked for the 20th which matched the date the email was sent. He then checked the code. It read 22, 65, 66, 83, 105, 118, 130, 137, 158 and the numbers went on. He began counting the words in the body of the email. The message was short and clear:

> *proceed final assembly*
> *6pm deadline Saturday*

He checked the numbers again making sure there was no mistake. But there was none. It was finally time to assemble the last pieces of the weapon. In two days time on Saturday the 22nd of November his waiting would be over and he should receive his final orders to deliver the operational weapon.

Saif had already assembled the sturdy metal frame of the bomb. Standing just over a metre tall, the stainless steel struts had been welded into place and the wiring had been hooked up to the command module which included a small electronic keypad and a digital display. The weapon would be fused and armed with a simple six digit code entered into the command module.

Once armed, it would be triggered by an electronic timer relay. A secondary microwave-activated switch would also be installed allowing the warhead to be detonated remotely using the signal from a handphone should the timer switch fail.

While military nuclear weapons are complicated beasts because of their sophisticated safety systems to prevent unauthorised tampering, the design of the weapon Saif would be working on would be far simpler.

Most nuclear missiles and bombs dropped from an aircraft are designed to be denoted while still in the air to maximise destruction over the target area. A mid-air detonation at a height of between 100 and 1000 metres allows the blast of the explosion to bounce off the ground creating a shockwave that is more powerful and destructive than a surface level detonation. Both atomic bombs unleashed on Japan during World War II were detonated at a height of between 550 and 600 metres to achieve their maximum damage potential.

But an accurate airburst over the target area would entail the use of sophisticated barometric switches to detect the altitude of the falling weapon and radar detectors to complete the last part of the firing circuit which would then trigger the detonation sequence.

As his weapon was designed to be exploded at ground level, Saif would not have to worry about such complicated systems. A surface-level explosion is far less destructive as a significant amount of the blast and resulting shockwave would be directed into the ground. But this ground penetration has the added benefit of generating larger and deeper thermal shocks destroying even modern reinforced buildings. It will also maximise residual radiation within the target area making the scene uninhabitable for years if not decades to come.

Still Saif's creation with its plutonium core of 11 kilogrammes, would have twice the destructive power of the atomic bomb that destroyed Nagasaki. It would vaporise everything within a radius of 1.8 kilometres or a little over a mile. He was sure this would be more than sufficient to obliterate his intended target whatever it may be.

Working within the stuffy confines of his anti-radiation suit, Saif knew that the next part of assembly would be the most dangerous – installing the core of the weapon. Before handing the plutonium fuel, he would need to position one of the two semi-spherical primary explosive modules. Each half resembling a salad bowl was made of thick, hardened titanium. On the inside were 16 hexagonal shaped charges of high explosives.

Delicately he positioned the bottom bowl and secured it to the outer frame with a series of thick titanium rods. He tugged on them making sure that the upturned bowl was firmly locked in place. He then placed a thin curved sheet of tungsten carbide into the bowl. This neutron reflector would significantly increase the amount of nuclear fission when the plutonium core went supercritical upon detonation.

The core itself would be next. This, like the explosive sphere, had been delivered in two halves. Adjusting his thick gloves, Saif gingerly removed the first half of the core from its protective waterproof metal casing and carefully placed it into the bottom bowl so that it sat snugly on the neutron reflector. He then used a laser positioner to make the final adjustments. The fit had to be exact, calculated down to the last millimetre.

In the centre of this half sphere was a small round cavity just over one centimetre deep. Inside this little opening, Saif inserted the nuclear trigger – the discs of beryllium and polonium which were separated by thin gold foil. He then connected the three wires from the trigger mechanism to the command module.

With the bottom half of the core done, Saif began assembling the rest of the device. The remaining half of the plutonium core was put into position followed by the neutron reflector and this was finally covered with the other half of the primary explosive titanium shell. He checked the guide markings on the outside of the 'salad bowl' to ensure both halves lined up perfectly.

Any mistake in the precise positioning of these explosives

could result in the core failing to attain a supercritical state and this would stop the nuclear chain reaction. Finally he tightened the 36 titanium bolts which secured the two halves together using a computerised torque wrench. This ensured that each bolt was tightened exactly to the same degree.

He took a step back and examined his work. He rechecked his notes one more time making sure that he did not miss any of the steps. The nuclear heart of the weapon was now in place.

To prevent premature detonation of the weapon, Saif then installed the MSAD. The Mechanical Safing and Arming Device is essentially a safety module which holds a small initiating charge of explosives out of alignment from the main explosives now inside the nuclear sphere. Only when the six-digit arming code is entered correctly into the command module does the MSAD bring the command detonator into position with the main shaped explosives surrounding the plutonium core.

It took him another two hours to complete the wiring of the charges to the command module. When this was done, he connected the last two wires to a small but reliable lithium ion battery. A little red light began blinking on the console panel of the command module.

Saif smiled to himself. The heart of the weapon had started to beat. He watched the flashing red light, mesmerised for several more seconds before disconnecting the battery again. Now his job was almost done.

He knew that removing the plutonium from its shielded

casing would increase the chances of radiation leaking out and possibly being detected. Still this was a risk that he had to take.

He checked his watch. It was just after 2.30am. If everything went on schedule, he would have just one more day to wait.

24

CHANGI COAST, SINGAPORE – NOVEMBER 21, 0832 HOURS

As they had been doing for the last three days, the two fishermen cast their lines into the water and waited. They had been camped here long enough to observe the comings and goings of vessels at the Changi Naval Base just a few hundred metres away.

The fishing had been poor at this desolate spot along the Tanah Merah Coast Road just beside the SAF Yacht Club but still they were not alone. Several families who braved the uncertain weather of the last two nights, were camped in cheap nylon tents nearby and the stale smell of barbequed fish hung in the air.

Little white capped waves stirred the otherwise calm sea as the first American frigate was sighted still far out at sea. Soon the rest of the fleet was clearly visible on the horizon. Among the dull grey ships was the unmistakeable shape of a giant aircraft carrier.

The men continued fishing patiently for almost an hour as

one by one the warships turned the corner out of view as they entered the sprawling Changi Naval Base. The aircraft carrier was the last in, towed by a number of small tugboats. On its mighty flight deck high above the water, the wingtips of jets were clearly visible. The fleet had finally arrived.

Still the men waited another two hours just to be sure that their targets were still at the base. Then they packed up their gear and left quietly heading for their black Nissan van parked by the roadside 100 metres away. Walking across the grassy patch, they tossed the three small fish they caught earlier that morning into a rubbish bin. The little yellow and blue Snappers had served their purpose.

The men made their way to Changi Village – a sleepy recreational suburb located a 10 minute drive away. There, at a public phone booth, one of the men made a long distance telephone call to Riyadh.

25

RIYADH, SAUDI ARABIA – NOVEMBER 21, 0835
HOURS

Hassan held the sleek polymer note up to the light as he scrutinised the security thread and watermarks. Master printer Mr Omar had been very thorough to point out all the various security features incorporated into the new currency assuring him that it would be almost impossible for such notes to be easily forged.

But forgery was the last thing from Hassan's mind. He was satisfied that the first batch of the new currency had finally been printed and was in place for speedy distribution to banks across the region.

It had taken several months to get the design right with agreements from all the Seven Heads. The notes, he had stressed in his earlier meetings with the men, must not carry any religious symbols nor should they be representative of any one country from the region. The designs, while reflective of the spirit and the culture of the Middle East, also had to be readily recognisable and accepted by any country around the world.

After numerous aesthetic changes, it was finally agreed that the main design element on the front of the Gold Dinar would depict sketches of three children, two boys and a girl along with the value of each note. On the lower left corner was stamped the words 'Printed by the Eastern Star Reserve Bank'. This ambiguous name was chosen on purpose. Such a bank did not exist yet but it soon would. On the lower right hand corner was the note's individual 18-digit serial number separated in three sets of six digits. The reverse side of the dinar featured a charcoal rendering of a lone figure riding on a white horse in the desert as dusk approaches with a bright star visible in the darkening sky.

All ten denominations of the dinar – one, two, five, ten, twenty, fifty, one hundred, five hundred, one thousand and ten thousand – would bear the identical designs and dimensions. The only differences would be the large printed value of each note and its respective colour.

It had cost considerably more to print the polymer notes rather than the usual paper currency but the added expense had been well worth it. Each dinar with its gold border looked impressive and they would last far longer than the various types of paper money currently in circulation. The glossy finish and expensive look was meant to inspire confidence in the value of the new currency.

Hassan had worked closely with the printer in secret, adding a range of abstract symbols to the background designs. To all but a trained eye, these would go virtually unnoticed and that was the point.

Three hundred and thirty-five million notes of different

denominations had been printed and were kept securely in warehouses across the region. Over the coming months much more would be printed. Potentially worth billions, they were as of now worthless and would remain so until their time came.

Another piece of the plan was falling into place on schedule and Hassan was pleased.

26

POLICE HEADQUARTERS, SINGAPORE – NOVEMBER 22, 1600 HOURS

"How certain are they?" asked the Commissioner impatiently. "We can't afford to make a mistake with something like this."

"Well obviously the Israelis are not going to reveal their sources but they seem to be damn confident that the nuke is here, in Singapore, and the components have been assembled. We still don't know the timing or the target. All the Israelis can tell us is that it is of major western interest," said Brent.

"What the hell does that mean? It could be hotels, businesses, banks, our casinos, just about anything. Are they holding back on us?"

"I really doubt that Commissioner. They have nothing to gain. If Israel wanted to keep it a secret, they simply wouldn't have said anything at all. They are trying to find out more but that is as much as their intelligence people have gathered as of now," said Brent.

"Of major western interest …," said Gerald. "If this is in any way connected with the strike in Jakarta – two of the seven targets there were American – the school and the embassy. With a nuke, you are not going to target just one building. The Singapore American School is in Woodlands and that's a pretty isolated residential area with a small American population living in the nearby Woodgrove Estate. The US Embassy here is situated smack in the middle of a whole bunch of embassies so that's one possibility. A nuke would take them all out. We've got a couple of western-owned hotels in our shopping belt along Orchard Road and with the holiday crowds the casualties would be massive there …"

"What about Marina Bay Sands?" suggested Viviane. "That's American-owned. It's big, iconic, with a large casino. Muslim radicals would probably want to target that. Plus it was designed by an Israeli."

Marina Bay Sands is one of two integrated resorts in Singapore. It was developed by Las Vegas Sands and is reputed to be the world's most expensive standalone casino property built at a cost of S$8 billion. The resort which opened in 2010 features a 2,561-room hotel, along with a convention-exhibition centre, shopping malls, restaurants and even a museum.

"Brent didn't you say earlier that an air-burst is the most efficient way of detonating a nuclear bomb? The three towers of that hotel are about what … 200 metres tall? Is that high enough?" asked Viviane.

"Yeah that's high enough for an air-burst to maximise the damage for sure," said Brent.

"But there are lots of other potential targets here as well," countered Gerald. "If I were them, I would want the effects to be felt globally. Vaporising one school or one resort isn't going to do that. The Central Business District with all its banks, the Stock Exchange … taking them out along with all their computer records will cause global mayhem. With a nuke, you may be able to destroy both targets – the resort and the business district."

"We also have the American fleet in town," added Brent. "It arrived at the Changi Naval Base yesterday and should be leaving tomorrow. It's only here for some urgent repairs and a quick shore leave for some of their crew. I understand the Israelis have informed the Americans about this latest piece of intel. We are not sure as yet if they would order the fleet out any earlier."

Commented Gerald: "Yeah that fleet could be a target but then again, the trigger was intercepted here exactly a month ago. They couldn't have known at the time that a US strike force would even be sailing in here …"

"Unless it was all planned," countered Viviane.

"Meaning?" asked Gerald.

"That those exploding truck bombs, that whole attack in Jakarta could have been staged just to lure a US attack fleet to the region and then destroy it with a nuke."

"That's possible Viviane," said Brent, "but it's also a whole lot of trouble to go through just for that. If they had wanted to target the fleet, why not hit them at their Japanese home port in Osaka?"

"Maybe they didn't want to risk going that far away from their home base in Indonesia?" speculated Viviane.

"Alright people," interrupted the Commissioner. "There are targets aplenty here but realistically there is not a whole lot we can do based on the limited information we have in hand at this time.

"Brent, I want you to sit on the Israelis and see what more we can find out. I have already spoken to our Prime Minister and the Defence chiefs. All our military units will be put on an Ops Thunder alert until further notice. Stay in touch with the Americans especially their NSA and CIA people – they may have some leads. Also let's keep tabs on this American fleet. The sooner we get them out the better. It would be one less thing to worry about.

"Gerald, I want increased police patrols in the city. Get as many of our uniformed guys about as you can. Hopefully a higher level police presence might be a deterrent – it's a long shot. The orders to the terrorists … these have to be coming in from somewhere. Let's increase our monitoring of handphones and the Internet. Any progress with the interrogations of the JI members we have in detention?"

"Nope, nothing at all, but we are still pushing. I've also ordered increased security checks at the airport for both inbound and outbound passengers. If these guys are about to set off a nuclear bomb, they are not going to sit around here. They would have made plans to leave as soon as possible and be clear of the blast. We have two SAF commando strike teams on standby at the airport just in case," said Gerald.

"Viviane, I assume your people are still out looking for radiation hits?"

"Yup, we've been concentrating in the city area without any luck. We are now moving into the suburbs around Hougang, Toa Payoh and Ang Mo Kio focusing on the industrial sites there."

"Ok keep at it …"

"Commissioner?" said Viviane. "Look I know all this spy stuff is new to me but isn't there something else we can do to …"

"Like?"

"Leak something to the press …"

"Are you crazy?" said Brent. "Then we'll have a panic on our hands …"

"I wasn't suggesting," replied Viviane somewhat annoyed, "that we tell them everything! We could just have it leaked that we are investigating a terrorist threat and are closing in on the perpetrators … or well, something along those lines. It may just make those guys panic and maybe they'll abort and run …"

"Oh yes, brilliant. I'm sure that would scare them!" said Brent sarcastically. "What's to stop them from just setting the damn nuke off immediately?"

"Isn't that what they are planning to do anyway?" Viviane fired back. "If they do explode a nuclear warhead here and it gets out that we knew about it and we did nothing to warn our citizens …"

"So are you suggesting that we tell Singaporeans to head to their friendly bomb shelters and remain there for how long? A day, a week, a month?" asked Brent his tone still dripping with sarcasm.

Over the years, Singapore had invested significant resources in building a civilian shelter programme for times of war. Since 1987 under the Civil Defence Shelter Act, the government built numerous air-raid shelters in public residential estates, schools, community centres and other public buildings such as underground train stations.

"That's enough you two. Viviane, I'll consider your suggestion but that's not an operational decision it's a political one which needs to be made at the very top," said the Commissioner. "Like I was saying earlier, I want you to keep your teams at it around the clock sniffing for any radiation traces. Unless we can get better intel and soon, it may be our best hope yet."

27

ANG MO KIO INDUSTRIAL PARK, SINGAPORE –
NOVEMBER 22, 1630 HOURS

This was D-Day for Saif and he had been impatiently checking his email account all morning waiting in vain for that message to arrive. The mechanics from the car repair shop on the ground floor had already gone home as it was Saturday and the shop was closed at 2pm.

Saif looked at the weapon again as it sat in the centre of his office covered with a large blue plastic sheet. It was almost complete. The battery together with the mercury tilt switch – a simple yet effective anti-tampering device, would be added later after the weapon had been transported to its final destination.

While waiting for his last orders to come in, Saif tried to keep himself busy by cleaning up his office. He had already packed his two bags of clothes for his flight out of Singapore later that evening.

All his work-related papers except for the hidden decoding sheets had been gathered up and burnt in a small bin at the back of the building. He mixed the ashes with water and emptied the contents of the bin onto a grass patch.

Then, wearing overalls and a pair of thick rubber gloves, he spent most of the afternoon scrubbing down the office with a strong solution of bleach to remove any fingerprints and as much DNA evidence as possible. He cleaned every surface he could reach including the walls and floors. He paid particular attention to the old sofa which had been his bed to rest during the day. He removed any stray strands of fallen hair and cleaned the imitation leather thoroughly. Saif wanted to ensure that no traces of his presence were left behind should the police one day discover his hideout.

He had almost lost track of time when he heard the soft beep from his laptop. A new email had arrived. Hurriedly he read it:

Greetings Bro,

Good to hear from you again. I've been on the move pretty much these last few days trying to get all the details sorted out for the big wedding. Had to be on site at the hotel for the food tasting yesterday at 7pm. We had a good time. Jerry is thinking of getting some fireworks but that's gonna cost a lot.

According to the astrologer, the most auspicious time for exchanging of vows is at 10.30pm. I don't know how we are going to manage that but we will try. I hope you have booked your ticket home. Pam said she will try to make it but she is still stuck in Jakarta for work so we'll see how that goes. Still waiting to hear back from her. I hope she remembers to call us when she is at the airport from her Garuda flight or drop us an SMS when she is ready to go.

Can't wait to fire it up on this wedding. Just hope we don't have to abort cos the groom has gotten cold feet lol. Oh didn't tell you, the contractor had his assistants finally set the tent up on the lawn by the way and all is looking good. Well that's the updates from here. Hope to see you soon. Take care.

Andy

For the last time, Saif walked to the back of his office and retrieved the hidden brown envelope with the codes. As the message had been sent on the 22nd, he pulled out the appropriate sheet and checked the numbers – 11, 25, 32, 33, 34, 43, 44, 49, 53, 56, 76, 77, 98, 114, 124, 140, 142, 145, 151, 157, 161, 162, 163, 173, 179, 180, 190, 196, 200, 201, 228, 234, 237, 238 and the numbers continued.

Counting carefully, he decoded his last message. It read:

move out be on site at 7pm
time of fireworks at 10.30pm
ticket Jakarta waiting at airport Garuda
sms go fire it up
abort cold feet
assistants on the way

He checked the message again making sure that he had counted correctly every word in the body of the email. His orders were clear. He had two and a half hours to get the weapon on site and prime it for detonation. His final "Go" or "Abort" codes would be delivered via SMS. Saif himself did not know where the final destination would be. He was sure one of his assistants would have that last piece of the puzzle.

Twenty minutes later, the two fishermen accompanied by two others arrived at Saif's office. He did not know them but they gave the correct password.

"We have two vans waiting outside,' said one of them.

"Okay good. Now I want you guys to lift this very carefully and load it up. Keep your hands away from that steel ball. Remember, do not tilt it or knock this against anything. Then we still have much work to do here," Saif commanded the men who carried out his instructions in total silence.

Still covered in a plastic sheet, the weapon with its solid steel frame weighed just over 200 kilogrammes and was about the size of a large washing machine.

With great care it was wheeled out on a trolley and loaded into one of the two black vans which the men had parked in the driveway directly fronting the repair workshop.

The weapon was placed gingerly on a padded bed of styrofoam boards at the back of the van. Discarding the plastic sheet, the weapon's steel frame was secured with thick nylon straps to several metal anchor points welded to the sides of the vehicle. Saif supervised the men and was pleased that they worked quickly and efficiently.

He did not know if these men knew what they were carrying or the nature of the mission they were about to embark on. But that mattered little now. They each had a job to do and the clock was ticking. When the weapon was secured, Saif inserted the lithium ion battery to the main control panel to test that it was still working properly. He heaved a sigh of relief when a small red light began flashing. All the delicate electrical components were still intact and functioning correctly.

As the cabin of the van had no windows, there was no longer a need to cover the bomb with the plastic sheet. One of the men crumpled the sheet and tossed it into a rubbish bin in front of the workshop which was filled with old and discarded car parts.

After the van door was locked, Saif directed the men back up to the office once again. He wanted them to clean it up one last time.

He checked his watch. It was 5.15pm. Turning to one of the men who appeared to be the leader of the group, Saif asked, "Where is the destination?"

"It's the naval base in Changi. We have to leave here by 6pm, no later," came the abrupt answer.

Saif nodded. So now at last he knew. His bomb was to obliterate a military target. "Well it's better than taking out a civilian town," he thought to himself.

Back in the office, Saif told the men to scrub the room again while he logged on to the Internet from his laptop computer. He checked the flight listing for Garuda Airlines departing Changi Airport for Jakarta that night.

There was only one remaining flight scheduled to leave at 9.45pm. The timing would be tight. Arriving at their target destination in Changi at 7pm, he would only have about 20 minutes to prime and programme the weapon. He would then have to leave and be at the airport by 7.45pm to get his ticket at the airline's desk and check in for his flight. His plane would almost be in Jakarta when the bomb was activated at 10.30pm. Being just over 900 kilometres away, Saif knew he would be safe and well outside the blast and hot radiation zone.

He burnt the last codes and flushed the ashes down the toilet. Taking a screwdriver, Saif opened the backing of his laptop and extracted its hard drive. He submerged this for 15 minutes in a bucket of concentrated bleach to destroy the components inside. He them tossed the hard drive along with the rest of the laptop into a green canvas bag. Taking a large hammer, he struck it repeatedly reducing the shiny computer to a mess of broken electronics. The bag would be discarded later along the way to their destination.

The men were about done cleaning up the office and checking his watch, Saif saw that it was almost 6pm and time for them to leave. He took a last look around, making sure that the room was as sanitised as it could be. Perhaps the police may in time, stumble across his hideout but he would have been long gone by then and it would be much too late to reverse the course of events which had already been set in motion.

28

Every jolt along that rough dirt track frayed his nerves even further. Gingerly he turned to look back into the cargo bay of the old van.

She was still there, lying peacefully, looking almost serene in the stillness of the darkening evening. The thick nylon straps held her securely in place as the firm styrofoam base cushioned against the frustrating bumps of her final journey into oblivion.

On her main control panel, the little red light continued to blink reassuringly. Her heart was beating strong and all was well.

Saif felt better now knowing that his task was almost over and scanning the dark track before him, he knew that the end would soon be literally in sight any minute now. Taking a deep breath which helped to steady his nerves, he whispered to himself: "It is almost done."

While understandably nervous, he still enjoyed this time of the mission best of all – the advent to a kill, stealthily stalking the unwary foe, savouring the seconds before pushing that button. It was like a drug and Saif knew he was a hardcore addict who could never get enough of a fix.

Once again he turned to look out the window. All his senses were on alert – waiting and watching for anything that was out of the ordinary, anything which could upset these carefully laid plans. The element of surprise was after all, one of his greatest assets. But here, his target area was empty and there would be no one to stop him now.

They were less than a kilometre away from their objective – a desolate area of reclaimed land. Beyond the little trees planted along the fence in the distance lay their prize – the Changi Naval Base. In the hours to come this scrubland, if anything still remains of it, would be infamously known as Ground Zero.

These past few weeks had been a long and dangerous journey. The task was formidable, fraught with peril and uncertainty and yet he had done everything that was asked of him. He had done it well as a soldier should and now the mighty *Saif al-Haidar* with its plutonium core was finally ready to explode brighter than a star in the heavens above.

Thinking back over the short time he had spent in Singapore, Saif was proud that he had been chosen, destined really, for this mission. The history books would tell of this night that changed the world. It mattered none to him that those same books would probably never record his name or his role in it all. Simply to be picked from among all the others to be that singular instrument of total annihilation, that was enough of a reward for him.

This mission would surely eclipse even his greatest accomplishment to date – the crushing of the American Embassy in Nairobi, Kenya back in 1998. But that was many years ago – many years spent waiting in hope for his next assignment and the intoxicating adrenalin rush that came with it. Hiding in the shadows, this was simply the nature of the world he lived in – the world he belonged to, if only briefly.

Saif had waited a long time for this opportunity to prove himself yet again and tonight he was sure that everything would go as planned. He could see it all in his mind's eye – the brilliant flash of light that would unleash the unspeakable vaporising power of a nuclear firestorm. Unlike Nairobi, this time the fire and the glory will burn much brighter. And after it was all over, nothing would matter anymore. His job would have been done – his sacred mission complete.

A sudden bolt of lightning tore through the black sky and reflected off the calm surface of the sea in the distance. They were very close now. He could smell the salt in the air and straining his neck to see beyond the trees, he caught his first glimpse of the American warships anchored in the distance, oblivious to their fate.

Through the side mirror, Saif spied the subdued headlights of the second van with the other men travelling far behind them.

"Cowards!" he thought to himself. "Keeping your distance

will not save you from this. Nothing will ..."

As Saif was arriving at his destination, US President Theodore Monroe was in his office early to be briefed on the latest intelligence update provided by their Israeli allies.

"Is this all they can tell us? It doesn't say what the target is or when the strike will take place!"

"Mr President, that's the latest information the Israelis have," replied NSA's Director James Carron. "Our sources have not been able to provide any collaboration as of yet but we are working on it."

"Do we know how this intel came about, how reliable is it?"

"No Mr President, Tel Aviv isn't saying. They have not confirmed it either. It is still raw intel and they passed it along to us and the Singapore authorities immediately in good faith and in the interest of time."

"Our naval strike force in Singapore – when is that scheduled to leave?"

"It's almost 7pm in Singapore now," said Secretary of Defence Jeffrey Brown. "They were originally scheduled to depart at 8am tomorrow Singapore time. I've ordered the resupply process to be expedited. We can leave by 2am their time."

"Why the hell can't we just go now?" asked the President.

"Some repairs are still being done on two of our ships and some members of the crew are on shore leave for the day. We are trying to recall them back home. They were due to return at midnight ..."

"Kick some asses – do whatever it takes. I want those ships out at sea ASAP. They are to leave Singapore no later than midnight local time whether or not those repairs are done. If anyone is late getting back, we just have to leave them behind – understood?"

"Erm yes, Mr President."

"And where would the task force head to?"

"They would head east sir, away from Singapore and Jakarta, out to the open sea in international waters – it's the safest place for them to be ..."

"Alright, good, see to it. Do we have any other military assets in the country?"

"Mr President, we have our back-up strike squadron from the *George Washington* based on land – at one of Singapore's military air bases on the island's west coast," said Defence Secretary Brown. "They are conducting joint exercises with the Singapore air force practising ground strikes. They can't return to the carrier at this time – it has to be moving at sea for the planes to land safely and ..."

"Ok get them to rejoin the *George Washington* as soon as it gets out to sea. Bill, has the CIA anything to add?"

"Our people on the ground have not detected anything out of the ordinary," said CIA Director William Baldwin. "And satellite images show no unusual movements at the JI camp…"

"Why am I not surprised that our own agents keep coming up empty and we have to rely on the Israelis of all people to give us a handle on what's really going on!" said the exasperated President.

Calming down, he continued: "Okay gentlemen, I want the CIA and NSA to work closely with the Israelis on this possible nuke strike in Singapore. They seem to know a lot more about what's really going on. I expect to be informed the second we hear of any further developments – clear?"

Both men nodded.

"Kelly, do you have anything else to add?"

"State has been in contact with the Singapore Government," said Secretary of State and President-Elect Kelly Yee. "They are clearly worried and are scrambling – putting their military and civil defence on alert but with the fragmented intel we have, there is not much they can do but to hope for a breakthrough and … to pray."

"Yeah maybe that's about all we can do right now … pray," said President Monroe.

RECLAIMED LAND IN CHANGI, SINGAPORE – NOVEMBER 22, 1900 HOURS

The men had just stopped their two vans a few metres off the dirt track when Saif checked his watched. It was exactly 7pm and right one cue, his handphone beeped.

The SMS was short: FIRE IT UP

That was the GO word – the confirmation he needed to proceed. There would be no need for Saif to reply. He removed the SIM card from his phone and snapped it in two, tossing the pieces in different directions. He threw his handphone on the ground and taking a rock, he smashed it into pieces and scattered the broken fragments in the tall grass nearby.

As the four assistants watched, Saif gently opened the cargo door of his van. Placing his hands on the cold stainless steel frame of the bomb, he said a short prayer seeking divine blessing for the task at hand.

Then taking a deep breath, he carefully connected the small anti-tampering device with its mercury tilt switch to the main control panel. In a clear sealed glass tube, Saif watched the small bead of mercury as it settled in the left corner of the tube. Barely ten millimetres away were the two exposed electrical points. Should anyone try to move the bomb or drive off the van, the slightest jolt would cause the bead of mercury to move. If it touched the two electrical points, that would complete the firing circuit triggering an immediate detonation.

With the tilt switch securely in place, Saif turned to the main control panel and set the electronic timer for 10.30pm. He was finally ready for the last task of the mission – keying in the six digit arming code – 239499.

The flashing red light changed to a pulsating green while the arming code blinked twice on the display panel to confirm that the code had been accepted. The code then disappeared and was replaced with the countdown monitor which read two hours, 58 minutes, and 42 seconds. The nuclear weapon was now fully armed and primed for detonation.

With the outside of his hand Saif gently stroked the cold titanium sphere housing the plutonium core one last time. Even in the dim light of the darkening sky, she still looked beautiful with her shiny components glistening. He had done his part in giving her life and now it was time for her to do what she had been created for.

Carefully he closed the rear door and locked it. Checking his watch, he saw that it was 7:34pm. He turned to his left and he could still make out the outlines of several American warships anchored at the Changi Naval Base nearby.

There was no turning back now. It was out of his hands. Again he thought of his family – his wife and daughter. Would they be proud of him? Would they have understood that he had done it all for them? He did not have the answers but in his heart he felt that it was the right thing to do – the only thing a man like him could do.

He turned to the leader of his assistants. Saif had not even bothered to ask his name. In their world, names were dangerous. From his shirt pocket, Saif extracted a small sheet of paper. "This is the telephone number – 96944126. If for any reason the bomb does not explode at 10.30, simply call the number and it will detonate immediately. Understood?"

The man simply nodded and placed the slip of paper in his wallet.

"Okay get me to the airport and then you guys know what you have to do," said Saif to the men as they walked in silence to the second van. His part of this mission was now over.

29

ANG MO KIO INDUSTRIAL PARK, SINGAPORE –
NOVEMBER 22, 2048 HOURS

So far, the four NEST teams that had been driving around
the country hunting for ambient radiation in the air, had
turned up nothing but the luck of one was about to
change.

NEST Team Two turned its unmarked van into the Ang
Mo Kio Industrial Park and began testing the air when
they received a faint but positive hit. Slowly the van
continued to cruise the small estate with the detector still
deployed. The dial on their gamma ray spectrometer
spiked as it passed the Hoi Kee Car and Accessories repair
garage. The men inside exchanged excited looks but still
the van moved on for another 300 metres as the needle
began to fall.

Stopping the vehicle by the side of the road, one of the
men wearing a civilian jacket over his uniform alighted
carrying a small haversack. Slowing he began walking back
to the car workshop. As he neared the building, he heard
the small handheld radiation detector in his haversack

begin to beep softly. He stopped outside the locked workshop, lit a cigarette and looked around. The area was deserted as all the shops had long closed for the night. A crumpled sheet of blue plastic lay discarded in an open bin two metres away from the workshop's locked gates.

Standing before the bin, the officer bent down pretending to tie his shoelaces. The detector started beeping rapidly. The radiation hit was confirmed. A few minutes later, Brent's handphone began to ring.

CHANGI INTERNATIONAL AIRPORT, SINGAPORE – NOVEMBER 22, 2052 HOURS

With his passport and boarding pass in hand, Saif was waved past the Immigration Counter at the airport. He had been told that his boarding gate had been changed to Y32 located at the far corner of the terminal.

He still had some time to kill before he was due to board his flight for Jakarta at 9:45pm. Saif's thoughts were already on his next mission – the second bomb he would be assembling in Jakarta. He hoped that all the components were already in place so he could get started with the assembly as soon as possible.

Passing a Duty Free Shop, he went in and bought a carton of cigarettes. So far all was going according to plan and in less than an hour, he should be airborne and safe.

He had left the crowd of noisy passengers far behind as he headed for his departure gate. As he reached Gate Y32,

Saif saw that there were just a handful of people milling about in the waiting room. He had expected that the room would be filled with more passengers waiting to board the aircraft. An attractive hostess manning the counter smiled nervously and asked for his boarding pass. She avoided looking at him directly and his senses immediately told him that something just did not feel right. From the corner of his eye, he saw a group of men approaching him from the rear. He was about to turn around when it happened.

Everything that occurred in the next six seconds seemed to be in slow motion. He felt a hand on his back pushing him forward violently. As he stumbled and fell, more rough hands pressed him to the ground. Men grabbed his arms and held him down firmly.

"SAF Commandos!" came a commanding voice. As Saif strained his head to look behind him, he found himself staring into the muzzle of an automatic pistol which was just centimetres from his face. "Don't move ... you are under arrest."

ONBOARD THE *USS GEORGE WASHINGTON*, CHANGI NAVAL BASE, SINGAPORE – NOVEMBER 22, 2103 HOURS

The Task Force commander Vice Admiral Cyril J. Forrestal checked his watch impatiently. The encrypted orders from SECDEF – the Secretary of Defence was clear – he had to get his task force out of port by midnight and no later.

His men had been working hard to complete the urgent engine repairs to two of their ships and by the latest estimate that he had just received, they should have the work done by 11.30pm.

"At last count, we still have 124 personnel on shore," reported his Executive Officer.

"Any word from the MPs yet?"

"They are still checking the bars, fast-food joints and the usual hang-outs in the city but it may take them a while to get everyone rounded up," said the XO.

"We will begin casting off lines at 2330 as soon as the repairs are done. Anyone not back gets left behind. Make sure all commanders have someone to replace any mission-critical positions left vacant."

"Yes sir. Has Washington said why we need to bug out in such a hurry?"

"No they haven't. No explanation at all and that's worrying. My greatest fear is a repeat of the Cole incident. Make sure all our sentries know what to do. Let's not take any chances."

On October 12, 2000, the American destroyer USS Cole was attacked by suicide bombers while on a refuelling stop in the Yemeni port of Aden. A small craft laden with about 300 kg of explosives which was moulded into a shaped charge, pulled alongside the battleship and detonated its deadly cargo. The blast tore a 10 metre gash in the destroyer killing 17 sailors and injuring 39 others.

To speed up their departure, Vice Admiral Forrestal had instructed that both nuclear reactors on the aircraft carrier be brought up to full power. He also ordered that all personnel man their battle stations as a precaution. As live rounds were chambered into the fleet's anti-aircraft weapons, more armed Marines scanned the skies and the waters looking for possible intruders.

Forrestal had contemplated ordering some of his ships to depart immediately and get them out of port but as this was a small strike team, every vessel was needed to provide a tight security screen around the carrier. The fleet would all have to leave together as one unit, just as they had entered port.

Washington as usual, had been very cryptic in giving information to its frontline commanders. "SECDEF wants us to head east, the direction we had just come from instead of west to our assigned staging area," said the XO.

"Yes I know. I'm hoping this is just the usual muddle at the Pentagon. This had better not be another drill," said Admiral Forrestal. "As far as we know, our orders to hit that terrorist camp in two days still stand and we certainly don't need any screw-ups like this!"

APARTMENT BLOCK IN PASIR RIS, SINGAPORE – NOVEMBER 22, 2120 HOURS

Standing in the balcony of their apartment on the 20th floor, the two fishermen looked out towards the dark sea.

They had just returned after dropping Saif at the airport.

The four men had waited a few minutes in the airport's multi-storey carpark after he had gone. Then two of them, following the orders that had been given earlier, headed back on foot to the departure terminal. Their job was to secretly ensure that Saif boarded his plane on schedule and report back to Riyadh.

From their balcony in Pasir Ris, the two fishermen had a grand view of Changi Airport in the distance some eight kilometres away. They could see the bright lights of her control tower and watched as civilian planes landed or took off every 45 seconds.

A few kilometres beyond the airport lay the Changi Naval Base. The men could not see their prize but that did not matter. The mushroom cloud would be clearly visible soon enough.

They began setting up their video camera. It would run on internal batteries rather than be plugged into an external power source. By not using long external wires, the chances of their video equipment being destroyed by the EMP – the electromagnetic pulse radiating out from the nuclear blast, would be much reduced.

Their high definition video camera had been placed in a special housing – a heavy wooden box lined internally with a special coating of plastic and a sheet of lead to protect it from radiation. The camera lens looked out from behind a centimetre of reinforced laminated glass. The legs of the tripod securing the camera housing were held in place with 17 sandbags to keep it steady.

The men were clear about their orders. They had to film the explosion and then immediately smuggle the digital tape out of Singapore and into Malaysia. Once across the border, they would email the video to an address which had been given to them earlier.

The men checked their watches – they still had just over an hour to wait.

ANG MO KIO INDUSTRIAL PARK, SINGAPORE – NOVEMBER 22, 2213 HOURS

The strike team made up of commandos from the elite Special Operations Task Force (SOTF) took up their positions silently outside the deserted car workshop.

One group was poised to strike at the front door while the second breached the rear exit. Simultaneously both teams would move inside to secure the premises. Their orders were to take any occupants alive as any information they had could very well save the lives of thousands.

From across street, the workshop and the room on the second floor had been discretely scanned with the HIFER IV. The High Frequency Electronic Response device had been purchased recently by the SAF as part of its upgrading programme in electronics warfare. Essentially this sensitive scanner bounces both sound waves and radio signals into the suspected target area. The return signals from each are then merged by its software into a series of algorithms which are combined to form 3D images. It can, in effect, see through walls, wood, plaster, brick and even reinforced concrete to reveal void spaces, hidden objects or even people. The HIVER IV reported that no persons or suspicious objects in either the workshop or the second floor unit. But still the team could not afford to take any chances.

Accompanying the strike teams would be ordinance disposal experts along with several specialists in electronic warfare. Their job, if a nuclear weapon was found, would be to disarm and remove it.

Now the commandos dressed in black with balaclavas and assault rifles ready, were stationed just metres away from their assigned entry points. The strike leader turned to Brent who was beside him and waited for his attack order.

Gerald, who was in the unmarked command vehicle parked a hundred metres away from the workshop, had been on the phone with one of his police investigators stationed at Changi Airport.

Saif did not notice the concealed radiation detector as he entered the airport's Departure Lounge about an hour earlier. A small light on the machine immediately started flashing as it picked up the residue radiation on his clothes. Two undercover police officers then started trailing their suspect as Saif headed for the queue at the Immigration Counter. The officers had radioed ahead and commandos were moved into place to take down the suspect.

As planned, Saif was told that his departure gate had been changed when he reached the Immigration Counter. This was to separate him from the other passengers as a precaution in case he was armed.

While his arrest a few minutes later had been swift, none of the commandos noticed that they themselves were being watched by two men from among a group of departing passengers gathered nearby. Soon a call was being made to Riyadh in code to report that Saif had been captured.

Interrogated for an hour, their Egyptian suspect Saif al-Adel had told his police interrogators absolutely nothing. He had denied any knowledge of a nuclear device. However chemical swabs taken from his clothes and his hands revealed confirmed hits for residual radiation and well as SEMTEX 10 – a military grade of high explosives.

"Get him back to headquarters and guard him carefully. I want him kept in isolation," Gerald told his subordinate, "we will continue with the interrogation there as soon as I get back."

As Saif was bundled into the back of the police car, he looked at the digital clock on the dashboard. It read 10:24pm. He could feel the blood still dripping from the side of his swollen mouth. The interrogation had been brief but quite physical. Still he knew the throbbing pain he felt in his jaw from the repeated punches would end in exactly six minutes. He overheard that he was being taken back to Police Headquarters in the city and there was only one route to get there. It was time for Saif to make his peace with God for they would soon be driving directly into Ground Zero.

APARTMENT BLOCK IN PASIR RIS, SINGAPORE –
NOVEMBER 22, 2215 HOURS

The men had completed setting up the video camera and had pressed the small remote control button to start filming. They still had 15 minutes to go but their orders had been to start recording at 10.15pm just in case of a premature detonation.

The red light on the camera came on indicating that it was recording. The men then stepped back from the balcony. They knew that they were outside the blast zone and should be safe but still they took no chances and crouched behind a reinforced support wall as the minutes ticked by.

One of them had his handphone out and held that sheet of paper with the telephone number for manual detonation of the nuclear warhead. Once again the man checked his watch and waited.

ANG MO KIO INDUSTRIAL PARK, SINGAPORE –
NOVEMBER 22, 2215 HOURS

Brent too was checking his watch. It was time. He keyed the microphone on his headset and took a deep breath.

"Ops Thunder … all units … standby … standby … standby." He counted three seconds in his head and then gave the order "Go – Go – Go". Immediately he heard two near-simultaneous explosions as both the front and back doors were blasted apart.

Brent let the other commandos rush past him, not wanting to get in their way. He gave them a minute and then entered the workshop weapon in hand. All he saw were two cars with their hoods open. He knew more commandos were scanning the unit above for possible booby traps. Two minutes later he heard the team leader say: "Clear – Clear – Clear".

Viviane and Gerald had joined Brent as they ran up the stairs to the second floor office. Most of the commandos had taken their defensive positions, crouched by the windows, weapons pointing outwards. Other men were scanning the room for radiation.

"Sir, the bomb or whatever it is was here," SOTF team leader Captain Timothy Chan told Brent. "It's obvious from that smell of bleach that someone tried to clean this place in a hurry but we've got a few residual traces of radiation along with SEMTEX 10. We are still checking for prints. See the walls and part of the floor here ... it's still damp. Those guys couldn't have been gone more than a couple of hours."

Brent nodded in defeat as he surveyed the near empty office cursing fate for missing their target.

"Well there is nothing here now," said Viviane. "They seem to have cleared everything out. So now what?"

"My guys," said Gerald, "have arrested the owner of this

unit and they are picking up everyone employed in the workshop downstairs. We've also got that suspect at the airport. Now we turn the screws on these bastards and get them to talk, any way we can."

The room was quiet for a second and then it happened.

Viviane at first thought that it was a flash from a camera coming from one of the windows – but it was brighter, hotter and lasted for several long seconds.

"What the – " said one of the soldiers at the window as he shielded his eyes from the blinding flash. The eastern part of the sky shone bright as day. Gradually the white light dimmed only to be replaced by a fiery glow and then they all saw it – a red mushroom cloud was growing in the distance. For several seconds they stood there in shock, utterly mesmerised by the surreal scene before them.

Brent was the first to recover. "Get down – shockwave!" he screamed as he grabbed Vivianne and pushed her to the ground shielding her with his body. But his voice was drowned out by an angry roar as a hot gale-force wind swept across the island. The unthinkable, a holocaust feared for a generation, had just happened.

30

RECLAIMED LAND IN CHANGI, SINGAPORE –
NOVEMBER 22, 2230 HOURS

The internal timer on the main control panel counted down the seconds to zero. A simple beep was the only sound it made as a mere nine volts of electricity were released and coursed down the firing circuit to ignite the 32 electronic detonators – one imbedded in each of the shaped SEMTEX 10 explosive charges surrounding the plutonium core.

The core's thick titanium shell contained the initial blast from the high-grade explosives and directed the force inwards causing an immense implosion of the plutonium core inside the sphere. The shockwave squeezed and fused the 11.3 kilograms of highly-enriched plutonium into a white-hot mass about a third of its original size. The weapon's nuclear core had just gone supercritical.

It remained in this state for less than one microsecond longer as the temperature inside rose instantly to 10,000,000° Celsius – hotter than the surface of the sun. At the same time, the super-dense core was bombarded by a flood of neutrons initiating an unstoppable nuclear chain reaction. The increased pressure building up within the hardened titanium shell of the weapon triggered an instant and massive release of raw explosive energy.

The first indication of the nuclear blast was an intense burst of both gamma rays and X-rays followed by massive neutron radiation escaping from the core. The titanium shell, unable to contain the colossal pressure building up inside, blew itself apart. The gamma rays ionised the atmosphere around the device generating the blinding flash of pure white light. And for a few seconds, just as Saif had predicted, the mighty *Saif al-Haidar* shone brighter than an exploding star.

At that point of detonation, the entire warhead assembly along with all matter within a radius of 600 metres was simply vaporised. The energy then radiated outwards in an expanding shockwave of total and complete annihilation.

It took only two seconds for the giant mushroom fireball to reach 600 metres into the night sky. In ten seconds, the shockwave with its gale-force winds had already travelled over four kilometres destroying everything in its path. The massacre had begun.

Vice Admiral Forrestal was on the bridge of his carrier waiting for the final reports on the repairs to come in when he was struck by the blinding flash to his left just beyond the treeline in the distance.

Instinctively he covered his eyes and turned away as the shockwave tossed him into the air. Being just 700 metres away from Ground Zero, the mighty *George Washington* together with the rest of its fleet did not stand a chance.

The rolling wave of superheated air slammed broadside into the aircraft carrier blasting it apart. Only small chunks of twisted and melting steel remained scattered over a wide area. It was much the same fate that befell the rest of the American task force and another eighteen Singapore navy warships including two of its highly-prized diesel submarines anchored at the base.

The surface pressure of the shockwave pushed the sea back for almost 800 metres. But within minutes, the waters returned with a vengeance in a tsunami twenty metres high. The crashing wave smothered what was left of the Changi Naval Base before pressing its destructive power further inland.

Two kilometres away from the epicentre, Changi Airport was not spared as the shockwave flipped over airplanes waiting on the tarmac. The intense heat caused two of the three packed airport passenger terminals to spontaneously combust dooming those inside to a fiery death.

Within seconds of the nuclear explosion, five civilian passenger jets on their final approach to the airport began falling out of the sky like giant dead birds as the invisible gamma rays destroyed their flight control systems.

Changi General Hospital, the closest medical facility to Ground Zero was totally decimated along with many factories in Singapore's eastern industrial sector.

The nuclear inferno also laid waste to several key military bases including a number of infantry brigades, Singapore's elite commando battalion and two air force bases located on either side of Changi Airport. These housed the 145 Squadron which operated the country's frontline F-16D Fighting Falcons attack jets.

By military standards, this nuclear explosion was a relatively small one, estimated at about 27 kilotons – just slightly larger than the blast of 'Fat Man' – the atomic bomb that destroyed Nagasaki in 1945 which had an explosive yield of some 21 kilotons.

But as this had been a surface detonation, unlike the atomic blasts in Japan which were triggered in mid-air, about a third of the blast wave and the radiation it expelled was directed towards the ground, excavating a crater nearly 130 metres deep.

The thermal shockwave registered as a moderate 6.4 earthquake on the Richter Magnitude Scale, leveling buildings and rupturing underground gas mains, power cables and water pipes.

Ground Zero had been plunged into an unholy darkness illuminated only by the numerous fires and the towering mushroom cloud still growing in the night sky.

Major arterial expressways in the kill zone were demolished as the shockwave continued to radiate outwards.

Minutes earlier, handcuffed in the backseat of the police car, Saif's eyes had been fixed on the small digital clock on the dashboard which read 10:28pm. They were still driving along the East Coast Parkway and were just 10 minutes away from the bright city lights in the distance.

If they had another five minutes, perhaps they could outrun the shockwave but Saif knew there would be no escape. In his mind, he felt that it was better to die this way, to end his life by his own hands. His conscience was clear as he muttered a short prayer pleading for divine mercy for his soul. He knew his family would be waiting for him on the other side in Paradise and this thought comforted him in his final moments.

The clock now read 10:29pm. Turning to his captors he said: "It is too late now my friends. Pray for your souls and for your families. We were all good soldiers. We did what we had to do but our fight is done. It is finished."

The two escorting officers simply ignored him as the clock on the dashboard ran down the final seconds to 10.30pm.

Saif struggled to turn around in his seat as he wanted to see it for himself. And through the rear windscreen, he caught just a fleeting glimpse.

The star that he had created had exploded in a heavenly light beyond all mortal description. For him the very gates of heaven had just opened, welcoming home its faithful son. It was the last thing he ever saw as the light seared his retinas leaving him blind. He did not feel the shockwave flipping over his vehicle nor the roaring fires from hell which consumed what was left of it. He was at peace with his maker, ready for the final judgement of his earthly deeds.

The rolling shockwave took out the island's eastern

housing estates of Bedok, Tampines and Marine Parade, home to some 700,000 people.

Most of the victims had been home in their high-rise apartments when the weapon detonated. Their towering blocks, built so close together in land-scarce Singapore, fell like giant stack of playing cards pushed by the unseen hand of the shockwave.

In just minutes, these bustling suburban towns were reduced to a desolate and burning wasteland.

For most, the hand of death came swiftly in the fiery wind. The few who stubbornly clung on to life suffered massive third degree burns as the air around them was spontaneously set alight by the intense heat of the nuclear firestorm that swept over them.

They lay crushed and abandoned under the debris of their once proud and expensive homes, now reduced to melting concrete. Some survivors buried deep underground would linger on in limbo for minutes. The less fortunate would survive perhaps just a few more hours far beyond the pain threshold of consciousness. But for all of them, death was simply inevitable.

A few more who were caught in the open and were somehow unlucky enough to still be alive, were blinded by the piercing flash of the explosion and left deaf by the intense pressure of the shockwave which ruptured their ear-drums. These pitiful few would stagger on like zombies – blind and deaf, impaled by shards of falling glass and stoned by debris raining down from the buildings crumbling around them. There would be no one to hear their screams for help. It had only been less than five minutes since the explosion but already for all of them, it was much too late.

Still the nuclear nightmare was only just beginning.

In ten minutes, the ugly red mushroom cloud had reached its peak of 21,000 metres. And soon Singaporeans would experience their first snowfall of sorts in history.

As the hot materials in the cloud cooled and condensed, highly radioactive fallout in the form of dirty ash-laden specks of ice began to drift down across the island.

In the first seconds since the nuclear detonation, an estimated 50,000 people had perished. Thousands more lingered close to death, soon to be entombed in a thick suffocating blanket of radioactive ash.

Beyond the 10-kilometre hot zone, the slaughter of the innocents continued. Hundreds of people were trapped in their vehicles when the EMPs caused the engines to quit. They faced the dilemma of staying in their cars and buses which provided a limited amount of protection or to run for better shelter in a nearby building amidst the heavy ash fallout which was beginning to cover their vehicles.

Even those further from the blast zone would not be spared from the effects of the invisible radiation. The stronger ones may survive a few more weeks as their withered bodies slowly shut down. The radiation would destroy their cells, making it impossible for them to replenish the blood and fluids they had lost. Their stomach linings would be devastated, causing massive internal bleeding and severe diarrhoea. They would slowly waste away, praying for the warm comfort of eternal sleep.

Amidst the utter carnage, one building on the outer fringe of the death zone remained standing, virtually unscathed. The thick stone walls built nearly two hundred years ago had protected her from the gale-force winds and the fires of the nuclear abyss.

Slowly the lone priest emerged from his spartan room at the rear of the church, close to the Hall of Repose where wakes for the dead were held.

Dazed, he shuffled barefooted into the courtyard of the old church. Father Michel Bata stared unbelievingly at the scene before him. The night sky glowed an angry red and the air was thick and burning hot.

Once surrounded by tall buildings, many now lay broken in ugly heaps of smouldering rubble as if they had been sliced in two by Death's giant scythe.

Coughing violently from the hot falling ash, he spat out thick globs of blood as he felt a burning sensation grip his lungs. His old brain simply could not process what had just happened. It was a scene from hell, of this he was sure. The priest crossed himself praying aloud for strength amidst the utter silence that engulfed him. And then it dawned on him – he had one more mission to accomplish.

Stumbling along, he dragged his weary body forward towards the tower. He could barely see now as the falling ash grew thicker but still his weathered hands knew the old stone walls well.

It took him fifteen long and painful minutes to get to where he needed to be. Groping in the near darkness, he reached for the thick ropes and began pulling as hard as he could, just as he had done each day at noon to summon the faithful.

Cursing the slowness of his dying body, he finally heard the sacred brass bells toll their hollow peal. For all those who were still alive and who could still hear, the Cathedral of Saint Joseph which had survived two world wars offered a glimpse of hope and refuge for the people of this crippled nation. The heavy wooden doors of the old church would once again remain open to anyone who needed her help and the shelter of her mighty walls.

People had expected to hear the sirens of the Emergency Warning System – a series of loudspeakers mounted on buildings across the nation by the Singapore Civil Defence Force. These were meant to be triggered in the event of an enemy air raid but still this night, when they were needed most of all, they remained silent.

Many had been crushed as the buildings they were attached to simply collapsed. Others had their delicate electronics destroyed in the EMP wave rendering them totally useless.

As the lone church bells rang, other sounds of life would soon begin to fill the air. Sirens from emergency vehicles stationed well outside the blast zone could be heard in the distance sprinting to help. But none of those rushing in so bravely would be prepared for the hellish scenes of death shrouded in smoke and fire.

31

SITUATION ROOM, THE WHITE HOUSE,
WASHINGTON D.C. – NOVEMBER 22, 1145 HOURS

Just a few minutes earlier, President Monroe was seated behind his desk talking on the telephone as the doors of the Oval Office sprang open. Four Secret Service agents rushed in. More agents with weapons drawn were now entering his office. "We have to leave now Mr President," said one man as other agents grabbed their Commander-in-Chief by his arms and ushered him to the security of the underground Situation Room.

Seconds later, President-Elect Kelly Yee, her feet barely touching the ground, was similarly bundled into the shielded bunker by the Secret Service.

"I'm sorry about that Sir … 'Mam," said Senior Special Agent Jason McBride, "but we have an emergency. It's just protocol that we …"

"My God, they have actually done it, Mr President," interrupted Secretary of Defence Jeffrey Brown. "They have exploded a nuclear bomb in Singapore."

For the second time in barely two weeks, the President sat transfixed before the bank of television screens in his command centre as the first ghostly images of the nuclear blast in Singapore were replayed for the world to see.

It was just over 90 minutes since the explosion and the true extent of the devastation had yet to be uncovered. The high radiation fallout and the intense fires had confined rescue workers and the media to the outer fringes of the blast zone.

But even here, some seven kilometres from Ground Zero, one thing was abundantly clear – several densely populated suburbs had been simply levelled and the loss of life would be in the tens of thousands if not more.

The President had just gotten off the telephone to leaders in Singapore offering his condolences and any help the United States could provide. At last he spoke to his senior administration gathered in the Situation Room. "It's too late. Too late to speculate if there was anything that we could have done over the past few weeks to stop this," he said gesticulating to the muted television screens.

"Our strike task force?"

Secretary Brown shook his head. "As far as we can tell Mr President, the entire Changi Naval Base has been destroyed. It was only about half a mile from the point of detonation. We have a squadron of jets stationed on the other side of the island. It will be making a BDA, a Battle Damage Assessment, in about two or three hours to survey the damage when radiation levels have fallen a little. We'll know more then."

"Just half a mile away? So our Task Force was the main target?"

"It would seem so Mr President. It was either the Task Force or the naval base itself or Changi Airport. All three were in the epicentre."

The President nodded as Secretary Brown continued: "As you have promised the Singapore Government, we will be dispatching medical and humanitarian aid. The first Charlies from Japan and the Philippines will be arriving there in about six hours. The navy hospital ship *Comfort* will be leaving Hawaii tomorrow. It should arrive in Singapore in about four to five days along with other medical support vessels."

"What do we know about their casualties?"

"The Singapore Government has put the current death toll at about 50,000 but that's only a very conservative estimate based on the number of high-density housing estates that were within the blast zone. We estimate that in the end, the total number of casualties including those who are being exposed to intense radiation even as we speak, could reach between 250,000 and half a million," said CIA Director William Baldwin.

"We understand that their military and civil defence units still haven't been able to get within three to four miles of Ground Zero because of the hot fallout. Most of the injured that have been extricated so far, have third-degree burns and shrapnel blast injuries in addition to massive radiation poisoning.

"A majority of the population living outside the immediate blast zone are now being moved into underground shelters. From our satellite pictures, the city centre itself appears to be mostly intact but there may be serious structural damage from the thermal shocks which registered as a moderate earthquake. We anticipate that moderate to severe damage was done to their underground power and utility grids along with significant disruptions to computers and cell phone lines. But as this appears to be a surface blast, the electromagnetic pulse was not as severe as it could have been. Food and water supplies are likely to be highly radiated as well.

"The main concern now is with the radiation fallout. With the current monsoon winds, the clouds are moving north, away from Singapore. It could hit the Malaysian capital Kuala Lumpur in under 12 hours. As you can expect, the region is in a state of panic."

The President nodded, still deep in thought. Turning to Defence Secretary Brown, he said: "We need to assemble another strike force before this thing gets even more out of hand. We cannot allow this to go unpunished. What do we …"

Just then, President-Elect Kelly Yee cut him off. "Mr President, something is happening … you got to see this," she said turning up the volume of the television monitor tuned to the live Al Jazeera feed.

32

BREAKING NEWS, AL JAZEERA NEWS BULLETIN

The news reader was clearly flustered as he was interrupted in mid-sentence by an urgent voice screaming through his earpiece as he repeated news on the nuclear explosion in Singapore.

Regaining his composure, he read off his teleprompter: "And this just in … *Al Jazeera* has, in the last few minutes, received an unverified claim of responsibility for this evening's nuclear terror attack in Singapore."

The screen switched to an obviously homemade video recording which had been emailed to its headquarters in Doha, Qatar.

Yusman bin Iranto stared directly into the camera. Neither his face nor his voice betrayed any hint of emotion. Behind him clearly visible in the frame, a Russian-made AK-47 assault rifle was propped up against the wall.

Speaking in English, he began reciting the speech written by Hassan which he had rehearsed a thousand times in his mind.

"Today the world has witnessed the power of the mighty *Saif al-Haidar* – the Sword of the Lion. This was just a small demonstration of the power we now possess.

"The tiny island nation of Singapore was selected to be an example of the revenge we can unleash at will. Its government had chosen to be on the side of the infidels and fight against our brothers in the Middle East."

The scene then changed to show the footage taken earlier by the fishermen. The dark outline of the airport with the sea in the distance was suddenly illuminated by a blinding flash.

Seconds later as the glow receded, a red fireball emerged on the horizon, growing into a tall mushroom cloud. This was the first the outside world had seen of the actual nuclear explosion less than two hours earlier.

Subdued voices of the two men cheering in the background could be heard as Yusman continued: "This bright star, rising from the nuclear detonation, is an example of what we can now do to any city, anywhere in the world.

"It promises to be a new beginning. For too long America's greed has enslaved our Arab brothers, robbed the oil from beneath our feet, bleeding us dry. You brought nothing but war and bloodshed to our peoples. You have installed your armies on every shore. In your lust for money and power, you have turned man against his brother – Arab against Arab, keeping us divided, keeping us weak. You have stolen the holy lands of Palestine and have given it to our eternal foe, the Israelis.

"America has been the bully and the aggressor for far too long but today, with one sweep from this mighty star, sacred, burning justice has been levelled against you. Your reign of intimidation, murder and terror has ended."

The footage then returned to Yusman as he faced the camera: "Mr Monroe, you now have a simple choice to make. You can choose to live in peace with us as your equals who deserve your respect. Do this and this war will end, here and now – that is our promise. Let this war be over and the chapter closed. You know as well as I do, there can be no winners in such a battle. So let us hope there can be some survivors so that mankind lives to see another morning.

"But if you continue to persecute us, we will soon strike back with weapons far more destructive than what you have witnessed today. We will take out your cities one at a time starting with Tel Aviv and then who knows … maybe Washington, Chicago, London, Sydney or Paris …" and his voice trailed off.

"We know you will soon be sending aid and humanitarian assistance to the people of Singapore. It is only right that you do this, for you were the one that had put Singapore in such mortal danger by sailing in your nuclear task force.

"We will allow you to do this, to send aid to help the injured and to comfort the dying. We too have known the sorrow of war and death for far too long. But beyond this, you are to withdraw all your troops from the Middle East.

Leave our lands and our oil alone. We need not your money, your politics or your moral lectures.

"To my Arab brothers I say onto you, take back Jerusalem now. That land is yours, by history, by faith, by right. It has always been yours. Reclaim the land of your fathers for the day of reckoning is at hand."

33

RIYADH, SAUDI ARABIA – NOVEMBER 22, 2335
HOURS

Sitting in the crowded tea shop, Hassan watched the repeat of Yuman's video on the small television set. It had already been aired several times that night along with Arabic subtitles. And each time it was repeated, it never failed to draw in closer, a growing crowd of rowdy supporters.

"Do you see how the mood has changed?" he asked his aide Abdalla Saeed as they watched the people stare in fascination at the television screen.

Television cameras slowly panned the surreal, apocalyptic scenes of modern suburban towns in Singapore leveled in an instant by the nuclear firestorm of destruction, a sight unseen in over 70 years.

Heaps of charred and unrecognisable corpses were uncovered as giant slabs of concrete were slowly removed from the collapsed stadium of the Singapore Sports Hub. The home Lions XII team was playing a league football match against a team from Malaysia in their new open-air complex before a capacity crowd of 65,000 fans when the bomb detonated just seven kilometres away.

At hospitals across the country, Singapore's modern and efficient medical services simply collapsed into disarray by the sheer number of critically injured survivors in need of urgent help.

The crowd in the tea shop jeered, as thousands of Singaporeans with bags in hand were filmed attempting to flee into Malaysia; but there too the tide of fear was growing as the winds pushed the radioactive clouds further northwards.

"Look at them," said Hassan gesturing to the crowd gathered around the television screen who cheered as Yusman's video was aired once again. "Just a few hours ago, they were so afraid and look at them now." Earlier the previous evening, Hassan and Saeed had gone out on the streets of Riyadh soon after news broke of the nuclear blast in Singapore.

The mood then was very different. There was clearly fear and uncertainty in the people around them as crowds speaking in hushed tones, gathered around television sets throughout the city.

"Who did this?", "Was this a terrible accident?", "Was it the Russians?", "How would America respond?" These were the questions on everyone's mind. Many felt the attack in Singapore would herald the start of a new world war – the advent to a nuclear battle seemed to be on the horizon. Many felt that it was simply inevitable.

But since Yusman's video was released, the mood slowly shifted from worry and uncertainty to a new-found confidence about their future. Slowly those watching half a world away began to realise that they need not fear the United States anymore. Someone – a man most had never heard of – had struck a crippling blow on their behalf. The US was no longer the lone superpower, looking down with contempt and disdain on all the others. No, the rules had suddenly changed in their favour.

The crowd turned to jeer and shake their fists as a small convoy of US troops huddled inside their armoured vehicles, drove past the tea shop kicking up a cloud of dust.

"See for yourself," said Hassan, "see how confident they have suddenly become. It is so easy to manipulate people because they believe in what they see and what they are told. People were born to be led by their emotions and not their heads."

34

SITUATION ROOM, THE WHITE HOUSE,
WASHINGTON D.C. – NOVEMBER 22, 1300 HOURS

"We will allow you to do that – on humanitarian grounds! Who the hell does this little peasant think he is, dictating terms to me," thundered President Monroe after he watched a repeat of Yusman's video on television.

The President had earlier dismissed his advisors and now he was left alone with Kelly Yee, the President-Elect, to plan how the nation would respond. He felt she should be here and have an equal voice in the decisions made in this room for in a few short weeks when she assumed his office it would all rest on her head.

"He's was just taunting you, Theodore. You know that," replied Kelly.

"Yes of course I know that but I … the United States will not be blackmailed and held hostage by these … people. We need to respond, quickly and decisively with overwhelming force and impact," said the President slamming his palm on the table.

"So you have already dismissed his offer of peace then?"

"Kelly do you believe him? Do you really think that JI will suddenly stop their murderous ways and then what, overnight we become the best of friends?"

"No of course I don't believe him but that's not the point. If we strike back now and they make good on their promise to nuke another city or two, we are the ones who will be blamed for spurning this offer of peace however dubious it may be. They are already attempting to turn the tables on us. Suddenly we are the bad guys, the bullies, the provocateurs, the terrorists. That view is just going to be strengthened if the first action the world sees from the White House is a massive military strike in retaliation, in blind anger and revulsion.

"There must be another way," continued Kelly, "a way to negotiate. We can't deal with them, at least not directly and openly. It goes against everything we've been saying for years that the United States will never negotiate with terrorists."

"But isn't that what you are suggesting?"

"No, what I am saying is that we evaluate this possible avenue of mediation for the sake of peace and we do it quietly and off the record."

"And just who or what will this intermediary be?"

"I don't know yet ..." replied Kelly softly, shaking her head.

"Look Kelly, I don't like this any more than you do but as

President I don't have the luxury of sitting back and waiting for a channel of communication to suddenly appear. We need to strike back hard and cut off the head of this beast before he gets any stronger."

"If I were you, Mr President, I would be very careful about making such biblical references. We don't need that religious card complicating matters further."

"I wasn't even thinking of the Bible!"

"Yeah well cutting off the head of the beast, that can be interpreted as being from the Scriptures – you know, Satan as the Beast. Many people are going to jump on such a reference whether or not it was intended.

"Besides, as things stand now we don't even know where this Yusman character is holed up. The only target we know for sure is some remote jungle site, just a tiny training camp. Wiping that out would hardly right the balance and you will be violating Indonesian airspace – the largest Muslim country on earth."

"But it would be a start, a step in the right direction. Indonesia has been harbouring these damn criminals for far too long. If they want to go the way of Afghanistan and Iraq then we will take that country apart piece by piece!"

"Right and then you'll be no better than Bush – rushing into war with Iraq with no idea how to end it. More than a decade of misery and thousands of American lives lost and we are still no safer are we?" said Kelly.

"So what are you saying – we should do nothing, negotiate

– surrender?"

"You know that's not what I mean. We have to strike back. We have no choice in that, but it needs to be a meaningful strike beyond sending in a few million-dollar cruise missiles to blast apart some little jungle huts. We don't know for sure if they have other nukes at their disposal or where these might be. We need time to find that out. It could just be an empty threat, a psychological bluff to level the playing field. But for now, we need to play the hand we have been dealt. No, the only way to reassert the authority of the United States is to take out this JI leader and his command structure so there won't be anyone left to push that button. We need to be quick and ruthless."

"So we are in agreement then on the attack?"

Kelly nodded with a sigh but added, "Yeah I guess. But we need better intel and the locations of Yusman and his command structure. In the meantime I still want to try and find someone we can negotiate with for a long-term solution."

The President nodded realising that no matter which path he now chose, history would still blame him for failing to stop this attack during his watch. Finally he said: "You know Kelly, all of this is going to drag on well into your administration."

"Yes I know," she responded lost in thought.

"What happens if it's not a bluff and in a few months down the line, they go after our cities with another nuke or two? What then?"

"Then we have little choice but to respond in kind. We circle the wagons, dust off our tactical nuclear weapons and be ready to launch pre-emptive strikes against any country that continues to harbour these madmen. One tactical nuke can take out six city blocks – a big bang but limited in its damage and fallout. Still, unless we can defuse this and soon it could very well be an all out war."

The President recalled his senior advisors representing the Department of Defence, the Pentagon, Homeland Security, FBI, CIA and the Strategic Air Command.

After reviewing the events of the past hours and the military options available, the President continued: "Striking back is a foregone conclusion. We do not have any choice. What we need are the high-value targets. For the moment, all we have is this, a pathetic excuse for a target," he said pointing to the television monitor showing a satellite image of the jungle camp in Indonesia.

"This JI leader Yusman bin Iranto – that's the one we want along with any and all senior members of his organisation. I want all of you to pull out the stops; I need good, actionable intel be it electronic, satellite, field agents – good, reliable and timely intelligence so we can assign target strikes.

"Until that time comes, we will be keeping a low profile. They will be expecting us to talk, to vent our anger but we will bide our time," he said nodding to Kelly, "at least for the next few days. I will make the appropriate comments but we will give nothing away. Our silence will either make them more uneasy or lure them into a false sense of complacency. But gentlemen make no mistake about this – I need a target list quick and the clock is ticking."

General Bradley Myers, Chairman of the Joint Chiefs of Staff at the Pentagon was the first to respond. "Sir, in the light of this nuclear attack, are we moving DEFCON to Fast Pace?"

DEFCON is the defence readiness condition of the US armed forces. With alert posture scales descending from five to one, it is currently set at DEFCON Three codenamed Round House – a medium state of readiness. It had only been moved once to DEFCON Two's Fast Pace on October 23 1962 during the Cuban Missile Crisis. DEFCON One codenamed Cocked Pistol means nuclear war is imminent and the US has never moved to this alert level in its history.

"No officially we will stay at Round House – at least for now. But for all intent and purposes we are on a war footing. We need to start moving our assets. Alright General, what's the plan?"

Standing up, General Myers began outlining his battle strategy. "We must assume that these terrorists have operatives watching our movements at our military facilities. Conventional wisdom dictates that we begin moving our fleets and primary attack squadrons from Japan and Pearl because they are the closest assets to Indonesia.

"However I would recommend that we leave our bombers on the ground and our fleets in port, at least for the time being. They will of course be on high alert and can be mobilised quickly at a later time should we require secondary reinforcements in the theatre.

"For the primary strike force, we will use our fleets which are already far out at sea as these can't be tracked easily."

Calling up a map on one of the Situation Room's computer monitors, General Myers pointed out the locations. "As our primary targets still remain unknown, the plans need to be flexible to accommodate different strike packages and developing situations.

"Essentially we will have three staging areas. From the west we will move the *USS Ronald Reagan* and Carrier Strike Group Fifteen which is now off the coast of South Africa to here in the Indian Ocean. It's far enough away from commercial shipping routes to be out of visual and radar range to maintain the element of surprise. With aerial refuelling, our strike jets will still be well within reach of land targets in Indonesia.

"From the east, the *USS John C. Stennis* and its Carrier Strike Group Three now off the coast of the Vietnam will move to a positive control point here, about 400 nautical miles north-east of West Malaysia. We will position two of their nuclear strike subs closer to land, here … and here. As a precaution, I have also instructed the boomer *Nebraska* to move into position here in the South China Sea."

A boomer is a submarine specifically designed to carry and launch if necessary, ballistic nuclear missiles. The *USS Nebraska* (SSBN 739), an Ohio class submarine carries 24

Trident nuclear missiles with a range of 12,000km.

Continued the General: "From the south, we have four Spirits with their aerial refuelling tankers currently based just off Darwin, Australia. These B-2s will be escorted to their strike points by the surviving F-18s from the *George Washington* now based in Singapore."

"How long will it take to get these assets on station?"

"The bombers are in place now and our subs can be there in two days. It will take four to six days for the fleets to be on station, Mr President," said the General as he retook his seat.

"Alright do it. While we still have to identify our proposed targets, I want you to work out possible scenarios and I want to review the initial ORBATs by tomorrow.

"Gentlemen let me make this very clear. I want us to strike hard and fast – with conventional munitions only. I want the targets to be wiped out and I want our people to come back safe – understood?"

The General nodded. This meeting had troubled him. He had answered the President's questions as best he could but he still couldn't shake the nagging doubts as to where this country was heading.

Abruptly he stood up again and adjusting his uniform, the veteran soldier faced his Commander-in-Chief squarely and said: "Mr President, I have a duty to caution you sir. While we can, with air and naval assets, strike at just about any target we are assigned, we must avoid at all costs allowing this situation to escalate. We simply cannot afford to become entangled in a ground war with Indonesia.

"Vietnam was just a little sliver of jungle compared to what awaits any ground forces attempting to invade the Indonesian archipelago. Their armed forces may be small and quite antiquated in terms of equipment but the country sir," he paused, "it's thousands of islands, impenetrable muddy jungle and it has a huge Muslim population. For all the advances in technology any large-scale land offensive in such an inhospitable terrain would require well over a million boots on the ground. Such a war will be protracted and exact a terrible toll on US soldiers with absolutely no guarantee of victory."

President Monroe nodded, scrutinizing the soldier before him before he continued: "I appreciate the frankness General and a ground war is something I too want to avoid at all costs."

Offered Vice-President John McKenzie: "If we need to, perhaps we could threaten political and economic sanctions, maybe even a trade embargo if it comes to that. I tend to agree with General Myers. The military options at this stage are limited. The country is just too big to even try and enforce a naval blockade."

The President winced knowing full well how futile these threats would really be. Still he knew that his options at this stage were few. "Alright Kelly for now I want you to speak to the Indonesians and impress upon them how precarious their situation is. They better start cooperating with us and handover whatever information they have about these terror groups operating in their backyard if they know what's good for them."

Monroe then turned to his economic advisor Tim Drysdale who had been seated among the backbenchers at the meeting.

"Tim, I need a detailed analysis of our trade with Indonesia including what assistance we are providing their government and their military. I know that their main currency earners are petroleum and palm oil. Find out their main imports. Find me their Achilles' Heel and do it quick."

Moving on to James Carron, the director of the NSA and CIA director William Baldwin, the President continued. "I am depending on both of you to get the intel on the whereabouts of Yusman and the other leaders, their training camps and hideouts. Do whatever it takes. We only have four to six days until the fleets are in position to strike.

"And James, get on the line with our Israeli friends. They are now as much of a target as we are. See what they really know. I'll speak to their Prime Minister a little later today, I'm sure he has his hands full right now. No, this chapter is far from over."

35

EASTERN SINGAPORE – NOVEMBER 25

It had been three days since the nuclear attack and while the fires had largely been extinguished, many of the dead were still buried under mountains of rubble.

Like Israel, Singapore had a system of compulsory military and civil defence conscription for decades and with the country still paralysed, thousands of reservists were recalled back to active duty.

All non-essential construction work on the island was immediately halted as equipment and expertise were redirected towards the mammoth rescue effort still underway.

Roads leading to Ground Zero were cleared as hundreds of burnt out vehicles were towed away or simply pushed aside. This allowed the civil defence teams in their anti-radiation suits to penetrate deeper into the heart of the disaster. Victims were still being pulled out, many barely alive but as the hours turned to days, the number of survivors had dwindled.

The sickening stench of death hung thick in the air as four hundred civil defence officers of the Third Rescue Brigade, who were specially trained for search and rescue operations in hazardous environments, led the way. Each man wore a small radiation detector around his neck or clipped to his equipment belt. These would emit a series of beeps if ambient radiation exceeded safe levels.

Using life detectors and trained search dogs, they slowly probed the remains of each crumbled building for any signs of life as they inched their way deeper, getting ever closer to the epicentre.

Small red flags were used to mark the locations of bodies and body parts which would be retrieved later. The scope of the disaster became visibly apparent as media cameras filmed hundreds of these little flags waving silently in the breeze.

Several schools on the fringes of the hot zone were converted into temporary morgues. Each body was numbered, photographed and had tissue samples taken for DNA testing. Still the authorities knew that given the scope of the disaster, it would take months if not years to positively identify each and every victim.

As the nation still recoiled in shock and horror, government leaders many of whom were rushed to command bunkers across the island, had little choice but to order the mass burial of the dead whose bloated and irradiated bodies would soon pose yet another health risk.

The country itself remained in a state of lock down. Fighter jets circled the skies imposing a no fly zone for all civilian air traffic with the exception of those carrying humanitarian and medical aid which was pouring in from various countries.

Thousands of civilians remained in underground shelters within various public housing estates, train stations and schools. Medical authorities warned that they would need to remain there for at least another two weeks before the ambient radiation dropped to safe levels.

To stem the initial stampede of people crossing the border into Malaysia, the government there ordered a halt to accepting any more refugees from Singapore who were turned back as they tried to cross on foot at the two land bridges connecting the countries. But their efforts could not stop the radiation clouds from blowing further northwards towards the Malaysian capital.

Just as in the early stages of World War II, the Cathedral of Saint Joseph in Victoria Street was once again converted into a temporary triage centre for the injured and a morgue for the dead. It was one of the few buildings which still remained intact close to Ground Zero.

Covered in sheets before a life-size statue of the crucified Christ on the cross, the dead in their dozens were laid out in neat rows along the centre aisle of the old church awaiting mass burial.

Among them, with his bloodied hands clasped together in a final fervent prayer, lay the body of Father Michel Bata. He had continued pulling on the ropes to ring the church bells for 15 minutes until with raw and bleeding hands he collapsed from sheer exhaustion and died quietly from a massive overdose of radiation.

Viviane was at the church supervising the treatment of the injured when she was told that the body of the old priest had been found earlier that morning in the bell tower.

Kneeling beside him, Viviane slowly pulled the sheet down to reveal the face of a man she knew so well. Placing a gloved hand on his chest, she recalled fondly images of the kindly priest who had baptised her in this very church. She had seen him often when she studied at Saint Anthony's Convent just beside the church years later.

He was of course much younger then and many girls harboured a secret crush for this gentle young man. He never seemed to remember her name, for she was just one of hundreds of students at the mission school, all dressed in the same blue uniform. Still, with his wavy brown hair which matched his flowing robes, the priest was never without a smile – a smile she had always felt was just for her. And so today, even as a tear rolled down her cheek from behind her surgical mask, she returned that innocent smile for an old friend, one last and final time.

36

RIYADH, SAUDI ARABIA – NOVEMBER 25

A new-found confidence and self-belief was sweeping the Arab world. Yes, it was time to kick the foreigners out. The riches of the land would be theirs alone.

An anti-American backlash was just beginning. The journalists, who had been recruited earlier to the cause, got down to work. They began writing their stories and commentaries urging their governments to stand firm against the Americans. Demonstrations against US and British oil companies carefully planned months in advanced, were set in motion before scores of television cameras.

In the days to come Hassan would be one of several prominent businessmen who would be quoted in the media as supporting the growing wave of public opinion that the Arab and Muslim world must unite in launching a common regional currency and reject the acceptance of US dollars in all future transactions within the Gulf region.

Such 'public opinion' was of course just a ruse. It did not

exist – not yet. But once this idea was seeded in the public's mind, supported by the powerful local business communities and trusted religious leaders, Hassan was confident the people would soon rally behind them.

Soon crowds would form outside banks demanding that US dollars should no longer be regarded as legal tender in the region. Clerics preaching in mosques throughout the Gulf would up the ante proclaiming that the continued use of American notes was an affront to their faith.

The idea of establishing a new common Arab currency similar to the Euro was after all not a new one. As far back as 2009, nations of the Gulf Co-operation Council including Saudi Arabia, Abu Dhabi, Kuwait and Qatar had floated the idea of establishing a unified currency which would have meant an end to oil priced in American dollars.

The plan, which was later shelved for reasons that were never fully disclosed, had received political support not just from the Arab world but also from finance ministers and central bank governors in Russia, China, Japan and Brazil.

Hassan could not believe how smoothly everything had been going. The only minor hiccup to the plan so far had been the arrest of Saif in Singapore just prior to the attack.

The two observers at the airport's Departure Lounge had watched from a distance as Saif was handcuffed and taken into custody. They immediately called their handler in Riyadh. But by the time Hassan had been alerted, the scheduled nuclear detonation was only minutes away. He decided to wait and see what happened.

It was obvious that the police in Singapore could not stop the bomb from exploding. Hassan was unsure if Saif was still alive. Either way, that mattered little. Already a replacement bombmaker had been dispatched from Manila to Jakarta to assemble the next weapon.

Hassan's main worry now was not the United States but Israel. How the Jewish state would respond to its old enemy going nuclear was still a major uncertainty. An age-old religious divide was always volatile and unpredictable and when emotions and tensions between faiths peaked, anything could happen.

Still he need not have worried for Jewish zealots would soon be helping his cause more than they would ever know.

37

JERUSALEM, ISRAEL – NOVEMBER 25

Thousands across the Jewish state tuned in to their radios and television sets for word on how the US would respond to the nuclear attack in Singapore and the direct threat made against Israel.

Many had expected a swift reprisal but as hours turned to days with no apparent moves from the White House, a growing number of dismayed Israelis began to feel betrayed, that their mighty American ally had simply abandoned them in the cold to fend for themselves against a faceless enemy now in possession of a nuclear arsenal.

The Israeli Government also appeared to be playing a waiting game, unsure of what to do next. While appealing to its people to remain calm in the face of this nuclear threat, it also issued a strong warning to the Palestinians living in its territory that any violence by them would be met with swift and decisive force.

Its army had been placed on heightened alert, with reinforcements rushed to the volatile occupied regions of the West Bank and the Gaza Strip. Border security was also increased with armour units being placed in strategic locations to protect this small country.

The Israeli Air Force, the IAF, was busy scrambling its fighters to their defensive positions across the nation. What the Jewish State feared above all was a combined assault similar to that of the Six Day War in 1967 when it was attacked simultaneously on three sides by Egypt, Jordan and Syria.

Internally Israel was also worried about an armed uprising by the Palestinians and other Arabs living in the country and in its occupied lands. Numbering over 1.5 million or about 20 percent of the population, any organised insurrection could easily engulf the nation in chaos and bloodshed.

The mood among the F-15 pilots of Squadron 117 at the Ramat David Air Base in northern Israel was tense as they were briefed on the possible perils facing the country.

The older pilots had seen it all before. They and their predecessors had been fighting for their lives and right to exist as a nation since *Medinat Yisrael* or the State of Israel was born in 1948.

But even the younger pilots like Lieutenant Eli Mautner knew firsthand the cost of the struggle. Like his fellow aviators, he too had friends and relatives killed by the many Palestinian rocket attacks on Israeli villages over the years. Even as a boy, he had watched in disbelief and cold anger as Palestinians filmed by television cameras danced and jeered in the aftermath of each bloody attack on civilians. Mautner vowed then that he would do everything he could to protect his beloved Israel from the murderers brazenly walking around free and unrepentant in her midst.

But today such thoughts of revenge were far from his mind. During the hour-long briefing, Lieutenant Mautner was assigned to fly CAPs – combat air patrols above Jerusalem and the surrounding region. Normally this would be a routine operation but with the raw tension sweeping the globe, all eyes would be on Israel as the next likely target.

Mautner would be one of four pairs of fighter jets that would be in the air, flying low and clearly visible from the ground. Each pair would racetrack their assigned waypoints, making slow continuous circles for three hours until relieved by a new team. If trouble broke out, the fighters on CAPs would be the first to respond. More combat jets, with veteran pilots already strapped into the cockpit seats, would be on standby at the end of runways all across Israel, ready to back them up within minutes.

The aviators were told to expect trouble. Their multi-role F15 Strike Eagles were loaded not just with air-to-air missiles but also guided bombs for precision ground attacks if that became necessary. It was almost 8pm and time for Mautner and his fellow airmen to take to the skies once again.

Sensing fear and hesitation from the government they utterly despised, the mood among many Palestinians in Israel was already one of jubilant victory. One nuclear weapon detonated so far away in support of their cause, had given them a new sense of belief that the city was now theirs and that the time to retake Jerusalem as prophesised in the books of their faith, was at hand.

Flocking to the Al-Aqsa Mosque near to the Dome of the Rock earlier that morning, the Palestinians gathered in the hundreds as they listened intently to their clerics who urged them to assert their historic rights to this troubled land.

The brewing tension of the last few days was about to reach a tipping point that very night as a group of men made their way silently to the small Church of Saint Anne located in the heart of the Muslim quarter within the Old City.

This Roman Catholic Church was built in the 12th century near the remains of an earlier Byzantine basilica. Its weathered stone walls had been raised over a grotto believed by Crusaders to be the birthplace of Anne, the mother of the Virgin Mary.

For many long decades, the Palestinians had regarded this tiny church located in the area which they controlled, to be an affront to their faith – a visible thorn in their sides. And today a few men had been called upon to strike the first blow in the retaking of Jerusalem.

The planning had been swift but well coordinated. The heavy vehicles needed were already in place less than a kilometre away, hidden in several warehouses.

At 10pm the men and their equipment arrived at the deserted church. The nine bulldozers and hydraulic excavators immediately got to work attacking its stone walls with fury. They would only have minutes to inflict as much damage as they could and then escape before the authorities arrived.

The sturdy support pillars of the tiny church were struck first with all the brute force these mighty machines could muster. The men who had gathered to watch, cheered as the high vaulted ceiling came crashing down. They had just taken the first steps in asserting their authority over this ancient land. And even before the dust had settled, the men threw their Molotov cocktails setting fire to the crossbeams and pews of the old building which had stood there proudly as a beacon for the Christian faithful since 1138.

It was over in less than 20 minutes. As the sirens from the police vehicles rushing to the scene grew closer, demonstrators stationed down the hill blocked their path as planned. This gave the men along with the heavy construction vehicles a few extra minutes in which to escape back into the night. The culprits, who would never be identified, were jubilant that a new chapter in their long history had been written.

Crowds of residents soon gathered to watch the spectacle as police and firemen fought to control the blaze. But already for the little church, it was a lost cause.

Flying over West Jerusalem, Lieutenant Mautner was 20 metres below and to the right of his squadron leader Captain Ariel Aviram when they were informed of the attack on the church.

Turning starboard in tight formation, the flight descended to 1,200 metres to survey the damage from above and also to ensure that the roar of their twin-engines could be heard by all on the ground, reminding the crowd below that IAF was up and on alert.

Even using their night-vision cameras, there was little for the pilots to observe – just the smouldering remains of what was once a beautiful Romanesque building with acoustics so perfect that it became a well-known pilgrimage site for soloists and choirs, especially sopranos and tenors.

Mautner switched his right cockpit display to his infrared gun camera. The images were clear enough to make out the fire and the people gathered around it. As civil defence teams valiantly fought the blaze, he could see the crowd jeering at the firemen and raising their fists in defiance.

He knew the church well having visited it a number of times over the years. While situated in the Muslim quarter of the old city not far from Herod's Gate, it was a treasured place for both Christians and Jews like him.

It had a small courtyard with two large trees. As a boy, he and his younger sister Sharon had played in the shade offered by those old oaks. That had always been a vivid and happy memory for him, until now.

Eight hundred years of history had been obliterated that night and Mautner once again felt like he had been stabbed in the heart. Another one of his few treasured childhood memories had simply been erased amidst the taunts of the murderous Palestinian hordes who had gathered to watch the old church die so violently and with such indignation.

Without thinking, he eased back on his throttle slowing his jet down just above stall speed as he watched in seething anger, the ugly crowd illuminated by the flames, continue to jeer and dance.

There was little the two jets could do but to circle the scene and ensure the roar of their engines could be heard by the growing mob below. Over their military radio, the pilots heard the reports of riots breaking out all over the country.

A few minutes later, Captain Aviram was ordered to head north to the Palestinian stronghold of Ramallah in the West Bank where more gangs of angry Arab protesters were taking to the streets.

Ramallah, the one-time seat of the Palestinian Liberation Organisation, was still a hotbed of terrorist activity and unrest. The two jets patrolling that sector needed help after taking small arms fire from the ground. Mautner was told to remain on station above Jerusalem and report any changes to the scene below.

Captain Aviram confirmed receipt of his new orders. Rolling his jet sharply to the left, he gunned his engines and pointed his American-made Eagle towards the West Bank.

A growing sense of foreboding now overcame Mautner as he was left alone with his thoughts. He could feel the anger boiling inside. His country was once again being stabbed from within its own borders by its old enemy. He felt helpless, like a reluctant spectator strapped to his seat forced to simply observe the events as they unfolded below him, unable to stop this senseless carnage.

And then it suddenly occurred to him – he was seated in a fighter aircraft, probably one of the best in the world; an aircraft which in over 40 years of service in many combat theatres, had never been lost in action.

He had pledged his life to protect the weak and the defenceless. That old church had stood her ground peacefully surrounded by the unfaithful for centuries. She had endured the repeated desecrations and the filthy Arab graffiti which stained the pure white walls of her courtyard and yet she forgave, never closing her gates to anyone.

But today, she was killed and her body left to burn in the streets as the murderers stood there unrepentant, sneering at her defiled and twisted remains in her final minutes of agony. This little church, just like the country that Mautner loved so much, was slowly being ripped apart.

He felt he had to do something now before it was all too late. He was in the perfect weapon to strike back and the perfect target that would silence these murderous Palestinians was just minutes away.

It was impossible to miss the Dome of the Rock. Brightly lit, it stood out clearly as a beacon over the city and was just a few hundred metres away from the now smouldering ruins of the Church of Saint Anne.

Known to Arabs as the Qubbat As-Sakhrah, the Dome of the Rock occupied a prime position on the revered Temple Mount. Muslims claimed that their Prophet Muhammad ascended to Heaven from this very spot accompanied by the Archangel Gabriel.

This majestic shrine with its distinctive golden dome was believed by many to have been constructed on the site of the biblical Temple of Solomon. The First Temple built by King Solomon took seven years to construct and was completed in 957 BC. It stood for about 400 years before it was destroyed by King Nebuchadnezzar II of Babylon in 586 BC. The Second Temple built on the same site, was completed in 515 BC. Later King Herod the Great enlarged the building and created the famous Western Wall which is also known as the Wailing Wall, one of the most prominent sites in the Jewish faith.

Over the next two centuries, the Jews revolted twice against the oppressive rule of their Roman overlords who finally ordered its army to demolish the Second Temple in 70 AD. The Dome of the Rock, the first Muslim masterpiece, was built some 600 years later in 687 AD by Caliph Abd al-Malik, half a century after the death of the Prophet Muhammad.

And there it had continued to stand defiantly on what the Jews and the Christians regarded as a holy place central to their respective faiths.

But even as Israeli troops protected this Muslim shrine, secret Jewish organisations had been preparing quietly for decades to reclaim this holy site which they felt was rightfully theirs.

One organisation was better prepared than all the others. Calling themselves the Sons of Solomon, its ranks included architects, religious scholars, bankers, several high-ranking government officials, military officers and hundreds of wealthy and devoted supporters.

Over the years, the Sons of Solomon had painstaking drawn up detailed construction plans for a Third Temple based on the descriptions in the Torah and the Bible. Ancient religious garbs had been carefully recreated right down to the precious stones of the High Priest's breastplate by its sister organisation – the Daughters of Solomon.

Over 150 sacred vessels including the Holy Menorah were restored and in some cases, recreated based on historical documents, sketches and similar artefacts recovered from archaeological excavations in various places.

Even the giant blocks for the building's sandstone walls and stained glass panels had been cut, labelled and were carefully stored in dozens of warehouses ready for use at a moment's notice. For the Sons of Solomon, their centuries-old vigil would soon be over.

It would be wrong to say that Mautner's mind had snapped. He clearly was not insane. His thoughts were crystal clear. The belligerent Palestinians would never allow Israel or her people to be at peace. They were his nation's crown of thorns constantly drawing fresh blood even before an old wound had healed – leaving scar upon scar until a festering abscess was all that remained.

The voices in his head shouted down the blaring of his radio which called out to him repeatedly to report his position. The urgent voices of his flight controllers had simply merged into the background of his twisted thoughts.

Unconsciously he eased back further on the throttle trying to slow down the images racing through his mind. Distracted, his jet drifted west away from Jerusalem as the 23-year-old pilot struggled over the choices now before him.

He took a deep calming breath. Mautner now felt that he was following new orders – orders from a higher authority. He began to feel a burning sensation in his chest, a fire he could not explain. He did not know if he had consciously made that decision or if it was made for him but he had been trained to fight back and now was the time and behind him in the distance, was his golden target.

He felt that burning pain in his chest get stronger and then the F-15's shrill stall warning alarm jerked him back to reality. He had set the throttle too low and with insufficient air flowing across his wings to generate lift, Mautner's Eagle was about to fall from the sky.

He was still flying west and away from Jerusalem when instinctively he pumped up the power. Executing a wide turn, he headed back to the old city as his jet began climbing to its launch altitude.

On the left display screen in his cockpit, Mautner called up his ordinance stores. Cycling through the various air-to-air missiles and ground attack munitions at his disposal, he selected a single GBU-15 and pressing a button, he armed his chosen weapon.

Then keying in his digital map on his right display, Mautner moved the curser to his target and highlighted it. An invisible infrared beam locked on and began 'painting' his objective.

He was now approximately nine nautical miles from the Dome and had reached his minimum launch height of 8,000 metres for a shallow angle of attack. His weapons computer which was calculating continuously his speed, altitude and range to the target, then told him it was time.

In his digital Heads-up Display, the word 'FIRE' flashed in green and without hesitation, Mautner hit the pickle button releasing the 900kg weapon.

The unpowered bomb fell silently from its rails and began gliding towards its mark following the jet's infrared targeting beam. Steering to port while still 'painting' the target, Mautner held his breath and began counting down the seconds to impact.

Sensors in the weapon instantly began making their final corrections adjusting the angle of the bomb's tail fins to guide it to its target. Against the night's sky, the falling GBU was silent and virtually invisible to anyone watching from the ground.

Its flight was short, lasting only 23 seconds. The Guided Bomb Unit, GBU-15, impacted at a low angle, striking just below the golden dome. This weapon had been designed specifically to destroy buildings and reinforced military structures. As it penetrated the outer wall, the bomb detonated its payload of high explosives. The massive concussion generated within the confines of the Dome, blasted apart its walls and shattered its support columns. With the main bulk of the shockwave directed upwards and outwards, the sacred bedrock on which the shrine had been built remained virtually undamaged.

The blinding flash of the explosion lit up the night sky. Mautner's jet was rocked by the pressure wave of the blast as he overflew his target. He swung his Strike Eagle around to make another pass and survey the damage. Amidst the smoke, a large gaping hole in the ground was all that remained of the golden dome and the walls it supported. In mere seconds, Mautner had just demolished one of the most sacred and recognisable shrines in the world.

He felt neither elation nor guilt, just an overwhelming sense of nothingness. Fate had placed him at this turning point in history. The decision had been made. He did what he felt he had to and now it was time to accept the consequences that would inevitably follow. He knew full well that it would not just be his career that would be over, his life too would matter little now.

Turning his jet northwards towards the Ramat David Air Base, Mautner headed home, savoured the dying minutes of his flying profession. A stray thought entered his mind, to end it all here and crash his plane into the Mediterranean Sea to his left.

"Suicide – that would just be too easy. It's a coward's way to die and I am no coward," he told himself. He would not be like the Palestinians, running away after a fight. Mautner would face the consequences head on, whatever they may be.

Taking another deep breath, he executed a tight barrel roll, a quick spin of his jet. It was, to a fighter pilot, a sign of victory. Sadly there was no one there to witness it, to understand the sacrifice to history that a young, loyal patriot had just made.

But even before he landed some 25 minutes later, the Sons of Solomon were already making their urgent calls. Their moment of destiny had arrived and now was the time for action. Generations had waited for this fateful day and the rebuilding would begin immediately with the rising sun.

38

JERUSALEM, ISRAEL – NOVEMBER 26

As dawn broke over Jerusalem, the Israeli Army was already out in force. Within thirty minutes following the attack on the Dome of the Rock, heavy battle tanks and armoured vehicles were moved into their defensive positions, blocking the streets leading to the Temple Mount. Residents living within two kilometres of the attack site had been ordered to evacuate immediately "for security reasons".

The Israeli Government had acted swiftly imposing a strict curfew within Jerusalem. Everyone had to stay indoors as the heavily armed soldiers patrolled the streets. Telephone lines across the city were disconnected as the Israeli army began jamming television and radio broadcast signals as well as Internet access. Overhead military jets patrolled the skies imposing a no-fly zone over the city essentially to keep media helicopters from snooping on the construction work which was about to begin on the old hill.

In essence Jerusalem was being locked down and isolated. It was the first step in the government's plan to restore order and to begin rewriting history.

Already media speculation was rife that the blast which destroyed the Dome of the Rock had been set off by Jewish fundamentalists in reaction to threats made against Israel following the attack in Singapore.

At 9am as the world watched with growing anxiety, an Israeli government spokesman issued a brief statement on the events of the previous night: "Yesterday at approximately 10:32pm, a group, suspected to be Arab terrorists, detonated a series of large explosive devices within the Dome of the Rock.

"These simultaneous blasts completely devastated this holy and historic shrine. It also killed an undetermined number of people in the vicinity. We believe the same culprits were responsible for the demolition of the Church of Saint Anne which occurred several minutes before their attack on the Temple Mount.

"The strike on the church was apparently a diversionary tactic aimed at luring security forces away while the terrorists planted their explosives in various parts of the Dome.

"The resulting blast and the shockwave it generated also damaged various communication relay facilities within the Old City. Security forces are currently sifting through the rubble as they believe a number of large unexploded devices may still remain buried at the site. For this reason, the Government has imposed an evacuation zone of two kilometres and tall security barriers are being raised to protect and contain this crime scene.

"These senseless acts of violence and religious sacrilege were aimed at inciting public unrest in Israel following the nuclear terrorist strike in Singapore.

"Already we have received one unverified claim of responsibility for the twin attacks of yesterday. Israeli authorities are currently conducting an urgent investigation to identify and bring to justice those responsible.

"As a precaution, an indefinite curfew has been placed on Jerusalem. We urge all citizens and visitors to remain indoors. Any acts of civil unrest will be strenuously countered …"

The GBU-15 had done its job well in demolishing the shrine without causing any significant damage to its holy bedrock.

The barren rockface situated one level below the shine was littered with debris but remained intact. This outcrop of stone is central to three major religions. The Jews believe that this was the spot where Abraham stood ready to sacrifice his son Isaac to God. Christians regard this ground to be site of the Second Temple of Solomon where the baby Jesus was presented and where he later preached.

For most of the 12th century when the Crusaders

controlled Jerusalem, many believe they had excavated numerous caverns beneath this bedrock and hid priceless artefacts of their faith including the Ark of the Covenant – a golden chest containing the actual Ten Commandants written in stone by the finger of God and presented to Moses, as well as the Holy Grail, the mythical cup of the Last Supper.

Muslims hold this rock to be the exact location from which Muhammad's winged horse leapt into the sky towards heaven. The rockface is even said to bear the imprint from one of the horse's hooves. They also believe that an angel will come to this very slab of stone to sound the trumpet call of the Last Judgement at the end of the world.

On the southern side of the rock is a series of weathered steps leading down to a small cave. Known as the Well of Souls, it lies directly beneath the sacred foundation stone and has been well documented in a number of Jewish and Islamic legends.

Slowly Yoram Kessel descended the ancient steps carefully looking for signs of damage. As a senior member of the Knesset, the unicameral legislature of Israel which was located in Givat Ram, Jerusalem, he was the first top government official to enter the site following the attack the previous night.

 "Good, good. It is all still here. Everything seems to be still intact," he remarked to an aide. "Let Shimon know he can begin work at once. We do not have much time."

Shimon Tzabar like Kessel was a ranking member of the

Sons of Solomon and was its chief architect. In the hours since the attack, the top echelon of the organisation had gathered to plan the move that they, like their fathers and grandfathers before them, had prayed for. It was time to rebuild the temple and everything that was needed was ready. The Knesset, meeting in secret just hours after the bombing, had given its approval. That too was not unexpected as many of them were staunch Jews and also members of the SOS.

Given the current nuclear threat that it was facing, the Jewish State simply felt that it had nothing to lose by taking advantage of this opportunity to rebuild the temple. They felt its construction would rally Jews from around the world to protect their homeland.

The Israeli Government harboured no illusions that it could keep the rebuilding a secret for long. Even with the curfew in place and high plywood barricades screening the hilltop, this site was simply far too visible for the work to go unnoticed. Protests, riots, even suicide bombings from within its borders were more than likely to occur over the next few weeks.

But Jewish security forces had dealt with these on an almost weekly basis since Israel came into being. The government was confident these demonstrations could be contained however bloody they may prove to be.

What this tiny state still feared most was a revenge attack from its surrounding Arab neighbours. Tens of thousands of army reservists were recalled to active duty as reinforcements were rushed to strategic border points.

Israel then played its trump card. In a special news report carried by the *Hebrew Times*, the government for the first time openly admitted what the rest of the world already knew. Splashed across its front page was an undated file photograph showing rows of ballistic missiles loaded on mobile launchers being moved across the desert on training manoeuvres.

According to the report, each missile identified as the Jericho III, was fitted with an operational nuclear warhead. Details on the number and range of these weapons were withheld but the effect was no less chilling.

An unnamed government official was quoted as saying: "Israel will not be the aggressor in any conflict but we will do everything within our power and capabilities to defend ourselves from any terrorist group or any country that seeks to threaten our peace or the continued existence of this State."

The message to the outside world was clear – if Israel was attacked, it would have nothing left to lose in launching these nuclear missiles.

The Jewish propaganda machine of disinformation had already been set in motion earlier when it blamed terrorists for the attacks on the church and the Dome. The government had hoped that by shifting the blame for both attacks on unnamed Arab terrorists, it would divide and weaken Palestinian support.

Soon more reports would be leaked to the media complete with evidence implicating a range of terrorists' organisations for the bombing on the Temple Mount.

These included al-Qaeda, Hezbollah, ISIS, the Palestine Liberation Organization and Jemaah Islamiya. The media would suggest a number of reasons why such organisations would want to attack one of their own sacred sites. All these were designed to create confusion, distrust and disarray. No one would know the truth of what had really happened the night before.

As Yoram Kessel was emerging from the Well of Souls after his inspection, at the Ramat David Air Base, the body of Lieutenant Eli Mautner was being carried on a stretcher to an awaiting ambulance.

Months from now in a closed-door session, a military court would rule that he had committed suicide by shooting himself in the head, possibly as a result of a failed relationship with an unnamed woman. No details of this case would be released to the media. The only witness to the attack on the Dome had simply been silenced.

Protected by the Israeli army, workmen on the hill got down to business. Debris from the old shrine were quickly but carefully removed. Whatever recognisable pieces of the golden dome that could be salvaged, were packed away along with fragments of the elaborate tiles and mosaics which had adorned the walls of the shrine for well over a millennium. These would be returned one day to Muslim clerics as a small gesture of peace and conciliation when tempers had cooled down.

But for now, all effort was concentrated on the rebuilding of the temple. It had to be done swiftly but to the exacting measurements as described in their books of faith. Already surveyors with construction blueprints in hand and working under the direction of architect Shimon Tzabar were plotting the exact locations where the cornerstones were to be laid.

From warehouses across Jerusalem and beyond, dozens of covered flatbed trucks had begun hauling in the first stone blocks which had been cut and prepared decades earlier. Work would continue throughout the day and night for weeks to come. It would not stop until the temple was completed and was once again the beating heart of Israel and the Jewish faith, just as it had been foretold in the Torah.

39

As the first giant blocks of stone were being lifted onto the Temple Mount, Saeed waited patiently for Hassan. Beaming with pride, he could not wait to tell him the good news.

"So what exactly did you tell them?" began Hassan when they met a few minutes later.

"Exactly what you told me to say – that I am an emissary for a person who is willing to provide the US government with information on the whereabouts of Yusman."

"Did they ask for proof?"

"Yes of course. I gave them the photographs of Yusman, the ones I took of him coming out of his hotel here and the unedited copy of his video just as you had instructed."

"And?"

"And they were very keen to meet with you, erm I mean

the informant – of course I didn't tell them your name. They wanted to set up a meeting immediately. But I told them that you would only speak to her. It took them a while, almost two hours, but they have confirmed it for tonight – that would be afternoon in Washington. We have to be at the embassy at 10pm and then, they will put the call through."

"Good, you have done your first mission well. American agents from the embassy would have no doubt followed you back here and will soon be tapping all telephone calls, emails and Internet traffic so be careful what you say and do from now on," cautioned Hassan.

"Was this part of the plan to destroy the shrine?" asked Saeed pointing to the television set which was showing images of the destroyed Dome of the Rock and the riots that were breaking out in various parts of Israel and the demonstrations across the Muslim world.

"No Saeed. The church was the only target we had. This … this was just a huge bonus, a gift to our plans."

"But who did it then?"

"I don't know Saeed. Not everything is made known to me."

"Is this the start of the war you said would come?"

"No, it has yet to begin. This is just the sound and fury – a howling wind of anger and despair by people who do not know what to do next. They need a mission and that my friend, is coming soon."

40

VATICAN CITY. NOVEMBER 26, 1334 HOURS

As Saeed reported to Hassan about his meeting with officials from the American Embassy in Riyadh, the Holy Father was preparing to deliver a statement on the horrific events of the past days in Singapore and Israel.

Pope Peter II, more commonly known as Petrus Romanus or Peter the Roman for his Italian pedigree, was elected to succeed the very popular Pope Francis who died in May, six months earlier.

For more than 2000 years, none of the popes before him had chosen the papal name of Peter probably out of respect for the original apostle Saint Peter who, according to the bible, was commanded by Jesus to be the rock on which the church is built. That order made Saint Peter the first Pope.

But Pope Peter II picked the name precisely out of great respect and admiration for Saint Peter. He reasoned that for far too long, the Roman Catholic Church had been distracted by the affairs of the modern world and lost sight of its true purpose in preaching the faith and guiding the faithful just as Saint Peter had done in those troubled early days.

Broadcast over Vatican Radio, Pope Peter II now delivered his message of peace and hope to a frightened world: "Despite the terrible loss of life suffered in Singapore and earlier in Jakarta, and the senseless destruction of sacred sites in Israel, I urge all parties involved and affected by these tumultuous events, to exercise restraint and to pray for wisdom and harmony. Resist the pressure to exact revenge for any escalation of this conflict would only endanger the peace of the entire world …"

Whilst understandable, the Vatican's neutral stance did nothing to defuse the growing tension around the globe. The Pontiff knew full well that the world was looking to the Church for its response to the destruction of the Dome of the Rock and the disturbing rumours that Israel was scrambling to build the Third Temple of Solomon in its place.

Politically the Vatican was caught in a quandary. Weighing in on either side be it for the Muslims or the Jews, was simply not an option. The Pope had evaded giving a direct response to the deteriorating situation in Israel and his silence on the issue had not gone down well with either side.

The Muslim world had largely dismissed Israel's claim that the attack on the Dome was carried out by Arab terrorists and interpreted this resoundingly hollow response by the Catholic Church to mean that it did not disapprove of a

Jewish temple being hastily constructed in secret over what had been a sacred Muslim shrine.

To the Jews who were already feeling increasingly isolated, the lack of support from the Vatican on the reconstruction of Solomon's Temple had caused a major rift between these two religions which by virtue of their overlapping history, had been on cordial terms for decades.

As he knelt down to pray in his private chapel, the Pontiff could feel the weight of recent events on his shoulders. Once again he bowed his head and pleaded for divine grace and good judgment. Dark images of wars and nuclear firestorms raced through his troubled mind as he sought refuge in the depth of his unwavering faith and in the ancient words of prayer.

Finally the voice in his head spoke telling him what his heart already knew. The answers he so desperately sought had already been written. All he had to do now was to understand the divine messages revealed by the prophets of old and prepare his flock for the events still to come. He needed to consult the *Sacrum ordinem Scolarium*.

A scholar of history, Pope Peter II understood better than most that the Vatican, seat of Papal power, was a vast multifaceted organisation caught in a time warp. On one hand, the Church was rightly obsessed with the age-old rituals and obligations of faith rooted in its rich history spanning more than 2000 years. On the other hand, it endeavoured to remain relevant in a modern world, to shepherd its global flock of over one billion Roman Catholics guiding them through the complicated and uncharted perils of life in the 21st century.

The Pope firmly believed that the answers to the challenges and dangers facing the world today were written in the books of the Bible, the Torah and other ancient holy texts handed down over the generations. All that was needed now was for these to be studied with modern eyes and interpreted to reveal the wisdom of the ages.

One of the first changes he instituted as Pontiff was to revive the *Sacrum ordinem Scolarium*, the Sacred Order of the Scholars. It was first established in 1347 by Pope Clement VI who reigned during the Black Death pandemic which killed between one and two thirds of Europe's population from 1347 to 1350. Pope Clement VI believed that a cure for this unholy plague could be found within the massive volumes of religious texts which had been carefully catalogued and stored within the *Archivum Secretum Vaticanum*, the Vatican Secret Archives.

The other task he charged the clergymen of the *Sacrum ordinem Scolarium* was to decipher when and how the world would come to an end. Among the learned men drawn into this secret organisation was a noted astronomer to study the heavens. It was a common belief at the time that just as the Magi followed the Christmas Star to Bethlehem, so too a special star appearing in the heavens above would herald the End of Times.

Over the centuries that followed, this order of scholarly monks was sidelined as a succession of Popes found themselves struggling to cope with the day-to-day demands of papal administration. Pope Peter II had revived the *Sacrum ordinem Scolarium* and staffed it with some of his most learned priests from around the world. They included religious scholars, academics, political observers, economists and one noted astrologer.

But even as the Pope was anxious to find out how these men interpreted the tragic events of the past two weeks, he felt a growing sense of dread as to what he would be told.

41

OVAL OFFICE, THE WHITE HOUSE, WASHINGTON
D.C. – NOVEMBER 26, 1445 HOURS

"Basically Hassan told me that he had contacts which could pinpoint Yusman's location giving us two maybe three hours of advance notice," said Kelly.

"And how reliable is this information?" asked President Monroe.

"Well he seems to know what he is talking about. He knew some details of the Jakarta attacks that were not released to the media. He was also able to produce an unedited version of Yusman's video tape. It said essentially the same thing but he had mispronounced a few words so they probably had to reshoot it."

"Mr President this could very well be another trap," warned CIA Director William Baldwin. "This whole Jakarta attack was a set up right from the start to get the task force into Singapore so it could be destroyed. They could just be playing us yet again."

"Yes, thank you very much. That possibility is fairly obvious now to everyone in this room!" said the President bluntly. "But, if it's not a trap, what does he have to gain by helping us?"

"That was the question I put to him directly," continued Kelly.

"And?"

"His reply was that he was just after the money."

"You mean the reward? I thought this guy was rich!"

"Well a $10 million incentive for information leading to the capture of Yusman isn't exactly loose change. But it's more than that. According to Hassan, several Gulf States are banding together to release a common currency, one that will be used throughout the region and beyond. Anyone who wants to buy oil from the region would have to use this new currency. He said an announcement would be made very soon."

"Yes it's been speculated in the papers more of late. These guys have been talking about it for years now but they could never reach any consensus. More than a decade on and the Euro is still struggling. What makes them so sure they can pull off starting a successful regional currency from scratch?"

"The situation in the Middle East is very different, especially now since the attacks," said Kelly. "We've been branded as the bad guys, the aggressors. All these riots and the calls from religious clerics across the region to stop using American dollars are putting significant pressure on governments to do something if they want to stay in power.

"You simply can't ignore the enormous strain religion brings to bear on politics and the hearts of men. That's quite different from the situation in Europe. Besides, the governments of the Gulf know their crude is going to run out in less than two decades so switching to a unified currency now while they still can play the oil card, it just makes sense."

"Tim, where would that leave us?"

Presidential Economic Advisor Tim Drysdale, who had been expecting this question, rose from his seat to answer. "If that were to happen sir, it will be nothing short of a game-changer.

"If all countries who buy oil from OPEC or at least the Gulf states are compelled to use this new currency, then the standing of the US dollar would be weakened considerably. Countries in the Gulf have enormous buying power and therefore influence on world trade. Under these conditions, introducing a new and powerful currency is likely to trigger a psychological paradigm shift. As people mentally swing from thinking of oil prices in US dollars to this new currency, they will similarly, over time, stop thinking of trade value in US dollars but in these new dollars.

"If it's just the Gulf States pushing this new dollar then its effects may be limited to just the region but there is also the China factor to consider.

"It's no secret Beijing wants to displace the Greenback as the sole global currency but they are reluctant to put the Yuan up in its place because they still want to control the value of their own currency and keep it low for obvious trade advantages. Now if China, the world's largest economy, accepts this new currency and starts using it externally instead of the Greenback then this new dollar or whatever they call it could emerge as a serious rival which could, over time, supersede the US dollar as the international currency of choice. In short Mr President, it would give them control."

"What do you mean?"

"All of this is simply speculation right now but if this currency takes off and is used throughout the Muslim world, if China and other major economies back this currency, then theoretically those who control the value of this currency can inflate or devalue it at will and that could well wreck our economy."

"How?" said President Monroe.

"If they drop the value of their currency, then every export from the US will suddenly be seen as more expensive. We could simply be priced out of the market. With fewer external buyers, our industries would not be able to survive if they were only serviced by domestic demand and may well collapse. If they inflate the value of their currency, then just about everything we import, oil in particular, is going to be a lot more expensive. Domestic inflation could well go through the roof."

"Can we do anything to discredit … to kill this currency in

its infancy?"

"From an economic standpoint, no. We can't stop any country or a group of countries from starting a new currency or banding together for regional economic gain."

"But if they just start printing paper money indiscriminately, it is virtually worthless right? I mean it's not backed up by gold or anything."

"Neither is ours, Mr President. A currency has value only if it is guaranteed by a country or group of countries and the people using it have faith in its promised worth."

"How likely is this to happen?"

"Well Mr President as you yourself said, the Gulf States have been talking about this for years. But it's not something they can do overnight. Even such basic things as finalising the look of a common currency, that alone took the EU years to reach an agreement. And then you have the national legal hurdles to be crossed and the logistical nightmare of printing, distributing and gaining regional and international support. They would need a central bank to coordinate things and a very strong PR campaign to get it off the ground. A currency is useless unless people believe in its value. So even if they are moving in this direction, it will take a lot of planning and coordination and if they are only starting now …"

"How's this for a PR campaign?" asked the President nodding towards the television screen which was replaying images of the nuclear destruction in Singapore."

"Mr President, if that's their idea of a PR campaign just to push a new currency then it's the lowest form of evil I can think of. I cannot even begin to contemplate …"

"Alright, alright," said President Monroe raising his hand and cutting the man off in mid-sentence. "Let's monitor this closely and respond when or if it happens. So Kelly, coming back to Hassan, what's his angle with this so-called unified currency?"

"Well he's a businessman and all he wants to do is to make money, or so he says. He seems pretty certain that the unified currency is something that's going to happen sooner rather than later. To him, the attacks in Singapore and the situation in the Middle East with Israel, all this will just cause more political instability and that's just bad for business. He says he has no love for these terrorists but in his line of work he hears things which he wants to pass on to us. If we are to believe him, he says the sooner we get this affair with Yusman over and done with, the quicker things can get back to normal."

"Kelly, do you believe him?"

"I'm somewhat inclined to. It's a big risk for Hassan to stick his neck out like this. If he's trying to lure us into a trap, then he'll know that he'll never do business again and we will put a price on his head. Besides what other options have we got?"

Turning to the other men present, the President asked: "Yes, gentlemen, do we have any information on where Yusman or his henchmen are right now?"

The directors of the CIA and NSA shook their heads. "We are still working on it but there is nothing definite as yet," said Director Baldwin.

"We need that target list and time is fast running out. Brad, when will our strike teams be in position?

"Our attack submarines with their Tomahawks have been lying in wait just off the Indonesian coast for two days now as is the *USS Nebraska* in the South China Sea," said General Bradley Myers, Chairman of the Joint Chiefs of Staff at the Pentagon. "The two carrier groups will be in position by 1800 hours tomorrow. Our Spirit bombers out of Australia are ready to go at any time. All we need are the targets."

"Mr President, there is another development," said James Carron, the director of the National Security Agency. "Singapore has identified what they believe to be a second terrorist camp about 320 miles south of the first camp that we had pinpointed. An NSA satellite is due to make a flyby in about three hours so we will know more then. And Singapore wants in."

"What do you mean they want in?"

"They know we are going to be striking back and they want to take out this target themselves, a measure of revenge for the nuke strike. They are not asking for our permission. They are telling us in advance what they intend to do, alone if they have to."

"Jeffrey?"

"Well sir, we can't stop the Singapore government from deploying whatever forces they still have left," said Secretary of Defence Jeffrey Brown. "But still, we should work with them and coordinate the strike for a simultaneous hit. If they strike first, it could very well mess everything up and we lose the crucial element of surprise when we launch."

"But does Singapore have what it takes to carry out such an attack on their own?"

"Oh yes. They may have lost their Fighting Falcons, the F16s, in the nuclear attack when two of their airbases were hit but they still have the F15SGs, modified versions of the Strike Eagle at another base and their pilots are excellent. They are not battle-tested as yet but they have been trained well."

"Kelly as Secretary of State, can you ask the Singapore Government to back off? If they have a target, we can help to take it out with our cruise missiles. They don't have to send their people into harm's way and risk a bloody nose."

"State has received the same report and I was on the line with their Government earlier today," said Kelly. "They are determined to strike this second target themselves – on their own if they have to. For them it's a matter of pride and an act of revenge so they are very determined to get their hands dirty on this one no matter what."

"Alright Jeffrey, you and the DOD are to work with them. Tell them, erm … no, make that request Singapore to hold off for now until we are ready to launch simultaneous strikes. We need confirmation on the whereabouts of

Yusman and his gang. That is the priority, these training bases are secondary targets. Clear? Kelly, when can we expect to hear from Hassan?"

"He said he should be able to get back to us within 48 hours."

"General Myers, when this is all over, I want absolute confirmation, irrefutable evidence that Yusman's been taken out. We need to show the world that we had struck the right targets. So what's the plan?"

42

RIYADH, SAUDI ARABIA – NOVEMBER 27, 1835 HOURS

Saeed handed over to Hassan the decoded email from Yusman and waited patiently for his reaction. While the message was only four lines long, Hassan took his time reading it.

Finally he gave the printout back to Saeed. "Reply in the usual fashion to confirm the meeting," he said with a sigh knowing that he was about to send his faithful friend to his death. "I will be in my study and I do not wish to be disturbed by anyone."

"Is there anything wrong?" asked Saeed.

"No, I'm just tired and need some rest," came the reply just as Hassan shut his study door. Hassan could feel the burning sensation in his chest again and it seemed to be growing hotter. Unconsciously he rubbed it but he knew that would offer no relief. The pace of events was certainly moving faster now and the pain inside would only get stronger.

The plan so far had been going even better than he could have hoped for. Hassan did not trust the Americans but there was little choice in the matter. The time had come again for them to unknowingly play their part and if they screwed up now, then everything that he had worked so hard for would simply fall apart.

He had to ensure that the Americans would launch an all-out attack on JI. There was always a chance that the outgoing-president would lose his nerve. He could choose to back off and wait, preferring to leave this decision and the responsibilities that came with it to his successor. That would simply spoil everything. Hassan needed to make them an offer the Americans could not refuse – the chance to intercept a second nuclear weapon – one headed their way.

Picking up the telephone on his study table, he made the call to the US Embassy. This part of the plan would, for the next few days at least, be out of his hands.

OVAL OFFICE, THE WHITE HOUSE, WASHINGTON D.C. – NOVEMBER 27, 1125 HOURS

"Hassan contacted our embassy in Riyadh a few minutes ago. We've got the target list and GPS cordinates," said Kelly as she walked into the Presidential office that she herself would occupy in less than two months.

"What have we got?"

Opening a map on his table, Kelly pointed to the spot.

"Yusman and all his senior JI commanders will be here at a meeting tomorrow at 10pm Jakarta time, that's 10am our time. He says it's a small isolated farmhouse, just one level. The place is about 560 miles north-east of Jakarta. I've sent a CIA team from our embassy to stakeout the place. They will make the visual confirmation before the attack as we can't afford to just go on Hassan's word alone. The meeting site is about 150 miles from the first terrorist camp here. Then further south about 120 miles, here at this river bend, is the second camp identified by the authorities in Singapore. We are getting satellite pictures of this meeting point now. We should have them in about two hours.

"How accurate is the intel on this JI meeting?"

"I'm not sure, so far all we have is Hassan's word. Maybe the CIA has more info but I haven't heard from them yet."

"Get Myers and the others to the Situation Room in 20 minutes and let's go through this in detail."

"Yup but hang on, there's more. According to Hassan there is another target. A container ship left Indonesia heading west. He says it's carrying a second nuclear weapon, probably bigger than the one that struck Singapore. He's not sure where it is heading."

"What! A second nuke? Do we at least have the name of the ship?"

"Yes and NSA is checking on that now to determine its approximate location."

"Okay, tell them I expect a detailed strike package ASAP. Given the time of this JI meeting, we have less than 24 hours to put it all together."

"My ground team should be in place in about three hours and we'll keep the target house under observation. They will make the positive identification of Yusman and the other leaders while the SEAL team is inbound," said CIA Director William Baldwin.

"What if your guys get spotted?" asked the President.

"They won't. They are all ex-Army HRT Rangers. They know what they have to do."

"And if Yusman doesn't show up or they can't make a positive ID on him?"

"Without positive confirmation, my recommendation is that we abort this part of the mission. However we will still continue with the strikes on the two training bases."

"And that Russian tanker?"

"Mr President, we still have no evidence apart from Hassan's word that there is in fact a second nuclear device or that such is concealed on that ship. It's one hell of a leap of faith," said James Carron, the director of the National Security Agency.

"I am well aware of that James," replied the President.

"But if he is correct about this JI meeting," offered Baldwin, "and we would know that before we launch against the ship, then we would have to assume that he is also right about this possible nuke."

"Is there any way that we can secure that nuke … safely?"

"I'm afraid not Mr President," said General Myers. "Out in open water, we would not have any element of surprise. We would have to assume that someone on board that vessel has the ability to detonate the nuke should that ship be boarded by US forces. Given its approximate location, the blast may trigger an ocean-wide tsunami just like the one in 2004 that killed about a quarter of a million people. A surprise attack … destroying the target swiftly from a safe distance before it can be activated, that's the only option. We will take it down over deep water so we would never know for sure one way or the other if there was in fact a nuclear weapon on board."

"We've seen what these people are capable of," said President Monroe. Again he was haunted by that single image of the burnt hand of a child from the bombed school bus in Jakarta. "And they have already used one nuclear weapon. Can we really afford to risk not acting on this information and let a second bomb slip through our fingers? History will never forgive us if we do nothing."

Looking at Kelly and the others gathered in the room, the President continued: "This one is my responsibility and mine alone."

Then turning to General Myers, the President commanded: "Track that ship down. If Yusman turns up at this meeting, then we will have to assume that Hassan was right about this second nuclear weapon. Then General, I want you to destroy that ship. I don't want any traces left behind. Understood?"

43

THE *USS RONALD REAGAN*, INDIAN OCEAN –
NOVEMBER 28, 2217 HOURS

The *USS Ronald Reagan* together with the Carrier Strike
Group Fifteen had been patrolling in international waters
west off Sumatra in Indonesia when it picked up its target
on radar six hours earlier. Still well out of visual range, the
convoy began to shadow it from a distance of 120
kilometres.

According to the NSA report which the *Reagan's*
commander Admiral David G. Thomas had received, the
MT Khekov, a small Russian-registered container ship had
left the port of Sibolga in western Sumatra and was headed
to Durban in South Africa with a crew of 27.

The container ship now classified as a bandit – an enemy
vessel – had been designated the codename Tango Zulu
and Admiral Thomas was ordered to keep tracking it until
the target was over deep waters and clear of other
commercial shipping traffic.

Helo One, a Sikorsky SH-60B Seahawk helicopter was

dispatched earlier from the *Reagan* to fly 300 metres from the *MT Khekov* to visually confirm the ship's identity. There was no mistake.

Overhead an EA-6B Prowler jet was waiting in a holding pattern, circling high above the clouds. Its pilots were ready to start jamming the target's radar and communication systems to prevent any distress calls from being transmitted.

The *MT Khekov* still had another eight kilometres to go before it cleared the continental shelf and the sea depth plunged to more than 1,900 metres. This would be the old ship's cold, dark tomb well beyond the reach of all but the most expensive of salvage operations.

Seated in the Combat Information Centre of the *Ronald Reagan*, Admiral Thomas had been in secure radio contact with the destroyer *USS Higgins* which was patrolling the western flank of the carrier's fleet protection screen.

"Do you have a firing solution for engaging Tango Zulu?" he asked.

"Affirmative, Harpoon is locked and ready," came the response from the *Higgins*.

"Confirmed – stay tight on weapon's hold," said the Admiral. It would only be a few minutes more.

SOUTH CHINA SEA – NOVEMBER 28, 2232 HOURS

The two stealth Black Hawks had been flying low over the sea for more than an hour since leaving their carrier the *USS John C. Stennis*. Now barely clearing the canopy of the Indonesian jungle, they were just minutes away from their objective.

THE CIA team on the ground reported that four vehicles with 13 occupants, one visually identified as Yusman, had arrived at the target house seven minutes earlier.

With their low acoustic signatures, the modified UH-60 Black Hawks came in low and fast. Hovering just six metres off the ground, the SEAL teams fast-roped down and hit the ground running. One team, landing in the garden fronting the target house, moved quickly to the front door. The second team from the other helicopter landed in the sprawling rear garden of the premises and covered the exit for possible escaping targets.

Blasting apart the front door with explosives, the seven-man SEAL insertion team then tossed in several flash-bang grenades. Crouching low, the team waited for the explosions. The deafening blasts and the blinding flashes of the burning magnesium had caught the JI commanders in the house completely off guard.

The head of the strike team codenamed Manta Ray Leader was the third man through the door. The first two SEALs had already entered and took their defensive positions, one to the right of the door, the second to the left.

Their targets had been sitting around a large dining table which was strewn with papers. Most of the men, still in shock from the stun grenades, just stared in utter disbelief as the black-clad commandos burst in on their meeting.

It took only seconds for Manta Ray Leader to scan the faces of the targets before him. He recognised Yusman in a heartbeat as he centred the laser targeting beam of his Heckler & Koch MP10 assault weapon squarely on the man's chest.

Yusman's eyes widened as he saw the red laser dot move to his heart. In his final seconds of life, Hassan words came back to haunt him: "The Americans will hunt you down and with my help, they will get you eventually." This was the ultimate sacrifice demanded of him and one that he was gladly prepared to make for the sake of the cause and his faith.

Yusman knew that there was no point in trying to run. Instead, in his last act of defiance, he straightened his back and looked at his killer in the eye. Then taking a deep breath, he awaited the inevitable. The pause was brief – a three-second burst of automatic gunfire and his body was tossed backwards. Yusman was dead well before his torn corpse came crashing to the ground.

Simultaneously the rest of the SEAL team followed their orders to the letter, quickly dispatched the remaining terrorists where they sat with double shots to the chest. They were told to avoid headshots if possible as it would complicate visual identification later on.

The strike, done in almost business-like precision, was over in seconds. As three commandos stood over the bodies splattered with blood and bits of human tissue, the other four searched the house for more targets but they came up empty.

"Whiskey One … Manta Ray Leader," said the team commander as he keyed in his microphone. "Coyote is down. I repeat, Coyote is down. Extracting in 10."

Coyote was the codename for Yusman and their mission was almost over. They had been on the ground for barely four minutes.

The team knew what they had to do next. Yusman's body was quickly photographed and bundled into a plastic bodybag. His remains would be taken back by the team for DNA identification.

Meanwhile other commandos including those who had been guarding the rear of the house began their systematic search in silence. All the documents on the table along with three laptops and an iPad Mini were seized. Plastic number tags were placed on the chest of each dead terrorist as they were photographed. The men were also quickly fingerprinted and blood samples were taken for DNA testing later.

Searching the bodies, the commandos recovered their wallets with identification papers. Four thumb drives and 15 hand phones were also found and collected. The search of the hideout itself and the parked cars outside revealed nothing of any obvious intelligence value. Still the team took detailed photographs of the scene and the licence plates of the vehicles.

Ten minutes later and both teams were back in their helicopters flying low, barely clearing the treetops. They would be "feet wet" and safe over the sea in less than six minutes.

On the floor of the lead helicopter, in a black bodybag on which the commandos rested their feet, Yusman was on his final journey. He had played his part and his mission, like that of his killers, was over.

SOUTH CHINA SEA – NOVEMBER 28, 2232 HOURS

Some 400 kilometres away, a squadron of four F-15SG Eagle attack jets from the Republic of Singapore Air Force had just crossed the Indonesian beach and headed inland over the jungle.

The pilots had been flying for more than 50 minutes after lifting off from Tengah Air Base in Singapore. They had been refuelled in mid-air just before they entered Indonesian airspace.

Flying low to avoid detection on enemy radar, they headed for their target 36 kilometres away. They were shadowed by another group of fighter jets. Flying some five kilometres behind them, Lieutenant Commander Robert Green was leading his team of seven F-18 Super Hornets from the now-destroyed *USS George Washington*. Both groups of fighters had taken off together from Tengah.

Although the nuclear attack in Singapore had destroyed about a third of the country's advanced air force, the island's government had demanded that Singapore pilots take the lead in this strike. National pride was at stake and it was time for payback.

The US had reluctantly agreed to this condition and had its squadron of Hornets tail the Eagles to provide cover in case they ran into trouble with the Indonesian Air Force.

As the four Eagles closed in on their target, the second jungle training camp that Singapore had identified, the commander of the American carrier *USS John C. Stennis* issued the attack order to one of his fleet submarines lying in wait just off the Indonesian coast.

Rising silently to its launch depth, the nuclear-powered *USS Seawolf* fired in quick succession, four Tomahawk cruise missiles before submerging again to its cruise depth and heading off to the safety of deeper water. The guided missiles were timed to strike the first terrorist training camp just as the Singapore fighter jets began their assault on the second camp.

Captain Chow Wai Leong, codenamed Raven, the lead pilot of the Singapore squadron activated his Sniper ATP Surveillance & Ground Targeting pod and readied his team as they entered the launch envelope some 22 kilometres from their target.

The jets which had been flying at near treetop level to avoid radar detection, had pulled up to 6,000 metres, the minimum required height to launch their weapons. This was the most dangerous part of the mission as flying at that level would make them plainly visible on enemy radar.

"Raven Patrol – Raven One … go weapons hot," said Captain Chow to his team as he armed his AGM-154

JSOW, a fire-and-forget precision guided ground attack weapon. The jets now flying in a staggered line three metres apart, waited for his attack order.

On his Heads-Up Display, Captain Chow watched as his computer calculated the exact time for weapon release. The targeting information and GPS coordinates of the second terrorist camp had been fed into the single four-metre-long Joint Standoff Weapon slung beneath the fuselage of each Eagle.

The HUD displayed the countdown to the last second and then the word FIRE flashed in green.

"Raven – launch, launch, launch," said Captain Chow as the JSOWs of the four fighter jets left their rails and began gliding silently to their assigned targets.

"Egress now," said Captain Chow as the F-15SGs flying in perfect battle formation, executed a sharp starboard bank and dove for the cover and safety of the treetops.

The JSOWs were now less than 15 kilometres from their targets. Guided by satellites and an inertial guidance system, the missiles with their stubby wings took just minutes to reach the terrorist camp. While still in mid-air over the target, each weapon released its payload of 145 small bomblets saturating the camp in a series of deafening explosions.

Deadly shrapnel tore through the small camp killing all the sleeping militants as fires reduced the makeshift wooden buildings to untidy heaps of smouldering embers. The destruction was over in seconds and the little island nation of Singapore which was sometimes described as a shrimp with teeth, had exacted it's a measure of deadly retribution.

Two hundred kilometres away, it was the same scene of overkill as the four Tomahawk cruise missiles fired by the *USS Seawolf* destroyed the other terrorist training camp in a series of deadly surgical strikes.

"Raven, this is Foxbat. You have two bandits, MiG-21s, your seven o'clock high, Angels Three Five."

The American squadron had picked up two Indonesian Air Force MiGs that were scanning the skies searching for the low-flying Singapore fighter jets that were now desperately scrambling to reach the safety of the sea.

"Foxbat – Raven, we are erm … twelve minutes from feet wet."

"Raven – err, roger stay on course, keep your heads low. Doesn't look like they have spotted you guys yet. We'll pop up and let's see if we can give 'em a heart attack!" said Commander Green as he led his squadron from their tree-top cruising height into a steep powered climb.

The seven American Hornets immediately formed two attack groups as they levelled off and headed directly towards the on-coming MiG fighters.

Keying his microphone, Lieutenant Commander Green announced, "Unknown aircraft, this is a squadron of Super Hornets from the United States Marine Corps. We will be heading into international waters. Do not engage us."

Still the two aging Indonesian fighters continued with their head-on approach and were now just 20 kilometres away.

"Maybe these idiots don't understand English," said Green to his wingman on his right. Just as he was about to reissue his warning to stay clear, one of the Indonesian jets opened fire unleashing a three-second stream of cannon fire.

The old Russian-built fighters were still well out of gun range and Green was not sure if this was just an act of bravado or a seriously mistimed attack on his squadron. Still Green's orders were strict. He was not to engage any enemy aircraft except in self defence. Washington did not need more headaches with Indonesia now.

The Singapore Eagles had, by this time, passed well below him and should be over international waters in about four minutes. Green knew he still had to stall the enemy MiGs for a while longer.

Switching to a secure radio channel, he ordered his jets to fall into a staggered line formation and activate manual control of their M-61 Vulcan canons. On his orders, the seven Hornets all opened up with an impressive barrage of 20mm cannon fire aimed above the heads of the approaching two Indonesian jets.

With streams of glowing red tracer rounds flying just metres over their cockpits, both Indonesian jets immediately executed a hard left bank and dove for cover.

"Snake Eyes – lock in hot – hold fire," commanded Green coldly as the American fighters trained their AiM-9 Sidewinder missiles on the two hapless jets.

Alarms blared within the cockpits of the two Indonesian MiGs as their computers registered multiple radar locks from the pursuing Super Hornets which had just entered effective missile range. Knowing they were seriously outgunned, the Indonesian pilots ejected a string of anti-missile flares as they turned their jets around and headed home.

As Green watched the two MiGs disappear into the night sky, he checked his watch. The Singapore warbirds he was protecting were now safely over international waters. This was not quite the fight that he had been training for but still, he was happy to have done his part.

"Return to base," he ordered as he executed a wide turn and headed north, back to Singapore.

THE *USS RONALD REAGAN*, INDIAN OCEAN – NOVEMBER 28, 2246 HOURS

The *MT Khekov* was now well clear of the continental shelf and with no civilian traffic for more than 150 nautical miles, Admiral Thomas gave the order for the patrolling Prowler to begin its jamming of the bandit's radar and communication systems.

The container ship, unaware that it was being targeted for destruction continued on its assigned course heading. Noting no unusual movements from the bandit, the *Ronald Reagan* gave the *Higgins* its attack order.

"You are cleared to engage Tango Zulu. Fire when ready," said the *Reagan's* Executive Officer to the *Higgins*. Less than a minute later, a cloud of fire and smoke enveloped the destroyer as it let loose a single RGM-84A Harpoon anti-ship missile at the doomed container vessel far beyond the horizon.

Travelling at a speed of more than 800kph, it took less than two minutes for the sea-skimming missile to find its mark. The *Khekov* did not stand a chance as 220 kilogrammes of high explosives blasted the ship, breaking its keel and splitting it in two. Within seconds, it had begun to sink taking with it the nuclear weapon hidden in one of its many containers.

Six minutes later, the Sikorsky helicopter swooped in low for a damage assessment flyby of the choppy sea with its night-vision cameras.

"Sir, Helo One has confirmed target is destroyed and sinking fast. Limited floating debris but two lifeboats are in the water. Standing by for S&R," said the *Reagan's* Executive Officer.

"Negative XO, there will be no Search and Rescue on this one. Get rid of the lifeboats and then recall Helo One. Our job here is done," replied the Admiral.

"But sir?"

"XO," said the Admiral his voice rising, "fill those damn lifeboats with little bullet holes and recall Helo One to the deck – understood?"

"Aye sir," replied XO as he relayed the orders to the crew of the Sikorsky.

The Admiral's orders direct from the Pentagon were that no survivors were to be left alive to tell of the night's assault. Sinking a commercial ship manned by a civilian crew would be next to impossible for Washington to explain. The rough ocean would take care of the remains, whatever was left behind.

44

Within hours of the attack, rumours were already spreading throughout the US capital of American military action in South East Asia when the White House hastily called for a press briefing.

The reporters had barely taken their seats when President Monroe entered the room to deliver his prepared statement in person.

"At 10.30am today Washington time, military operations by the US Armed Forces were carried out in Indonesia in response to the recent terrorist attacks in Jakarta and the nuclear detonation in Singapore. The targets were a terrorist training camp and a house in which 13 top JI commanders were meeting to coordinate yet another attack.

"I can confirm that among the terrorists killed in that hideout was Yusman bin Iranto, the leader of the outlawed JI sect in Indonesia and the mastermind behind the nuclear attack in Singapore.

"In today's operation, US forces also destroyed a second nuclear weapon which was being prepared for use. No radiation was released and the weapon's intended target remains unknown at this time. We believe that apart from the weapon detonated in Singapore, this was the only other nuclear device in the hands of these terrorists.

"A squadron of F-15SG attack jets from the Republic of Singapore Air Force in a simultaneous strike, also destroyed another terrorist training camp in Indonesia.

"These operations were carried out without any injury to civilians and all personnel involved have returned safely to their respective bases.

"I wish to repeat what I had said earlier that the United States will not hesitate to use whatever force it deems necessary to seek out and destroy any terrorist organisations that threaten the peace and security of this country or its citizens. We urge all nations to join with us to eliminate this scourge …"

The White House had refused to divulge any further details about the attack which destroyed the nuclear weapon or disclose where this had occurred. A spokesman would only repeat what the President had told the media earlier that radiation was not released and there were no civilian casualties.

There was no mention of the *MT Khekov*. Five days later, the ship's owners in Moscow would issue a statement that the vessel has gone missing and was presumed to have sunk in rough waters off the coast of Sri Lanka in the Indian Ocean. A search of the area would fail to locate any debris or survivors.

45

DOHA, QATAR – NOVEMBER 29, 1030 HOURS

The announcement from the White House a day earlier that it had killed terrorist leader Yusman bin Iranto in a raid in Indonesia could not have come at a worse time. Many in the Arab world saw this as confirmation that America had once again spat on the olive branch of peace which Yusman offered and resorted to reassert its dominance of the world by brutal military force.

Leaked pictures of Yusman's battered body, which the White House claimed were crude Internet fakes, only served to fan the flames of anger which were spreading throughout the region.

Over the past week spurred on by Yusman's video, thousands of Muslim demonstrators from Asia and the Middle East had taken to the streets, calling on their governments to renounce all diplomatic and commercial ties with the United States.

The Arab media too was upping the ante. Reporters interviewed many prominent businessmen and influential politicians, all of whom supported the idea to conduct all future oil trades in a single unified Arab currency rather than in US dollars.

A recent series of crippling financial debacles originating from America had devastated the region which depended heavily on the stability of the American dollar for its foreign exchange earnings. Instigated by press interviews of the Seven Heads, calls grew louder for the Arab nations of the world to launch a strong new currency which would unify their nations and put America in its place.

Newspapers ran background stories and commentaries supporting the reintroduction of the Gold Dinar as a common currency across the region.

The idea of using the Gold Dinar was not new. It dates back to the seventh century when the Gold Dinar was introduced by Caliph Abd al-Malik bin Marwan and its name was derived from denarius, the Roman currency in use at the time. Originally minted as gold coins, they held their monetary value because of the rarity of this precious metal. The Gold Dinar remained the official Islamic currency until the collapse of the Ottoman Empire in 1924.

Over the years various attempts were made to reintroduce the Gold Dinar as a standard currency especially among the oil producing nations of North Africa and the Middle East. But each time a proposal was floated to replace the American dollar with the Gold Dinar, tragedy soon followed.

Shortly after then-Iranian Prime Minister Mohammad

Mosaddegh proposed in 1953 replacing the US dollar in oil trading, he was overthrown in a CIA-supported coup d'état. In Iraq, Saddam Hussein came under attack in 2003 at the exact time when he wanted to stop trading oil in dollars. In 2009, in his capacity as head of the African Union, Libya's Muammar Gaddafi had proposed that the economically crippled continent stop trading oil in dollars and adopt the Gold Dinar instead. He last repeated this call in 2011 shortly before he was forcibly removed from power and killed in the streets in an apparent mob attack.

Clerics interviewed by the media fully backed the idea of reintroducing the Gold Dinar claiming that it would be the only legitimate currency "not tainted by blood and the greed of the infidels".

As governments across this volatile region debated in private on how to defuse the growing standoff with the United States while at the same time appeasing voters at home, many realised that their political futures hung in the balance. There were fears that another Arab Spring offensive was on the cards and religious extremists including the unpredictable ISIS terror sect which appeared to be lending support to the growing unrest, would soon unseat them.

The destruction of the Dome of the Rock and the clandestine rebuilding of a Jewish temple that Israel was undertaking had stunned and horrified many Arabs. And now, this raid in Indonesia and the murder of Yusman whom many regarded as their champion and a martyr of peace was the final straw. The governments of the Arab world were left with no choice but to bend to the will of the people or risk watching the region descend into anarchy once again.

Over the past three days, Hassan and the Seven Heads had been busy in meetings with Arab leaders discussing the many details of how the new currency would be launched and administered. The plans were all in place and finally the approvals from the various governments were given. There would be no turning back now.

In the ballroom of the Grand Qatar Palace Hotel, the leaders of ten Arab countries – Qatar, Saudi Arabia, Iran, Iraq, Kuwait, the United Arab Emirates, Jordan, Egypt, Syria and Libya – gathered to announce their decision to the world.

In a joint statement they unveiled a unified regional currency to be known officially as the Gold Dinar. It would be administered by a new central bank, the Eastern Star Reserve Bank to be headquartered in Doha.

Hassan was named president of the reserve bank along with the Seven Heads who would form its board of directors.

"All banks across the region will begin issuing Gold Dinars from 9am tomorrow," said Hassan in his speech to over four hundred delegates and the world's media. "Details of the exchange rates against local existing currencies will be released after this briefing and we expect the full conversion to be completed within six months. During this transition period, existing national currencies will still retain their legal tender status. And for the time being, we will allow US dollars to be exchanged on even par with the Gold Dinar.

"However all exports of oil from our member countries will, from 9am tomorrow, be conducted exclusively in Gold Dinars which will replace the current use of American dollars. Those countries which do not recognise and accept our Gold Dinars as legal international tender, will be barred from making future oil purchases ..."

While this announcement was widely anticipated by the media, the speed of its implementation sent shockwaves around the world.

Within days, banks across the region began raking in millions of US dollars in exchange for the crisp new dinars. China and Indonesia were among the first countries outside the Middle East to formally recognise and support the new currency – the first of many to come.

46

The deadline which His Holiness had given Father Jacque Philippe to complete his report was an almost impossible one and yet the old priest had finished it just the night before.

Father Jacque, 72, had always been a happy and contented man. He was an assistant professor teaching economics at a university outside Milan for 15 years until at the age of 43, he could no longer ignore the call resounding in his soul and so he began his decade-long road to the priesthood.

His diminutive stature earned him the affectionate nickname of Little Poverello after the Franciscan song. Since his ordination, Father Jacque had been comfortable with life as a simple parish priest in a small town in Serbia. He was happy to put the world of economics far behind him and serve a higher cause.

But his idyllic life changed five months ago when he was ordered by the Vatican to relinquish his parish duties and report to Rome immediately. There he soon received his new orders to lead the *Sacrum ordinem Scolarium*, the Sacred Order of the Scholars.

Waiting outside the Papal Office, Father Jacque paced the corridor unable to sit still. His mind was still in turmoil as it had been for the past fortnight since he received this latest assignment.

"Facts? Where are the facts? It's all just speculation, conjecture and a series of coincidences perhaps. Is this what you have become Father Jacque – nothing more than just another advocate of rumours and conspiracy theories? Maybe if I had more time, it would be clearer. If only I had more time," he thought to himself as he clutched his report even tighter.

But his time was up as the doors to the Papal Office opened silently and he was ushered in for his audience with the Vicar of Christ.

Entering the small but comfortable office, the elderly priest knelt down and bowed his head. Pope Peter II who was standing next to the desk walked over and touched him on the shoulder. Father Jacque kissed the papal ring before the Pope spoke: "Come Little Poverello. I fear we have much to discuss and very little time left to do it."

The task which the Holy Father had set before Father Jacque was a formidable one. Firstly it was to examine the events of the past few weeks and advise the Vatican on the possible socio-economic and political repercussions on the Catholic Church and the *Istituto per le Opere di Religione* – the Institute for Works of Religion or as it is more commonly known, the Vatican Bank.

This, given Father Jacque's teaching background, was a more straightforward task. But the old priest was also directed to investigate if the tumultuous events of recent weeks were, as many people were beginning to speculate, signs that the end of the world as foretold in the bible and in other religious works, was at hand.

"There have been five key events over the past few weeks that I have examined and will present to Your Holiness today," began Father Jacque.

"Each one is more serious, more alarming than the one before. First we had the terrorist bombings in Jakarta on November 5 and then the nuclear attack in Singapore on November 22. This was quickly followed by the unrest in the Middle East with rising Muslim extremism. On November 25 the Dome of the Rock was destroyed in circumstances which still remain unclear and Israel began constructing what by all accounts appears to be the Third Temple of Solomon. And now we have the world in financial turmoil with the introduction of the Gold Dinar."

"So you feel the last is more serious than even an atomic bomb exploding in Singapore or the destruction of the Dome?" asked the Pope.

"I realise that this may sound cold, Your Holiness, but in terms of their ramifications on the world as we know it, then yes. The attacks in Jakarta and Singapore were terrible, simply catastrophic. But their impact on the world at large was limited. Already the international shipping lanes around Singapore are being opened and the radiation effects on the region were less severe than expected.

"The destruction of the Dome of the Rock and Israeli's rebuilding of its Third Temple has obvious biblical implications and significant religious ones as well. But still, it is the recent introduction of this Gold Dinar," he said holding up one of the new currency notes that was already flooding the world's banking system, "this now could very well impact the life of every person on the planet."

Father Jacque paused, waiting for the Pope to respond. However the Pontiff merely nodded and so the priest continued.

"The introduction of a new currency is in itself, not such an ominous thing. Governed responsibly and following rational economic doctrines, global commerce will in time adjust to using the Gold Dinar over the US dollar even as the fiscal dominance of the United States is severely blunted.

"Already we have seen mega economies like China, South Korea, Japan and Russia moving to accept the Gold Dinar perhaps if only to continue buying oil from the Middle East. But the Gulf States behind the dinar are not just global oil exporters. They are also major consumers of international commerce. These countries have started buying significant stakes in major global corporations from electronics to pharmaceuticals to alternative energy and more. In other words, they are very aggressively diversifying their assets and future revenue streams well beyond the business of oil.

"They have also been eagerly snapping up futures on a

range of agricultural produce – rice, wheat, grains, just about everything they can get their hands on. They have signed deals with a number of countries for massive desalination plants. Bartering with oil, Russia is building several nuclear power stations all across the Middle East. They are a military binge buying mainly ex-Soviet and Chinese hardware ranging from main battle tanks to missile systems, attack jets to high-tech cruisers and submarines. The region appears to be arming itself at an unprecedented level, getting itself ready for … something.

"Over the past two weeks or so according to press reports, their reserve bank has been raking in billions of dollars in major foreign currencies not just US dollars, exchanging these for Gold Dinars. If this trend continues, the sheer volume of foreign exchange in their hands would allow this grouping to manipulate exchange rates by dumping currencies, causing hyper-inflation at will and triggering global fiscal chaos."

"How then would this compromise the Vatican's financial position?" asked the Pope.

"Your Holiness, as you are aware, I am not privy to the full asset accounts held by the Vatican Bank. But as I understand it, the majority of the Church's wealth lies in its buildings, properties, gold reserves, works of art and priceless objects of religious significance. Even in a global financial crisis, these hard assets will still retain much of their present core value. On the other hand, our liquid assets, cash mainly in US dollars and Euros, that's a different story. We would be just as vulnerable as any other major conglomerate or country to deliberate and calculated currency manipulations."

"But what if we convert our liquid assets, our cash to gold? Would that not be more stable given the current climate and perhaps offer us some measure of protection against currency devaluations?"

"Well Holy Father, that's a difficult question to answer. In the short term it would seem a logical thing to do. Invest in gold and protect your dollar assets from risky exchange fluctuations. That is precisely what many countries are already doing and the price of gold over the past 10 days has gone through the roof. However in the long term, if there is a sustained global financial meltdown and the value of currency reserves plummets, there would be fewer buyers of gold about, be they wealthy individuals, companies or governments. And when, over an extended period of time, the demand for gold shrinks, it is simple economics that the price must fall – well, it would probably be more of a resounding crash than a fall."

Father Jacque continued but chose his words with even greater care. "But all this, Holy Father, is merely speculation. As I said earlier, it would all depend on how these Gulf States and its Central Bank choose to manage this new currency. But certainly the potential to cause reckless global havoc, for economic, political or even religious gain remains present."

The Pontiff met his eyes and nodded reassuringly. "I sense Little Poverello that you are troubled far beyond the possible economic or political ramifications of these events. We are the protectors of the faith, so speak freely with your heart."

"From a religious standpoint, there are too many troubling signs, from the *Books of Daniel* and *Revelation*, to ignore these recent events as a series of mere coincidences," said Father Jacque.

"Yes, go on. Tell me what you have to," encouraged the Pope.

Lowering his eyes, he said in a tone barely above a whisper: "I believe Holy Father that the Day of Reckoning is upon us as the Evil One walks the earth."

The Pope smiled and nodded again, acknowledging the obvious anguish of the priest before him. "The Day of Reckoning has always been on the horizon and the Evil One has stalked this earth for a very long time."

"But I believe, Holy Father, we are seeing the horrors of *Revelation* come to pass. The signs, they are all there."

"You realise," replied the Pontiff, "that throughout the history of man, every single generation felt that it was seeing signs of the coming end. They had misinterpreted a series of natural or manmade calamities or were swayed by what they had seen or heard. And so Father Jacque, tell me what these signs are that you now refer to?"

47

TEMPLE MOUNT, ISRAEL – DECEMBER 10, 0615
HOURS

As Father Jacque delivered his report to Pope Peter II,
work on the Temple Mount was stopped for the sacred
consecration ceremony.

Although the hundreds of skilled craftsmen had been
working on the site for only about two weeks, having the
large stone blocks and support pillars already carefully cut
and prepared years earlier, allowed the temple construction
to proceeded at a phenomenal pace. Already the shape of
the building as architecturally described in the *Book of
Ezekiel* was recognisable along with its majestic pillars and
high stone walls.

Israeli stonemasons had also over the years, carved in
stone the many decorations that would adorn this new
temple. Among the most iconic were the little cherubim
and palm trees. In these ancient religious motifs, palm
trees alternated with cherubs each of whom had two faces
– the face of a man turned towards the palm tree on one
side and the face of a lion toward the palm tree on the

other. The planners had done their work with meticulous care making sure that every detail described in legends of old was fully and faithfully reproduced.

The crowd of mainly high-ranking government officials, businessmen, Jewish community leaders and senior members of the Sons of Solomon, gathered at what would soon be the Eastern Gate of the Third Temple and waited for the consecration ceremony to begin. It was timed to coincide with the rising of the winter sun.

As the sun peeked over the horizon, the service began with songs from the choir of children assembled to the left of the altar. Then twenty-four little girls all dressed in white and each carrying a basket brimming with pure white rose petals entered the consecration area. They were followed by the twelve newly-appointed temple trustees, each bearing a sacred scroll.

As the trustees took their position to the right of the altar, the girls, arranged in a circle around the altar, began picking the rose petals from their baskets and throwing them into the air while the choir sang a psalm of thanksgiving. When they were done, the entire area surrounding the altar was covered with these fragrant floral offerings.

The bearers of the sacred scrolls then marched in a small circle around the altar seven times accompanied by chants from the choir.

When the seventh circuit was completed, the Chief Rabbi of Jerusalem Isaac Tzemah walked to the altar to light the perpetual lamp with a sacred flame that would never expire.

Rabbi Isaac began his sermon with the words from Scripture: "How beautiful are thy Tabernacles, O Lord of Hosts ..."

He reminded those present that this consecration of the ground and the soon-to-be-completed temple itself would focus the people of Israel on fulfilling the mission given to them on Mount Sinai – that Israel was a nation chosen by God himself and it must be as the Prophet Isaiah put it, a light unto all nations.

When the sermon and the ancient consecration rites were completed, urns filled with incense were then carried around the still unfinished temple watched by scores of workmen who removed their helmets and bowed their heads as the solemn procession passed by. Three hundred pure white doves, the winged symbols of peace, were released and slowly they circled the building as if bestowing their blessing on this new monument of faith.

Sadly there were no television cameras present to broadcast this historic event to the Jewish nation as the Israeli government had not even officially acknowledged that the Third Temple was being erected.

High temporary plywood walls were still screening off the Temple Mount as construction inside progressed at a hectic pace.

Beyond this hilltop, the Israeli army remained out in force sealing off this section of the Old City from the devout, the curious and the troublemakers alike.

The day curfew on Jerusalem had been partially lifted allowing citizens to return to work and school and to buy the necessities of daily life. However the night curfew remained in place from dusk till dawn.

The scores of pilgrims from around the world who were visiting the Holy Land in the advent to Christmas were turned away from the Old City gates and access to the Wailing Wall, a sacred site for Jews was restricted to just Israeli citizens.

The country-wide riots which the Israeli authorities had anticipated failed to materialise although two suicide bombings over the past week had killed more than 40 Israeli citizens including more than a dozen children.

Still, the tension around the Old City remained high even as Jews across Israel began to rejoice that the ancient promise of a new temple was now close at hand.

THE WHITE HOUSE, WASHINGTON D.C. – DECEMBER 10, 0045 HOURS

As the consecration ceremony on Temple Mount drew to a close, it was well past midnight in Washington. The lights of the White House continued to burn as scores of the nation's top executives grappled with the unfolding events in the Middle East.

"He may have been right about Yusman but I still don't trust him. I believe that it was all a trap," said President Monroe. "He baited us, giving us that information knowing that we would attack in force. Then once again we come off looking like bullies spurning this so-called offer of peace and giving them that political leverage to announce their new currency. Damn it, it was all planned and well coordinated and we walked right into it – again!"

"Theodore, we were the ones that wanted to go after Yusman no matter what, remember. We would have done it on our own if we could. We knew the risks and we took it," replied President-Elect Kelly Yee. "Hassan just gave us the information that we were desperately seeking and he did warn us about this currency announcement that was imminent. He didn't have to do any of that. He told us about this second nuke. We had no hard intel on this at all. Again, he didn't have to tell us anything."

So you actually trust him, even after all this?"

"I'm not saying I trust him but we need to start trusting someone because we are fast running out of friends in the Middle East. No one believes in us anymore and economically we are being sidelined. We thought the Saudis were our closest allies after all we did for them when Saddam Hussein threatened to invade, but even the Saudis are now keeping their distance. They, like many other Gulf leaders, want to know what we are going to do to redress the situation in Israel with the destruction of the Dome and the building of this new Jewish temple of theirs. It's going to cause nothing but trouble."

"Well, tell them the truth – that we are working with Israel for a peaceful resolution to this issue," replied the President.

"Damn it Theodore! There is no such thing as a peaceful resolution to any of this. It's not about politics anymore. It's all about religion and dubious claims to a mound of dirt in the desert that goes back 2000 years and then some. Nobody's going to give in now because nobody can afford to. With this deadly religious fervour sweeping the Middle East, no Arab politician who wants to remain in power can afford to back down on this one. He who blinks first is dead and everyone knows that."

"Well Israel is not going to budge either for exactly the same reasons," said the President. "They feel that they are the next terrorist target for a nuke attack so Israel has nothing to lose. To them, rebuilding this temple from the ruins of the Dome was just history and religion taking its destined course. I have spoken to their Prime Minister and he won't even consider any neutral ground. It's a stand-off and we are caught in the middle. So Kelly, where does this all leave us?"

"There are many things that we simply cannot change but there are some that we can. America needs to change. It's not going to be simple or easy but we can't keep going on our merry way thinking that we are the lone superpower, leading the world which will meekly follow in our wake. They got us over a barrel with this currency thing and they know it.

"They are dangling this oil card and we have no choice but to buy their Gold Dinars to purchase the crude we need. As long as they keep the value on par with the Greenback and continue production at current levels, we'll be okay."

"But we both know that's never going to last," said the

President. "It's only a matter of time before those Gulf States and their new Central Bank start tinkering with the exchange rates and then …"

"Yes I know Theodore. But I feel that we can still work with them. That's the direction that we need to go. It all boils down to money. We need to show them that they still need us as much as we need them. We need to give it time for tempers and religious ruffles to calm down. And we need to start making friends again."

"Starting with this Hassan guy?"

"I don't know. Maybe."

48

VATICAN CITY – DECEMBER 10, 0748 HOURS

"Your Holiness, you had charged the *Sacrum ordinem Scolarium* to look out for signs of the coming Armageddon, and everywhere we looked – not just in *Revelation* but from Samuel to Jeremiah, Isaiah to Ezekiel, the hints, the ominous signs, they were there, staring us in the face," began Father Jacque.

"We found in particular the obscure writings of Saul of Cyrene, the first century seer to be the most prophetically linked to the signs of recent events."

Some of Saul's writings were recovered in 1887 from an archaeological dig near the village of Shahhat in present-day Libya. Of the many scrolls found, several were later transferred to the Vatican Secret Archives where they were locked away by orders of Pope Leo XIII and few of these were ever studied.

Another cache of scrolls belonging to Saul of Cyrene were discovered much earlier during the time of the Crusades. These were taken by the Crusaders back to their base in

Israel where they were said to have been stored in secret beneath the Temple Mount.

Continued Father Jacque: "I could not get my hands on all the scrolls but of those that I was able to, Saul did appear to mention these present events when he wrote:

A second star, angry and red, from the east will rise.
Trembling in fear, the tribes witness a temple reborn.
Men will fall, seduced by the false denarius
As the advent of the riders of steed draw near.

"This seems to describe with chilling accuracy, the events of these past months. Remember what Yusman said in his video. His language was odd for a Muslim terrorist, maybe even biblical perhaps. He openly says the day of reckoning is at hand. He described the nuclear blast as a rising star. It's almost like he was talking of a second star similar to the one which led the wise men to Bethlehem, promising of a new beginning."

"But is not the star a symbol of their faith too?"

"Yes Holy Father, you are right, it is. But the star appears again here in the Gold Dinar, the new currency that is causing so much trouble and uncertainty in the world today. Look at the image on the reverse side. It shows a star leading a lone rider on a white horse through the desert. Could this be the first of the four horsemen that Saul predicted, the one who was also described in the *Book of Revelation* – the rider bent on conquest?"

"The Jews have come home to Zion. The Israeli army has now cemented its control over Jerusalem and they have reclaimed the Temple Mount. They are starting to build the Third Temple. We all saw on television the star in the nuclear explosion and with all the unrest sweeping the Middle East, there are growing armies on every shore. Mankind is being torn apart as man is turned against his brother."

Father Jacque paused to regain his composure. He hoped the Holy Father would say something now even if it was just to rebuff him on the shoddiness of the paper thin arguments he was presenting. But Pope Peter II just continued examining the note the priest had presented and said nothing.

"As you can see," continued Father Jacque, "the note has an eighteen digit serial number divided into three sets of six numbers – 6 – 6 – 6 – the mark of the Beast perhaps? The Church and its people have speculated for centuries what this mark of Satan could possibly be. It was written in *Revelation 13* that:

And he causeth all, both small and great,
rich and poor, free and bond,
to receive a mark in their right hand, or in their foreheads:
And that no man might buy or sell, save he that had the mark,
or the name of the beast, or the number of his name.
Here is wisdom. Let him that hath understanding
count the number of the beast: for it is the number of a man;
and his number is six hundred threescore and six.

"To buy and sell – it implies money. The mark on their right hands or foreheads – it is not a physical mark, a tattoo as some people had believed or that Hollywood films speculated about. The right hand could simply mean that which we do, the forehead for that which we think. I believe it simply means that the Beast will control everything we do and how we think. And everyone will unknowingly carry this unholy mark of the Beast in their pockets and in their wallets.

"Already we see this new currency is being accepted around the world. Initially it was just to buy oil but if recent newspaper reports are to be believed the Gold Dinar could, in the months to come, emerge as major global currency to rival and possibly even surpass the American dollar.

"There were 10 Gulf countries who have banded together to launch this new currency. They appointed seven people – even the newspapers have called them the Seven Heads – directors to run this new Eastern Star Reserve Bank.

Look here at this report from the *New York Times* just three days ago. One of these seven, Wilhelm Lustrafjorden, he talks about the need for world depopulation from the current seven billion down to a manageable 500 million. Hitler was the last person who tried something like this. Have you ever heard of the Georgia Guide Stones?"

"No," said the Pontiff.

"It's a recent but rather obscure American monument built in 1979 commissioned by some people whose identities still remain unknown today. The man who ordered the stones built used the pseudonym R. C. Christian. It carries a message, ten guidelines or new commandments carved into granite panels in eight modern-day languages. On top there is a shorter message in four ancient languages of Babylonia, Egyptian hieroglyphs, Sanskrit and classical Greek. One commandment specifically mentions depopulation and bringing down the world's population to a mere 500 million people."

"How would this be done?"

"It doesn't say. No one knows for sure," replied Father Jacque, "but Lustrafjorden in his interview goes on to cite what he himself calls the ten 'crowns' – the most important assets which would control the world. These include clean drinking water, electrical power, developing genetically modified foods, pharmaceuticals and vaccines, information technology and climate control. Already we see this grouping of ten countries investing heavily in these areas."

"These Seven Heads – they are rich and powerful men who have always worked in the shadows. None of them have openly accepted such obvious public positions as being on the board of this new central bank. None of them have openly given press interviews – so why now? I believe that it's because whatever they have been planning, it is coming to a head now and that's why they are suddenly emerging from the shadows.

"Seven heads, ten horns and upon each a crown – that again is directly from *Revelation*.

"John of the *Revelation* said he saw the beast rise out of the sea, having seven heads and ten horns, and upon his horns ten crowns, and upon his heads the name of blasphemy.' The head of the reserve bank Hassan Ahmad Khan – see the way he talks about a new beginning, about healing the world. There is just something about him that I feel can't be trusted.

"Here Holy Father," continued Father Jacque handing the Pontiff a large magnifying glass from his bag. "Look at the microprinting along the edges of this dinar. It's not just a pattern border as it may appear to the naked eye. It also contains various symbols.

"See, this one is of a fish with a line through it. It is the *Ichthys* – the ancient Greek symbol used by the early Christians. The line through it could represent a stake being driven through its heart perhaps. And this one here … it appears to be a flower but look closely, I believe it is an inverted *Triquetra* – an occult sign mimicking in reverse the Holy Trinity. Then take a look here at the four corners, that's an inverted cross, the *Petrine Cross* – the Cross of Peter …"

And Father Jacque abruptly stopped, unsure if he gone too far in his abstract interpretations. The *Petrine Cross* which is also known as the Cross of Peter derives from the Christian tradition which holds that Saint Peter chose to be crucified upside down as he felt he was unworthy to die in the same way as the Christ. However in some circles, the inverted cross is also thought to have satanic overtures.

As the Pontiff remained silent, Father Jacque continued: "The situation in Israel is growing graver by the day with the rebuilding of the temple. Our sources in Jerusalem tell us that they are ready to re-consecrate the land and the Third Temple itself, or at least its skeleton would be completed by Christmas. That's just two weeks away. It has been written, both in the Bible and the Torah, that the rebuilding of the Third Temple would herald the End of Days.

"I can't see the Arab world sitting still for any of this and doing nothing to avenge the destruction of the Dome of the Rock. The clash of religions – Muslims against Jews, is unavoidable and the Church will inevitably be dragged into this quagmire. Holy Father, I beg of you. We have to do something now before it's too late!"

Again the priest paused and this time the Pope spoke.

"And what do you suggest we do?"

"Warn our flock, warn the world, warn America not to deal with this Hassan and his unholy money. He could very well be the one – the Evil One that has been foretold."

"Do you honestly believe that? That he is what – the Antichrist? Consider how difficult a position the Church would be placed in if we were to speak out now. What if we are wrong?"

"What if we are right Holy Father? What then?" replied Father Jacque his eyes downcast and his voice barely above a whisper.

The Pontiff continued: "The writings of Daniel and the

prophets of old together with the warnings from *Revelation* have all been twisted and misinterpreted throughout history. Even the obscure predictions of Saul of Cyrene that you have cited, we have kept these writings of his secret for a long time – hundreds of years and with good reason. They contain far too many conflicts with the bible as we know it. You ought to know that.

"Even then, Saul's writings, his predictions, those few that have been leaked in books and more recently on the Internet, these were just like those scribbles of Nostradamus – these same vague verses have said different things to different men over the centuries.

"Every generation thought it knew, with complete and utter certainty, the identity of the Antichrist – from Nero to Napoleon, Hitler to Ayatollah Khomeini, to George Bush to Saddam Hussein to Osama bin Laden and … who's next? They were all wrong. The world did not come to an end then and I do not believe that it will now.

"Everyone and his brother has throughout history, speculated who this Antichrist might be. Did not Saint Malachy predict almost a thousand years ago that I was to be the last Pope, the Antichrist?"

In 1139 while on a pilgrimage to the Vatican, this Irish saint reportedly described in a vision, all the 112 future Popes who would ever reign. The last he said would be Petrus Romanus – Peter the Roman. He predicted the final Pontiff would 'feed his flock amid many tribulations; after which the seven-hilled city will be destroyed and the dreadful Judge will judge the people. The End.'

Since May when he was elected as Pope, the media was awash with speculation about Saint Malachy's predictions especially after Pope Peter II revealed his chosen name under which he would govern the Catholic Church. Some even went on to speculate that this final Pope would be the Antichrist, heralding the end of the world.

"So do you believe that Lil' Poverello?"

"No, of course not. You are the chosen one, the Holy Father, the Vicar of Christ," replied Father Jacque.

"But why do you choose to believe other predictions and yet not this one, made by a saint no less? Is his meaning not clear enough for you?"

The priest remained silent, his hands still trembling.

"Parables, predictions, prophecies, convoluted and abstract religious writings – these only offer us a glimpse of the future, little snapshots, vague hints of what may yet be to come," continued the Pope.

"They were not meant to be taken at face value. One cannot assemble these little fragments and put them together, hoping they will suddenly reveal God's masterplan for the future of mankind. God does not work like that. The future is not a game that can be revealed in advance by following some cryptic clues. These writings are simply markers, reminding us that the end is coming at a time that will not be revealed to us until the hour it arrives. Only then … only then will our eyes be opened. Only then, will we understand the magnificence of the Creator and be humbled by our mortal ignorance.

"But until that time comes, we have to remain vigilant. To keep the faith, pray and be ready. It is not for us to try and change that which has already been ordained no matter how terrible it may seem to us. It will all come to pass according to His will and not the will of man. No, I do not believe that Hassan is the Antichrist. Perhaps he may be the first of the Four Horseman," said the Pope waving the Gold Dinar in his hand.

"The first of four who according to the prophets of centuries past, must come before and pave the road. Perhaps … but here … here I speculate as do you."

The Pope paused before continuing: "But are we, mere mortal men formed from dust and the holy breath of God meant to interfere in a divine plan? Is this really part of His will for us to act now? Sadly, I have no answers. I need to pray and reflect more on this."

"I am sorry Holy Father. I have failed you in this task you have asked of me," said Father Jacque.

"No my son, you have not failed. You and the *Sacrum ordinem Scolarium* have done everything I have asked of you – as difficult and painful as it all was.

"You have given me much to think about. Perhaps you may be right and we should warn the Americans but even then, I fear that it may already be too late.

"As I pray Lil' Poverello, I want you to continue your search of the archives, I still believe the answer lies there, hidden and waiting to be revealed. God has not forsaken us. He will not abandon his children even in times of the bleakest dark."

As Father Jacque left the papal office, Pope Peter II resumed his reading of the morning's papers. One story caused his heart to skip a beat. Quoting unnamed sources, the paper reported that Israeli authorities examining some sealed rooms under the Temple Mount in Jerusalem had discovered a hidden library containing a number of ancient scrolls.

49

WASHINGTON D.C. – DECEMBER 18, 0647 HOURS

There were resounding cheers from Americans when they learnt of the raid that killed Yusman and wiped out much of his terrorist command structure in Indonesia. Across the US and in many countries around the world, people breathed a collective sigh of relief on hearing that a second and potentially more destructive nuclear weapon had been destroyed.

But the pride many Americans felt in their government's quick response to the nuclear attack in Singapore was soon displaced, simply overshadowed by the announcement of the new currency in the Middle East which once again threatened their very survival.

Although it was vehemently denied by the White House, the American media was quick to speculate on the suspicious timing of the Monroe's attack and the Arab world's unveiling of the Gold Dinar.

One noted US political columnist Simon McIntyre, openly accused the Monroe Administration of "recklessly digging

America into an even deeper hole from which it may never recover".

In his weekly editorial McIntyre wrote:

History will no doubt show that the raid in the Far East, successful though it may have been on the surface, was in fact nothing more than a feeble attempt by an out-going president to redress the numerous intelligence failings which have blighted his inept administration over the years.

American has never learnt the simple lessons it should have from its own recent history. We cannot use the sword to shape the world into an image of ourselves when we are afraid to look into that mirror and recognise our flaws. The world did not become a safer place when George Bush invaded Iraq to remove Saddam Hussein from power or when it toppled the Taliban regime in Afghanistan or when the Obama Administration killed Osama bin Laden in Pakistan and it certainly isn't today with the murder of Yusman bin Iranto in Indonesia.

Monroe unilaterally scoffed what may have been the last offer of peace on the table with his face-saving hunt for Yusman. His hurried attempt to draw revenge in blood appears to have done little more than to widen age-old religious fault lines radiating out from the Middle East that is now shaking the world to its very foundations.

With every wave of its powerful military sword, the US grows weaker and more isolated. So it should come as no surprise that several nations have now banded against us in launching a new oil currency which looks set to end the global dominance and respect of the US and its once mighty dollar.

Once again it will be the American people who will end up paying for the callous policies so prevalent on Pennsylvania Avenue. And with just a month to go in his term, all we can hope for is that President Monroe walks away quietly into the sunset where he can do no more harm. Kelly Yee will certainly have her hands full as Commander-in-Chief and whether she is man enough for the job, only time will tell.

Kelly threw the newspaper on the dining table in disgust. "McIntyre's an asshole. Let's see him run for office if he thinks he's so smart!" she said turning to her husband Victor as he continued to read the sports section on the latest happenings at the World Table Tennis Championship currently taking place in Oakland, California.

"Yeah he may be a pompous Republican ass," said Victor, "but he is giving an outsider's opinion, the same opinion that many people seem to hold. So what are you going to do about it?"

"What am I going to do?" replied Kelly with a rising tone. "I'm going to do my job at least until the 20th and then we shall see. Things need to change and they will."

January 20th is the date set aside for the swearing in of the new American President. Kelly knew that she had much work to do to redress America's economic slide and calm fears of a coming doom.

Already the US dollar had shed 34 points on Wall Street and pundits were predicting even worse to come in the New Year when the Christmas buying sprees were over. Speculation of an impending currency re-evaluation of the Gold Dinar was rife leaving investors jittery. The new currency just weeks old, had already been accepted by 27 oil-hungry countries across the globe.

"It's these damn rumours that could sink us," said Kelly under her breath as she continued scanning through the pile of newspapers on her table. There was just one man who could help put an end to this speculation and as much as she hated to, she knew that she could not put off much longer meeting him on equal terms.

"This feels like I'm striking a deal with the devil," she thought to herself as she looked at Hassan's photograph in the newspaper accompanying yet another article on the growing strength of the Gold Dinar.

Just then her handphone buzzed. It was her personal assistant at the State Department. An urgent diplomatic communiqué from the Vatican designated for her eyes only, was waiting for her.

50

As Kelly Yee made her way down to her office at the State Department in the Harry S. Truman Building, Hassan had just completed another exhausting work day at his new office in the Eastern Star Reserve Bank.

Since assuming control of the reserve bank three weeks earlier, his days had been filled with endless meetings. Dozens of prominent businessmen and corporate leaders from across the world queued up to meet him and establish good working relationships with this influential central bank he now presided over.

After some initial scepticism over how the Gold Dinar would be accepted beyond the region, it soon became apparent that many countries, eager to continue buying Middle East oil and compete for the host of lucrative business contracts up for grabs throughout the region, were readily embracing the dinar.

Member countries behind the dinar were now flushed with

new cash reserves. Immediately they began trawling the world's major industries striking deals to strengthen their economic, financial and military infrastructures.

An aggressive construction initiative financed in part by the central bank was also undertaken across the region which saw the building of dozens of new schools, hospitals, roads, desalination plants and power stations.

To boost spending and encourage its citizens to accept the Gold Dinar, financial institutions throughout the Gulf following directives issued by the Eastern Star Reserve Bank, began offering low-interest loans especially to individuals and small businessmen pushing domestic spending up to a level not seen in decades.

A carefully orchestrated social media campaign was also launched to inspire confidence among the people in their new currency. Clerics preaching in mosques continued to encourage the faithful to support their governments and use the new currency with pride.

Exhausted by his long work day, Hassan was glad to have some time to himself as he closed his office door after escorting out his last guests.

Standing in the plush hallway, he noticed Saeed, his

faithful aide busy going through yet another stack of papers at his desk in an adjoining office. The last few days had been hectic and Hassan had little time to talk to him.

Looking at Saeed now, Hassan was still unsure if this young man was really up to the task which lay before him. He still did not have a clue as to how significant the events of the last few months really were or his role in all of it. He needed to be told and his eyes had to be opened. The time for that was fast approaching.

51

Kelly Yee studied the document in her hands, trying yet again to read between the lines. The letter from the Pontiff had been brief and yet disconcerting to say the least:

Dear President-Elect Yee,

The events of the past weeks have indeed been deeply troubling. Both the United States and the Vatican have been forced to make some difficult choices.

I can only imagine the anguish your nation must have felt in having to deal with last month's terrorist atrocities in Indonesia and Singapore.

The situation on the Temple Mount in Israel and the tumultuous developments in the Middle East with the introduction of the Gold Dinar would undoubtedly be defining challenges facing your new administration.

While the Vatican has, over the years endeavoured to remain neutral in the political arena, the Church now finds itself in an untenable position to respond to these apparent conflicts of faith in the Middle East which has caused such terrible violence, distrust and uncertainty around the world. I fear the darkness of the coming weeks and months and I pray that the Unites States will respond with utmost vigilance and restraint for the sake of peace for all mankind.

My advisors have warned me that going forward the greatest peril in our midst is the uncertainty over the global financial system.

I therefore urge you to be cautious in your dealings with the Middle East as I fear their true motives have yet to be discerned and these could extend far beyond mere economic or political gain.

My prayers for peace remain with you.

From the Vatican, December 18

Petrus PP. II

EASTERN STAR RESERVE BANK, DOHA, QATAR – DECEMBER 18, 1834 HOURS

Kelly Yee was not the only one feeling overwhelmed by the recent events as she read the Vatican's letter. Hassan too felt he was fast running out of options. He had done everything that was asked of him and the stage had been set. Still he knew not how the final act would be played out.

"He is still too innocent, simply too young and inexperienced to take over from where I have to leave off. He should have been told long ago so he could prepare himself. How can he still not know, after all of this? There is so little time left and this is how he spends it," thought Hassan as he watched Saeed trying unsuccessfully again to chat up one of the many pretty young aides in his department.

Indeed, at least outwardly, Saeed appeared to have matured somewhat over these past few weeks. He looked dapper in his new dark grey suit and stylish haircut. It was obvious that he had been working hard to polish his image to match his new role which was to oversee the external relations of the central bank. But his view of the world and his role in it was still myopic in both substance and form.

"Saeed," called out Hassan. "A moment please, if you are not too busy."

The young woman who had been leaning against his desk chuckling over what must have been some insipid joke, quickly scrambled away trying to look busy when she heard the commanding voice of her boss behind her.

Embarrassed that he had been caught flirting, Saeed offered a meek apology. "Erm sorry boss, we were just talking ..."

U.S. DEPARTMENT OF STATE, WASHINGTON D.C. – DECEMBER 18, 1034 HOURS

"Your Holiness," began Kelly as she cradled the telephone against her shoulder and held up his letter. "Thank you very much for writing to me and for taking this call at such short notice. I am trying to understand what exactly your concerns are at this point in time."

"I am glad that you called Madam President-Elect. Some things are hard, even foolish perhaps, to put down on paper," began the Pontiff.

"To put it bluntly, there appears to be enormous scope for this grouping of 10 Arab countries and their central bank to manipulate the global currency market by adjusting the exchange rate for the Gold Dinar and thereby inflating the price of oil and with it, just about everything else. The repercussions could be potentially catastrophic to say the least."

"Yes, we are well aware of the seriousness of these recent developments and the United States is working hard to resolve these complex issues. However in your letter you mentioned that their motives may appear to go beyond economic or political gain. What exactly do you mean?"

"Your world is the political arena, mine is to uphold, protect and spread the faith. Are you a religious woman, Madam President-Elect?"

"The name is Kelly and no, sorry, I believe in a greater being but I guess … I'm not as religious as I ought to be."

"Are you familiar … Kelly, with the Four Horsemen of the Apocalypse?"

EASTERN STAR RESERVE BANK, DOHA, QATAR – DECEMBER 18, 1835 HOURS

"Tell me Saeed," began Hassan, "how do you feel the world is taking to our new currency?"

"It has been going better than we could have hoped for. Already we have almost 30 nations actively using the Gold Dinar to buy our oil and to compete for various business projects across the Gulf. Even the Americans, at least the American oil companies, are also using it. It has only been a few weeks but already we have built up a very healthy accumulation of foreign currency. With all the construction work going on here, the economies across the region are thriving and it is all thanks to you and your great vision."

Hassan ignored the transparent attempt at flattery. He had more important things on his mind. "You and I, Saeed, each of us was put on this earth for a very specific reason. Man and the Bible would see all of this, the events of these past few months, as a clash of religions, maybe even a battle of good versus evil … and you and I are most certainly not on the side of good."

"Huh? The Bible? Sorry, I don't follow you."

"Listen to me Saeed. You need to know the truth, here and now. My time is running out and I shall not be with you much longer but your time, it is just beginning."

"What? But where are you going? We've just started work here and everything is going so well."

"Where I am going, it does not matter. But what is to

come next, that matters. This plan I have spoken to you about, we – you, me and there will be others, we were sent here to complete a mission almost as old as time itself.

"Have you heard of the End of Days, the Apocalypse and the Four Horsemen who are to come?"

"The Christian book? You mean like the movie '*The Omen*'? Vaguely … I mean, I took a course at the university on theology and yeah it was mentioned something about the end of the world but I …"

"Oh no, it won't be the end, not for a while yet. Now listen very carefully to what I am about to tell you and this is for your ears only. The Four Horsemen will pave the way for the Coming. The Advent is upon us. I am the first messenger. The Bible calls me the Rider of the White Horse. Look at the back of that dinar note in your pocket. I am that rider. I am the one the old book calls Conquest. That is what I have done and my mission now is almost complete."

U.S. DEPARTMENT OF STATE, WASHINGTON D.C. – DECEMBER 18, 1036 HOURS

"Sadly I believe Kelly that we are now in the End Times as the Bible has predicted."

"Holy Father, are you talking about the end of the world and the emergence of the … what … the Antichrist?" said Kelly as she felt the blood draining out from her face. To anyone else, she would have scoffed at the very thought of it, the sheer absurdity of it all. But she was talking to the leader of more than one billion Catholics around the world and Kelly could not dismiss his concerns so easily.

"No, he will come later. First the Evil One will send four emissaries – harbingers of the Last Judgment. The first will be a rider on a white horse and he is called Conquest. The second called War will mount a red horse. The rider on the black horse called Famine will come next and he shall be followed by Death, riding on the pale horse.

"Kelly, I believe the first one is already here. Everything that we have seen happen in the last few weeks in Indonesia, Singapore, Israel and elsewhere leading up to the introduction of the Gold Dinar, it was all planned with the goal of conquest.

"Take a look at the Gold Dinar, his unholy image is there …"

EASTERN STAR RESERVE BANK, DOHA, QATAR – DECEMBER 18, 1837 HOURS

"Is this some kind of sick joke? We are not of the faith foolishly held by the infidels. Why do you now speak of the Bible? How could you even say such a thing? It is blasphemy to speak of such things!"

"Listen!" screamed Hassan as he grabbed Saeed by the collar dragging him out of his seat and pinning him down over the conference table in his office. "Listen to me and to what I have to say. Open your eyes. You know it is all true. Now … can you feel that burning sensation gripping your heart? That fire, that eternal inferno of the damned. It is only going to get stronger until it consumes you to the very dust from which you were made. Go ahead – tell me … tell me you don't feel it now."

But Saeed had indeed begun to feel something unusual stirring deep inside him as Hassan spoke. There was a slight pain in his chest, a slow burning sensation that was only getting stronger the more he heard.

"What have you done to me? Is this some kind of a trick? Something is wrong, let me go! I need to see a doctor" said Saeed attempting in vain to push the larger man away.

"Do you still not understand? Doctors cannot help you – there is no escape. That pain, it is only just starting, it will never go away but it will not hurt, not as long as you fulfil your destiny."

"My destiny?"

"I am Conquest. I have prepared the way for you. You … you are the second rider. Your name is War."

U.S. DEPARTMENT OF STATE, WASHINGTON D.C. –
DECEMBER 18, 1038 HOURS

"But I don't understand. If all this is planned, if as you say, that all this is ordained, foretold in … your Bible, then what do you expect me to do?" asked Kelly.

"I am sorry," said the Pontiff. "Truly I am Kelly. I do not

have all the answers. All we have are the murky predictions of that which is yet to come … and our faith which binds us eternally to the Cross giving us hope in an eternal salvation."

"But who exactly are you now warning me about … Hassan from the Central Bank? Is he the one you fear?" asked Kelly. Immediately she corrected herself. "I am sorry Holy Father, I meant to ask if he was the one you were … referring to?"

"You were right the first time," said Pope Peter II. He then went on to relate to the President-Elect the biblical signs as Father Jacque had reported to him a few days earlier. He told her of the terrible things to come – of faith and fate which could no longer be ignored.

EASTERN STAR RESERVE BANK, DOHA, QATAR –
DECEMBER 18, 1839 HOURS

Even after Hassan explained to him the events of the past weeks and how it all led to controlling the world's financial system, Saeed was still troubled.

"But I don't understand. Why couldn't we just have issued this new currency at the start if this was the goal? Why was all this deception necessary? Did all those people really have to die, in Indonesia and in Singapore?"

"Don't you see, it was the only way, Saeed. We needed to push America and Israel into a corner and force their hands. We needed to ignite the religious passion of our people across the region, to put their internal differences aside and band together against the Americans and against Israel. Getting the world to use our currency whether by choice or by necessity, that was the goal – it was a conquest. Many have tried before to launch the Gold Dinar and failed. This was the only way to get it done. It would never have worked otherwise."

"The destruction of the Dome of the Rock – that was one of our most holy sites. You planned that?"

"No, as I said before, I was not privy to that part of the plan but I can see it now. It made sense to force the hand of the Jews to go ahead and rebuild their temple."

"And why is that so important? It's just a building."

"No Saeed, it is much more than just a building, a temple. Beneath its sands lie many secrets. There is a library filled with ancient scrolls. It had been locked, sealed, for a long time because what they foretold was simply too terrible to be disclosed. But soon that too will come to light. The horrible secrets of the Church will be revealed."

"I don't believe you or anything that you have said. Look, I'll keep your secret. I promise I won't tell anyone but I don't want any part of your plans. This is all wrong. You picked the wrong person. You made a mistake," screamed Saeed as he stared defiantly at Hassan.

"I never picked you. I would never have picked you of all people," spat Hassan in return. "But I did not have a choice and neither do you. You have been chosen just as I was. There were no options for us. There never was."

"How do you know that? This all could just be a mistake?"

"It's no mistake Saeed. You feel that unholy fire burning inside you, don't you? I have had that same flame inside me for a long, long time. You know it's real and you know everything that I have said here is true. Soon that fire will speak to you. It will reveal your role and it will guide you to your destiny."

"And what if I do not obey – what happens if I choose not to listen, simply walk away?"

"You think I had a choice in any of this? You and I are simple men wanting simple lives but we were called to be disciples, to serve a higher cause …"

"I don't believe in the Bible or in any of its silly stories …" shouted back Saeed.

"You damn fool. It is not just the Bible, you can pick any religious book and it will tell you the same story of the end because there is only one story – only one end. You may not believe it now but in time you will. It is not a matter of choice. We have none. Our future is ordained and nothing will change it my friend," said Hassan as he helped Saeed to his feet.

Saeed was silent for a long time allowing what Hassan had told him to sink in. He could feel the fire smouldering inside him, getting stronger. "And what then is my role in all this? Am I to start a war?"

"You must not take the names we have been given in the old book literally. I did not conquer any land. I am not building any empires. My conquest was of the mind and spirit, to control people. War in your case, may or may not have to mean fighting, I don't know. War could simply be but a means to divide people just as Famine, the rider who will come after you may not refer to physical hunger but more likely, the hunger the world would feel when religion fails them."

"And what about Death – the last to come?"

"I am not sure but I think Death refers not to the end of life but rather the end of hope when the Christian cross crumbles. There are many things which have not been revealed to me Saeed. I have been told only what I needed to know. Perhaps more will be made known to you. Your mission and its details will be revealed soon, very soon, when your time comes."

"How?" said Saeed. "How was it revealed to you?"

"For me, it came in a dream a few years ago. It was more like a waking nightmare from the smoky depths of hell," said Hassan shaking his head, lost in his thoughts. "I too tried to resist for a time. I thought I could save my soul but I could not. We had been summoned even before we were born. We can't escape who we are, what we are and what we are to become. Eventually I accepted it, reluctantly, and my eyes were opened. Since that day, I was guided every step of the way and things just happened as I was told they would. Things which led me here, to this, and to you."

"And what about me? I still don't know my role. Are you sure you have the right person? I know nothing about leading a war – any kind of a war. Hell, I can't even pick up a woman – who's gonna follow me?"

"Your time has not come yet but it soon will. But before that, you need to see certain places for yourself … in Israel. You will leave tomorrow."

"Where in Israel do you want me to go? To the Temple Mount?"

"Yes, but first I think you need some solitude to find yourself and to accept your fate just as I have. Only when you have walked the paces of the barren wasteland and kicked up the ancient dust, only then will you understand your true destiny."

52

U.S. DEPARTMENT OF STATE, WASHINGTON D.C. –
JANUARY 19, 0942 HOURS

It had been a month since Kelly spoke to the Pontiff and she had tried hard to put that disturbing conversation out of her mind. Nothing ominous had happened and the world was still revolving. After the tumultuous events of November and December, January had been a comparatively quiet month so far.

Governments and global businesses were slowly adjusting to incorporating the Gold Dinar in their transactions with the Middle East. And despite the dire predictions of some economists, the American dollar had still maintained its edge as the leading global reserve currency even as the Gold Dinar began to consolidate its position in second place.

While she could not totally dismiss the fears of Pope Peter II, Kelly knew she still had a job to do.

"I don't have the luxury of hiding behind some age-old biblical predictions that no one can decode with absolute certainty," she told Victor her husband when they discussed her conversation with the Pontiff. "My job is to deal with the affairs of the real world, one in which things are neither black nor white but shades of dirty grey."

"So you don't believe in what he had to say?" asked Victor.

"I don't really think that's the point. I have to deal with what I can see and play the cards that I have in hand. Besides, he offered no real insight as to what I ought to do. It doesn't help any when someone just tells you to be careful and nothing more. What are we supposed to do? Run away and hide? Just ignore the entire Middle East or what – launch a holy war of our own? The Crusades ended long ago. If America is to weather this coming storm and bridge the economic and political divides we face, we need more friends not enemies. We simply can't afford to be held hostage by old religious differences and obscure predictions."

Putting her personal misgivings aside, Kelly had already offered her hand in friendship. She had spoken to Hassan on the telephone several times over the past weeks and he had assured her that the Eastern Star Reserve Bank was keen to work closely with her new administration and that there were no immediate plans to reassess the exchange rate of the Gold Dinar against the US dollar.

He seemed a serious and decent enough fellow. While determined to protect the interest of his bank's member countries, Hassan appeared to be very receptive in working with the US to maintain responsible fiscal management.

Indeed she had invited him to attend her Inauguration Ceremony in Washington – a ceremony which was now only 24 hours away. It would be good, well necessary at least she thought, to meet him face to face and so Kelly scheduled a short introductory meeting with him later that day in the Oval Office.

Her thoughts now returned to her inauguration address tomorrow and once again over a cold cup of coffee, she read the speech she had been preparing for most of her life.

53

NEGEV DESERT, ISRAEL

It had been almost a month now – a long time indeed to be left alone walking the barren hills of the Negev in southern Israel as he headed towards Jerusalem. This rocky desert was a melange of brown barren mountains interrupted by wadis, the dry riverbeds and deep craters surrounded by foreboding cliff walls.

It was said the biblical prophet Abraham had lived in the Negev for many years after being banished from Egypt. The Israelites, who fled from Egypt during the time of Moses, had also passed through the Negev during their 40 years of desert wandering before reaching the Promised Land to the north.

Even in winter it was still sweltering during the day but it was the bone-chilling nights that were the worst for Saeed. Huddled in his sleeping bag, one of the few luxuries Hassan had reluctantly allowed him to bring, Saeed had lost count of the times he had cursed his former boss for abandoning him here. He shouted vile obscenities into the night sky and swore out loud at whatever dark forces of evil destiny had led him to this place of desolate emptiness and despair.

This was the first time in his life that he had truly been left alone. This was a test of survival, of this he was sure. Perhaps if he failed, he would be left out of this unholy plan that he wanted nothing more to do with. Perhaps then, he could somehow go back to his old life.

But at the back of his mind he knew the stakes – to fail would mean to die out here in this damned wilderness and be forgotten by all as if he never existed, as if his life up to that point in time did not count for a damn thing. No, there would be no going back to his old life. He was sure the dream would come soon enough just as Hassan had promised. Only then would he know exactly the dimensions of the task that lay before him. But night after restless night, shivering in his sleeping bag, that dream of revelation simply eluded him.

He was still not totally convinced about all that Hassan had told him. Saeed had never been particularly religious but still he considered himself to be a good man. Try as he might, he could not come to terms with the fact that he had been chosen by some unnamed evil or demonic entity to play a part in a biblical story which until just a few days ago, he knew practically nothing about. It just seemed all too incredible to contemplate. The only proof he had was Hassan's word and that burning, nagging pain in his chest.

"This pain could be anything," he tried to reason with himself. "Maybe Hassan just planted that thought in my subconscious and it's all just in my head."

But Saeed had been down this road a thousand times before having the same imaginary conversation with himself and all it brought was endless frustration and bitterness.

"Even Hassan, he ain't a bad guy. Sure he's gruff and strict and short-tempered at times and drinks every now and then, but I've also seen him show pure kindness," recalled Saeed.

Every morning before he started work at his villa in Riyadh, Saeed would watch Hassan go out into his garden to feed the stray cats that were always waiting patiently for him by the Koi pond. And every time he passed a beggar in the streets, Hassan would always stuff some money in the man's hand quietly, without ever saying a word, almost like he did not want this act of charity to be noticed.

"There is no proof that anything Hassan has said of my role is real. Maybe he had it all wrong. Maybe he has lost his mind. Maybe I'm losing mine," Saeed debated with himself. Still there was no doubt that Hassan was behind the attacks in Jakarta that killed those children and the nuclear strike in Singapore and the destruction of the church in Israel and he betrayed Yusman to the Americans and now, now he heads a powerful central bank that can cause global financial mayhem almost at will.

"The dream Hassan promised, that remains the key. If it happens then I'll know where I stand and what I would have to do. If it doesn't come then I'll be free to walk away from all this," he reasoned desperately in his mind but in his heart, he knew all this was a lost cause.

"We don't have a choice in this – we never did" Hassan had said and these words continued to haunt Saeed as he stoked the fire by his sleeping bag, still unable to shake the chill from his bones.

While he lacked human company, Saeed had not been left totally alone. A pair of Golden Jackals, native to this desert had been shadowing him since he began his journey. One with a ginger coat was more active, always sniffing about his campsite at night. Saeed named him Prancer. The other had more of a greyish white coat like that of a wolf and he called her Cheyenne. Each day they would follow him for hours on end but neither would come close no matter how much he called out to them. Sometimes the jackals would disappear for the afternoon only to show up again by his campfire at night – still wary and still keeping their distance.

Getting food in this desert was unusual to say the least. On his second day in the Negev when he had exhausted the meagre supplies he had brought with him, Saeed spotted a Bedouin camp on the horizon. These are the last true desert nomads still living in small extended family groups herding their goats as they moved around the Negev.

Saeed had hoped for some Arab hospitality or that at least he would be allowed to buy some food and water. But when he was still a distance away, an elderly man emerged from under the black tent made of rough camel hair. The man left some food – raw meat from a recently slaughtered goat and a pitcher of water by a rock – before returning hastily to his tent. As he got closer, the women, almost in a state of blind panic, grabbed their children playing outside and ran into their tents as if afraid for their very lives. Even the goats bleating loudly, would scamper off as he neared the camp.

At first Saeed thought that maybe they were just wary of strangers. Here he was, a sweaty man in dirty jeans with Oakley sunglasses and a New York baseball cap followed by his entourage of two mangy jackals. But each time this same scene was repeated, he began to realise that it was not just mistrust in the eyes of these people of the desert. For some unknown reason, they were in mortal fear of him. They seem to have sensed something about him, a dark presence, one to be feared.

Still Saeed took their simple offerings and always left some money behind. He did not know that his payments were never accepted. The Bedouins would notice the next day the Gold Dinars he had left under a small rock by their empty pitcher. But they simply left the money there untouched, to blow away in the desert wind. They wanted nothing to do with this man and the curse he seemed to carry.

Saeed would cook the meat by his lonely campfire each night, throwing some scraps to Prancer and Cheyenne who still regarded him with suspicion.

But it was at night, after a long day of walking that Saeed would once again be left alone with his thoughts. At times he would clutch his chest when the pain inside seemed too much to bear. He could still feel the fire burning deep inside his very being.

Even without admitting it to himself, in the cold desert

darkness, Saeed had surrendered and accepted his fate. He still did not know what lay in store for him. All he had been told by Hassan was to head north to Jerusalem and so with two canines in tow, he continued walking.

JERUSALEM, ISRAEL – JANUARY 20, 0847 HOURS

Saeed did not realise it then but he had emerged from his cold desert sojourn a changed man. He had cast aside his innocent boyish demeanour, he was now a man and one who would soon have a mission. For the first time in his life he had known true hunger, abject solitude and overwhelming despair. A fiery confidence now took over, a self-belief that just weeks earlier he would have thought impossible. Now he finally understood why the prophets of old always sought refuge in the desert only to emerge energised and more resolute from the experience.

It had been three days since he arrived in Jerusalem. He spent this time recovering from his desert ordeal regaining the weight he lost and treating the sun blisters on his skin. And today the contact that Hassan arranged for him, had led him here to the Temple Mount.

Saeed simply hated this place for it was filled with the Jews he still utterly despised. Still he had to admit that the architecture of the temple was simply breathtaking, reminiscent of an ancient Egyptian sanctuary. Disguised as one of the many workmen complete with a laminated identification card hanging from a lanyard around his neck, he entered the temple's inner court which was also known as the Court of the Priests.

While many finishing touches still needed to be done, the building itself was almost complete. The marble walls and floors had been polished to a near mirror finish and the crossbeams in the high ceiling above made of the ancient wood Cedar of Lebanon, lent an aged charm to the setting.

Adorning the walls were the little stone carvings of cherubs and palm trees. Gold trimmings embedded in the marble pillars, sparkled in the morning sun streaming in through the high double wooden doors from the outer courtyard beyond. Much more work still needed to be done before the temple was complete but the attention to detail was awe-inspiring.

Saeed still did not know why Hassan had made him come here. If he was discovered, he would surely be arrested. But his forged papers identifying him as a translator, had allowed him to pass through the tight security checks of the Israeli army.

He had always held a fascination for languages, especially the old ones from a bygone age and during his days in the university, he taught himself to read the various forgotten languages common in his part of the world.

While recovering from his desert journey, Saeed had been busy on his computer researching the history and the significance of the original Temple of Solomon. And even though he had been brought up like all Arabs to curse the Jewish faith, he was fascinated by the story of the temple and its many legends.

Gazing up to the high golden altar, he saw that it had five candlesticks on each side and on the ground before it, was a gold censer with burning incense. To the right was an empty stone table covered in a rich cloth of red interweaved with fine gold threads. He was told this would be for the showbread, an age-old sacrificial offering.

To the left was a gleaming replica of the famed Golden Menorah standing over two metres in height. From his research Saeed knew that the original menorah built by Moses had been seized by the Roman army when they destroyed the second temple in 70 AD. A carving depicting the theft of the menorah still exists today in the Arch of Titus located just north of the Colosseum in Rome.

At the back of the altar, concealed behind a large curtain of red and purple, was the central focus of the entire temple complex – the *Kodesh Hakodashim* or the Holy of Holies. His research told him that no one, save only the most senior priests was permitted to enter this most hallowed sanctum.

At the far end of the Court of the Priests stood a circular barricade made of sturdy wrought iron. Looking down into a shallow pit, he saw for the first time the revered Foundation Stone. Although he had recently learnt the long history of this limestone outcrop, Saeed was less than impressed by the old weathered rock held sacred by the three great monotheistic religions – Judaism, Christianity, and Islam.

Saeed's reverie was interrupted by a voice from behind. Turning around, he recognised one of the supervisors he had been introduced to earlier that day. "This way," said the man who guided him down the flight of old winding stairs a short distance from the Foundation Stone.

The cave below was smaller than Saeed had imagined it to be. Its rough sides had been cut from the bedrock more than two millennia ago. A tangle of wires lay on the floor connected to little florescent lamps spread around the room. These provided the only light for the men working in the Well of Souls.

The men, talking in hushed tones, were photographing some ancient inscriptions found etched on one of the walls. Shuffling past them, Saeed saw two narrow passages leading away from the cave entrance and his guide led him down the left one.

Bending low, he squeezed his way past some of the smaller turns in the corridor until he came to a much larger room with an old heavy metal door. On it was painted what Saeed recognised to be the Crusader Cross – a large Cross Potent in faded yellow surrounded by four smaller ones in each quadrant.

"You will work in here," said the supervisor as he pushed open the unlocked door and entered the room. Inside, seven small wooden desks were placed in the centre where two other men were already at work, huddled over what appeared to be rolls of ancient manuscripts.

"This is your pile here," said the man handing him a pair of white surgical gloves. "Go through each one carefully so we can sort out the time period, the author and the genesis. We need to make some sense of all this mess those heathens have left behind and rearrange the scrolls in their original order."

These documents he was told had apparently been locked away for hundreds of years since Muslim conquerors took over the Temple Mount from the Christian Crusaders and built their shrine above. Many of the wooden racks against the walls stood empty, before an untidy heap of ancient documents scattered about on the floor.

"We don't know what they were looking for but we need to clean this up and sort everything out. Clear?"

Saeed nodded and got down to work. Carefully he looked through the many crushed scrolls. Some were made of ancient lambskin, others of papyrus and the more recent ones were of what appeared to be thick rough parchment paper which had turned brown with age.

Left alone to begin his work, Saeed tried to carefully arrange the bundle left on his small table. Touching one dusty scroll at the bottom of the pile, he instantly began to hear voices in his head.

At first these were just indistinct whisperings, barely audible but they soon grew louder. Blurry disconnected visions of fire and battle floated before his eyes as the burning sensation in his chest grew stronger.

For the first time since Hassan had spoken to him about his destiny, Saeed was beginning to taste fear. Disembodied screams intermingled with a chorus of harsh male voices now filled his mind.

Suddenly he felt a sharp piercing pain in the palms of his hands as if a white hot steel rod was being driven through them. Instantly his fingers clenched around the scroll still in his hand. The pain in his chest was getting stronger now as Saeed sat down. He could feel his heart racing as beads of cold sweat trickled down his head. He sensed the other two men in the room were watching him curiously but they said nothing and offered no help.

Saeed knew he was not hallucinating. It was all too real and it was happening to him. This was nothing like the dream Hassan had promised.

In sheer panic he shut his eyes tight willing the voices in his head to cease, but they continued taunting him. Above all the others he could hear one voice whispering directly in his ear with a fiery breath that raised the hairs on the back of his neck.

The sounds, garbled English words, appeared hauntingly familiar and yet their meanings seem to be just beyond his comprehension. They blended into the background which he could only describe as sombre, indistinct chanting.

With his eyes still tightly shut and concentrating hard, Saeed slowly began to make out a few whispered phrases here and there – 'Spores of fire', 'Know this', 'I am', 'Thorns of Rome', 'Har Megiddo', 'For Saul has written', 'Seek Ezekiel'.

And then as suddenly as it had all begun, there was silence.

Saeed looked up and saw the two men still watching him. Slowly, still shaking their heads, they returned to their work and he was left alone, sitting at his small table, clutching that scroll in his trembling hands and feeling like a fool.

Unrolling the ancient lambskin creased with age, the ink barely visible, he began to read the old Aramaic text written presumably by the hand of the Prophet Ezekiel.

Saeed's revelation had finally begun and soon he too would know the truth.

54

OVAL OFFICE, THE WHITE HOUSE, WASHINGTON D.C. – JANUARY 20, 1006 HOURS

Kelly did not know why she was feeling so awkward today, meeting President Monroe for the last time in the Oval Office. He had always been a close friend and a confidant. But the burden of his office had claimed a heavy toll, ageing him well beyond his years. Perhaps she thought that this was the curse one paid for holding such absolute power. Perhaps this was the same fate that awaited her.

"I couldn't be more proud of you Kelly. You have served America well and I know she is in good hands. I'm just sorry to leave such a mess behind, so much work still to be done to put this country right," he said grasping her hand in a final farewell.

In retrospect, his last gamble in taking on the terrorists was as much a failure as it was a success. He had demonstrated once again the military superiority of America and yet in so doing, he had exposed her very weakness – the dominance of the United States exists only in a deeply divided world, split by religion, by distrust and the defeated will of people which made them unable to alter the path of history.

The retaliatory strike in Indonesia had been the final straw for the Arab world and now its people had banded together, standing shoulder to shoulder in vast numbers, united by history and religion, intent on crushing the once mighty American dollar and the empire behind it. Monroe knew this would be the lasting legacy his administration would be remembered for.

Kelly nodded in response. She could sense his anguish, the internal torments that had plagued him over the past weeks. She felt sorry for this man who had once walked so tall, so self-assured in his own interpretation of what was right for him and the country he led with both passion and pride.

"America, Mr President," said Kelly, "owes you a depth of gratitude which she can never repay. You led with honour and distinction, guiding this nation through some of the most daunting times in our history. We could not ask for more of you."

President Monroe nodded accepting the compliment knowing that while it was well-meaning, it was probably in hindsight, undeserved. "Thank you Kelly, now I guess it is time. Good luck Madam President. I wish you well."

And with that, he stood up. Kissing her lightly on her cheek in a fatherly way he walked quietly out of the Oval Office for the last time, closing the door behind him.

Outside the US Capitol Building, Washington D.C. – January 20, 1030 hours

It was still a bitterly cold morning when Kelly arrived at the steps of the US Capitol building. Hundreds of flags fluttered in the frigid breeze as throngs of spectators huddled close together for warmth and waited anxiously to welcome the country's first woman president to the White House.

Flanked by her husband and their two teenage children, Kelly strode confidently to the podium where the Chief Justice of the United States, Luanna Judith Miller was waiting.

Placing her left hand on the bible and raising her right, she took the Oath of Office. "I, Kelly Kaileen Yee, do solemnly swear that I will faithfully execute the Office of President of the United States and will, to the best of my ability, preserve, protect and defend …"

Oval Office, The White House, Washington D.C. – January 20 1227 hours

It would be a long and hectic first day in office for President Yee. She had scheduled a series of brief 10-minute introductory meetings with various key officials and selected foreign dignitaries who would be crucial to her new Administration.

Hassan was the eighth in line to meet the new head of

state. He straightened his suit as he was ushered into the Oval office. Kelly had thought long and hard about whether he should be included in this select group. She remembered well the dire warnings of the Pontiff. Her predecessor too had been convinced that Hassan had tricked the US to strike in Indonesia at the exact time he intended to unveil the new Arab currency to rival the US dollar.

"I'm not totally convinced he had set us up but that's also in the past," reasoned Kelly earlier when she discussed the issue with several advisors some of whom would soon be inducted into her new Administration. "We need Hassan now to calm markets and to reassure the world that his central bank will continue to act responsibly in its fiscal management."

Hassan too realised the importance of this first meeting. Everything rested on him gaining the trust of this woman. "It could all still fail," he reminded himself. "The conquest is far from complete."

"I believe," said Hassan when they met in the Oval Office, "that we both want the same thing – economic prosperity and that simply cannot happen without trust and without peace.

"We have not made any adjustments to the price or volume of oil exported and we are still maintaining an even par trade between the dinar and the dollar. We have welcomed American contractors amongst others to bid for the many multi-billion dinar contracts to improve the infrastructure of the Gulf States. All this we have done for our mutual benefit.

"America needs friends in the Middle East," continued Hassan echoing a statement Kelly had made often during her election campaign, "just as we need friends here. From banking to IT to agriculture to defence, there are so many ways Madam President that we can continue to work together for the benefit of the United States and the Gulf region as a whole."

"Thank you and I look forward," replied Kelly, "to working with you, your Central Bank and the countries of the Middle East in promoting business growth, fiscal stability and regional peace."

"I wish you well Madam President and I am confident that this will be the start of a new and strong friendship," said Hassan as he stood up and shook hands with the woman who would be so pivotal to the success of his plans.

Hassan smiled to himself as he left the White House. It was all still going exactly to plan and his role was almost finished. Now it would rest on Saeed and the others to do their parts. Already Hassan could feel the fire in his chest was slowly fading. Soon he hoped he would be free of this curse, free to simply fade away as a mere pawn sacrificed to fulfil its fated task.

55

PLAINS OF HAR MEGIDDO, ISRAEL – FEBRUARY 19, 1745 HOURS

Saeed could not believe how peaceful it all seemed now. Sitting on a rock overlooking the small hill in the distance as the sun began to set, it was hard to imagine that this picturesque desert plain held such a murderous history.

In ages gone by, Egyptians, Greeks, Romans, Christian Crusaders, Israelites, and Mongols had all fought great bloody battles here, dying in their thousands and yet nothing remained today of their presence or their wasted sacrifices.

The scrolls had led him here. He had to come and see this site for himself, now before it was too late. The visions they foretold still haunted his dreams. In his mind, he could still hear the screams of the damned as their souls were consumed from within.

Plagued with guilt for the role he would soon play, he wondered if it would all be worthwhile, if more blood would be shed here, spilt in vain as in the other historic battles that had come and gone before. Still he felt that this time it would be different – it would be the final great act before the end.

Still lost in his thoughts, he doodled in the warm sand drawing a vertical line with his finger. Another smaller line intersected the first forming a small cross. Saeed looked intently at the symbol he had unconsciously drawn before rubbing it out and dusting his hands.

Four kilometres away on the other side of the hill, elements of Israel's elite Strategic Missile Forces were unloading their equipment. Soon they would begin their scheduled training manoeuvres, practising a mock battle that would become only too real.

Concealed under camouflaged nets, mobile launchers were being moved into position. Each one cradled a Jericho III, the black intercontinental ballistic missile. On its nosecone housing the warhead, the Star of David was proudly painted.

But these missiles did not contain a nuclear payload. Instead they housed something even more dangerous – billions of live anthrax spores that had been carefully engineered to resist all known forms of treatment.

The initial formula had been discovered more than a year earlier during a global outbreak of the disease.

It was triggered when workers digging a tunnel in Singapore stumbled upon a cache of Japanese war treasure that had been tainted with this unknown strain of anthrax.

Investigators from Israel who were called in to help, assisted in eventually tracking down the formula designed by a Japanese germ-warfare chemist Yasuji Naito of the Imperial Japanese Army. Since then, Israel working in secret with their Singapore counterparts, had developed an improved strain of the anthrax bacterium turning it into a super biological weapon.

Saeed knew it would not be long now. Soon Israel would be at war. He had met the soldiers the previous night and had given them the stolen launch codes. The flight of the Jericho from Israel would be short, lasting just minutes. Still it would be tracked on radar by all her neighbours like a giant fiery sword tearing across the dark skies. Of this he was certain. There would be no room for doubt that Israel had struck first, unleashing a biological holocaust of Jewish origin over the ancient city of Amman in Jordan.

The Arab war it would trigger would spread quickly with armies filling every shore, just as it was foretold. The United States would be put in an impossible position to respond. It would either have to side with its old ally Israel and risk the wrath of the world or stand with the Arabs in the war against Israel. And it would all begin here, on this dusty plain, with the simple turning of a launch key.

Saeed's thoughts of the battle to come were interrupted by a call from Hassan on his mobile phone.

"Why are you still there? It's not safe."

"Hey don't worry Hassan," he replied confidently. "Everything has been taken care of. All my meetings are done and I'll be home tonight."

"Good, don't risk staying there longer than you have to. There is still much work to be done here."

"Yeah I know. And Hassan …"

"Yeah?"

"I've found him!"

"Huh? … Who?"

"The next one …"

As Saeed turned to leave, he took one last look around Har Megiddo. Standing on a flat rock outcrop in the distance, he saw them – Prancer and Cheyenne. As their eyes met, the jackals let off one long howl and then they were gone, running off together into the sunset, their tails held high. Saeed smiled. It was like meeting old friends for one last time. "Live well guys and be safe," he whispered to himself as he lost sight of them.

It was getting dark now and he too had to go. He walked back to his car parked under some Date Palm trees a short distance away.

Not many people would have heard of this place – at least not by its Jewish name. 'Har' is the Hebrew word for mount or mountain but in the Jewish language that 'h' is silent. So Har Medido is pronounced as 'Ar Megiddo'. The world better knows this name in its Greek form – Armageddon.

AGOSTINO GEMELLI TEACHING HOSPITAL, ROME, ITALY – FEBRUARY 19, 1830 HOURS

As Saeed turned his flashy red BMW 316 onto the main desert highway and headed back to Jerusalem for the last time, Pope Peter II looking gaunt and deathly pale, had been left alone to rest.

In a special suite maintained by the Vatican for his exclusive use, the Pontiff had been warded for three days. In that time, his worried doctors had performed an exhaustive battery of tests to determine the cause of the Pope's apparent chest pains.

Initially they suspected that the most likely cause was *Angina Pectoris* probably triggered by a coronary artery disease. The Pontiff had described in detail, the burning chest pains he had experienced over the past week which left him feeling weak and breathless. His blood pressure too remained exceedingly low and he had almost completely lost his appetite. However all his tests including an electrocardiogram to detect a range of coronary obstructions and blood-borne diseases turned out to be negative.

Stumped, doctors advised strict bed rest and a change in diet suspecting that acute and prolonged stress may have triggered the symptoms.

They were partially right. Pope Peter II was indeed under tremendous stress. He had only described to his medical team the physical symptoms he had experienced. But there was more, much more, that he kept unsaid.

Pope Peter II had indeed kept much to himself. From the moment the Conclave elected him, he had been filled with doubts as to whether or not he should accept the papal throne. His predecessor, the humble Pope Francis, had done much to realign the Vatican with its original charter to focus on the poor, the weak in spirit and the disillusioned. He preached the simple message of love and charity. Pope Peter II wanted nothing more than to follow in these saintly footsteps.

But at that time of great uncertainly and anxiety in the Sistine Chapel as the secret votes at the Conclave were read out, Pope Peter II could feel a fire burning in his heart. At that time he assumed it was the Holy Spirit moving him to accept the heavy cross of the papacy. But now he was not so sure about the origin of those flames still consuming him slowly from within.

With the thick curtains drawn, the only light in the Papal Suite came from a small lamp on his desk nearby. He had asked that the lamp remain on as he dreaded the darkness and the spectres it seemed to conjure.

Despite the medication that he had been given to help him sleep, the Pontiff willed his weakened body to resist. The evil visions that had been plaguing him – of fires, disease, hunger and blackness – these were just too terrible to repeat even to his most trusted doctors. He was alone in his own private hell and even his faith was beginning to wane as the disembodied voices in his head grew increasingly louder.

One vision above all disturbed him the most. In what he could only assume to be a most vivid hallucination, he saw thousands of people in the square outside Saint Peter's Basilica kneeling in prayer, weeping tears of blood and wailing in despair. Their bodies were covered with the black and bloody scabs of anthrax. It was a new scourge of the old Black Death and it was on the hunt for souls once more.

People screamed in pain and tugged at their hair which came out in tufts. Dark menacing clouds gathered over the square as a light rain began to fall but it failed to wash away the dried blood which stained the ground.

The starving faithful with their distended bellies turned their vacant eyes to gaze at the Papal Apartment pleading for guidance and hope and assurance that they had not been forgotten – that their faith and that of their forefathers had not been in vain – an elaborate lie more than two millennia old.

"Forsake not the children. They have not sinned," cried out one woman as she lifted her crying infant with arms outstretched towards the only source of temporal salvation left in the world. But the small white windows of the Papal Apartment remained firmly shut as if deaf to the desperate pleading from the wretched throng of humanity below.

The biological war started by Israel had set the Middle East aflame. Across the world, scorching temperatures once casually dismissed as global warming, saw crops withering in the fields. As the ice caps melted, sea levels rose flooding the land and turning fresh-water lakes brackish.

Pope Peter II watched on helplessly as an unholy curse fell upon the earth. A famine of the spirit spread quickly through his flock. The end seemed to be closing in – a tightening noose he could do nothing to stop.

And now with a hot wind blowing from the dying sun in the west, he could almost hear the galloping hooves. The spectre of Death, his pale face still hidden, was fast approaching.

EPILOGUE

FOR IT WAS WRITTEN ...

I watched as the Lamb opened the first of the seven seals. Then I heard one of the four living creatures say in a voice like thunder, "Come and see!" I looked, and there before me was a white horse! Its rider held a bow, and he was given a crown, and he rode out as a conqueror bent on conquest.

– Book of Revelation 6:1-2

When the Lamb opened the second seal, I heard the second living creature say, "Come and see!" Then another horse came out, a fiery red one. Its rider was given power to take peace from the earth and to make men slay each other. To him was given a large sword.

– Book of Revelation 6:3-4

When the Lamb opened the third seal, I heard the third

living creature say, "Come and see!" I looked, and there before me was a black horse! Its rider was holding a pair of scales in his hand. Then I heard what sounded like a voice among the four living creatures, saying, "A quart of wheat for a day's wages, and three quarts of barley for a day's wages, and do not damage the oil and the wine!"

– Book of Revelation 6:5-6

When the Lamb opened the fourth seal, I heard the voice of the fourth living creature say, "Come and see!" I looked and there before me was a pale horse! Its rider was named Death, and Hades was following close behind him. They were given power over a fourth of the earth to kill by sword, famine, and plague, and by the wild beasts of the earth.

– Book of Revelation 6:7

ABOUT THE AUTHOR

David Miller worked as police investigator in Singapore for eight years before beginning his writing career first as a newspaper correspondent and later as a managing editor for a stable of magazines.

Over the years he has written a number of commercial books for both the public and private sectors.

His first novel *Year of the Tiger* was printed in August 2012. *Advent* was published in June 2013 and he is currently working on his third book to complete the series. He has also published two non-fiction stories in 2014 – *Bahau, the Elephant & the Ham* and *DutyBound*.

For more about the author, visit his website at www.dmbooks.org

A WORD OF THANKS

I am deeply grateful to Jan Tristram and Annette Douglas for their invaluable help in the production of this novel.

Readers, if you too have enjoyed *Advent*, please spend a few minutes penning your thoughts in a review on Amazon.com. Your comments are most appreciated. If you prefer to contact me directly and have your review published on my website, please email feedback@dmbooks.org

Cheers

David

Other books by David Miller

YEAR OF THE TIGER
*A WARTIME SECRET IN SINGAPORE TRIGGERS A GLOBAL
BIOTERRORISM NIGHTMARE*

During World War II, the Imperial Japanese Army under General Tomoyuki Yamashita looted untold amounts of gold and other valuables from across its occupied colonies in Southeast Asia.

But when the tides of war turned against Japan in 1943, much of this treasure had to be buried in secret. Over the decades, the search for the legendary Yamashita's Gold had been in vain until now...

A group of foreign workers digging a tunnel under the Padang in present-day Singapore stumbles across a treasure vault and inadvertently triggers a biological booby trap. An unknown strain of anthrax is released threatening a global holocaust. It is up to investigators in Singapore to decipher a cryptic clue left behind with the loot and halt this deadly plague.

Year of the Tiger
ISBN (ebook): 978-981-4358-89-7
ISBN (paperback): 978-981-4358-90-3
www.dmbooks.org

BAHAU, THE ELEPHANT & THE HAM

The Japanese Occupation of Singapore during the Second World War saw a group of Eurasians being sent to start a farming colony in Bahau deep in the unforgiving Malayan jungle.

Largely inept at working the land, many fell to disease and malnutrition. Others, unable to cope with the primitive conditions, simply gave up the fight.

Bahau, the Elephant & the Ham recounts with stark vividness and a touch of humour the day-to-day struggles of one ordinary family to beat the odds and eventually return home.

Bahau, the Elephant & the Ham
ISBN (ebook): 978-981-09-0244-5
ISBN (paperback): 978-981-09-0243-8
www.dmbooks.org

DUTYBOUND
A SINGAPORE WAR HERO REMEMBERED

This is a true story of a young police inspector who finds himself out of a job during the Japanese Occupation of Singapore. He begins to fight back in his own way and is soon lured into joining a clandestine Allied spy ring.

Working in disguise as a hawker, 22-year-old Halford Boudewyn is tasked to smuggle out from a POW camp classified documents which could prevent another major invasion planned by the Imperial Japanese Army.

DutyBound
ISBN (Paperback) 978-981-09-2389-1
ISBN (Ebook) 978-981-09-2390-7
www.dmbooks.org

www.ingramcontent.com/pod-product-compliance
Lightning Source LLC
Chambersburg PA
CBHW060152260626
47160CB00001B/236